WEAVER'S STONE

SHANNEN L. COLTON

For Aunt Wendy, who has encouraged and inspired me in all areas of life, but especially my writing.

CONTENTS

1 CAPTURE

It wasn't supposed to go this way.

Nils tore down the hallway, his worn shoes sliding on the polished floor as he rounded a corner. He threw a hand up to push off the wall and kept running, clenching the necklace in his other hand with gloved fingers. He could hear boot steps thundering much too closely behind him.

Another corner—he darted around it as quickly as possible, slid through an open doorway, and beheld with rapture an unguarded window. He threw it open and scrambled out into the cool night air, his stomach dropping at the distance beneath his narrow ledge.

Not down, then, he thought. His eyes darted back and forth, looking for the best place to re-enter the manor. *There. That balcony.*

He couldn't pause to consider the danger of dashing across the tiny shelf of architecture that stretched between him and his goal, not with the sounds of pursuit getting closer behind him. If he was going to lose them, it was now. He held his breath and ran until his feet were firmly planted on the balcony, then let it out in a wheeze, tearing off his black hood as he did. His blond hair might make him easier to spot, but he needed the air, he couldn't help it—

"Who's there?"

Fives. He really should've guessed the room inside would be occupied. Fancy balcony like this? It could only belong to one of the nobles. He looked for another landing, a place he could make another stupidly dangerous lunge for…

"I think he came out here!" a voice called from the window he'd just vacated. He had no time to think; he rammed his shoulder into the balcony door and flew inside.

The room was lit only by a small fire in the hearth. Nils' eyes immediately jumped to the extravagant four-poster bed, but it was unoccupied. Recently, it seemed, as the blankets were strewn about in all directions. *All right, so where is…*

He couldn't finish his mental inquiry before a hairbrush came flying at his head. It missed him by mere inches and smacked into the door behind him. He would've sighed in relief that it hadn't shattered the glass, but he didn't have time; a perfume bottle followed closely behind. He blocked it from hitting his face, but couldn't stop it from smashing to the floor, burning his nose with the sudden release of floral fumes. He winced. This encounter was much too noisy.

He whirled around, caught the next object—a small jewelry box—and finally caught sight of his assailant. She was a noble, all right, a young woman dressed in a frilly nightgown and armed with a candelabrum.

"Don't come any closer!" she squawked, brandishing the silver candle-holder.

"Quiet!" Nils hissed, eyeing the door leading out of the room. Was someone coming? Had they heard the perfume bottle smash?

"I mean it!" the noblewoman said, only growing louder.

Nils discarded the jewelry box, lunged forward, and grabbed her by the wrist. She nearly dropped the candelabrum, so Nils was forced to release the necklace he still carried, which hit the floor with a *tink.*

"Let me go!" the girl cried, flailing her free arm. Nils threw the candlestick back toward the bed, hoping for the best, and grabbed her other wrist, pinning both her arms against the wall. "Guards!" she shouted, and Nils did the only thing he could think of to quiet her mouth with both his hands already occupied. He kissed her.

The girl became still and silent as the grave. In fact, *grave* is exactly the word Nils would've used to describe her as he kept his lips pressed firmly against hers. He waited several heartbeats, waited to see if anyone had heard her scream. When all remained quiet, he hesitantly broke the kiss, afraid she would cry out at the first chance, but she didn't. She just stared at him, eyes wide as wagon wheels.

"You're alive," she said, voice barely more than a breath.

"Wha—?" Nils started to say, and then the dreaded noise filled his ears. Boot steps. His eyes shot to the door. How long did he have? He released the girl, bent to grab his fallen prize, and turned to run, but he'd barely taken two steps when the door flung open. Four guards poured inside, grabbing him before he'd even reached the balcony. One of them pried the necklace from his black-gloved fingers, and in the light from the hearth, he saw it: a hair-line crack in the solitary black stone. It had broken when he dropped it.

The necklace wasn't what he was looking for. He had done all this, and failed, for nothing.

A moment of numbness, then crushing dread spread through him as the guards hauled him from the room. The noblewoman was shouting something above their grunts and threats, but he didn't catch her words. In a blink he was out of her chambers and into the lamp-lit hallway. He traced the map in his head, trying to guess where he was in the manor house, but between his unexpected detour and his current state of panic, he couldn't seem to wrap his head around it.

Down a flight of stairs, through a grand hallway, now into a larger room. Another set of stairs before him, and there, descending...

It was Lord Dreygard himself, flanked by attendants, fully dressed and not looking at all as though it was the middle of the night. Did the man never sleep?

"What is going on?" he thundered. "What is this?"

"My lord, we've apprehended a thief," a guard explained. "He fled from us when we spotted him outside the third floor storeroom, and just now we caught him in Lady Raeya's chambers."

"In Raeya's—" Lord Dreygard said, his face becoming impossibly more furious.

Unholy fives, Nils thought. *She wasn't just a noble. She's the domiseer's daughter.*

"She is unharmed, my lord."

"She had better be. What did this *mudworm* steal? I assume you recovered it?"

"Yes, my lord." The guard hurried forward and presented the black-stoned necklace. The domiseer looked it over, eyes scanning every detail, before he stated, "Costume jewelry."

"Yes, my lord."

The domiseer's eyes at last flashed to Nils, who looked down at his feet. He could feel the heat of Lord Dreygard's stare boring into the top of his head.

"Execute him."

"What?" Nils said, head snapping back up. "No—you, you said yourself, it's merely costume jewelry. You'd execute a man over that?"

"You broke into my home, stole from me, and forced entry into my daughter's bedroom. You deserve worse than a quick death, but it isn't worth my time to bother with a more fitting punishment." Lord Dreygard signaled the guards to proceed.

"No, you can't—"

"Stop!"

Where Nils' words went unheeded, this new cry caused the guards to all but drop their weapons. Nils craned his neck around to see the young woman from before—Lady Raeya Dreygard—marching toward them, an untied robe thrown over her nightgown. A middle-aged attendant followed her, looking as embarrassed as if she were the one parading through the manor barely dressed.

"Don't lay a hand on him," Lady Raeya threatened the guards. "Father, you mustn't harm this man."

"And why not?" the domiseer demanded.

"He just kissed me in my chambers."

Nils grimaced. He didn't know what the girl expected, but surely that would just make the domiseer angrier, and yet...the man's face had gone still as stone.

"Show me," he said.

Show him what? Raeya approached Nils, and he almost could've laughed. It was just too ridiculous. "You aren't really going to..." he said, but as he looked back and forth between the girl and her father, he realized she was.

Some of Raeya's confidence faded once she was standing face to face with him. She glanced at his lips, then back to his eyes. "If I'm wrong about this," she said, "I'm sorry."

Once again, Nils had no idea what to make of that statement, but his mind went blank anyway as she leaned up and kissed him gently on the mouth. She kept her eyes closed afterward, shut tight like she was afraid to look. When she finally did, her lips parted in wonder.

Nils didn't think he'd ever stood in a room so quiet. He looked around, wishing he could shrink away from all the staring eyes. "What is it?" he stammered when he couldn't take the silence anymore.

Lord Dreygard was the first to thaw, but it seemed even he was only capable of one word. "Raeya."

"You saw, Father. You know what this means. And you know you mustn't harm him."

"If you think I'll let some lowborn, petty thief marry my daughter just because of this—"

"Father, he's the *only one!* You wouldn't, you *couldn't* execute him, could you? Could you really do that to me?"

The domiseer fought back his words, restricting his show of fury to the flame-light dancing in his eyes. Raeya seemed to take his silence as a victory, and turned to Nils with another look of wonder, followed by a timid smile.

"Wait, hold on," Nils said. "You...he didn't say *marry,* did he? Look, I'm not...I just *stole* something, remember?"

"That is unexpected, I'll admit," Raeya said, "but we can get past a mild act of thievery, I'm sure."

Nils looked around again. No one was countering her. "What...Are you all mad? Don't get me wrong—I'm all too grateful not to be executed, but why in Desna's season should a kiss mean I'm supposed to marry you?"

"Because you lived," Raeya said.

"How does that explain anything?"

"Because you are the only one who has lived." The girl's face grew solemn. "I've been cursed since my childhood. Any man who kisses me will die, except one." She looked back up at him. "My true love. I was afraid I'd never find you."

"True love," Nils repeated. "What, like…a soulmate?" He made one last sweep of the room, just waiting for someone to crack, to reveal this as the sick joke it was.

Nobody so much as twitched.

Unholy fives.

2 CURSES

Feren Dreygard, domiseer of Chanterey, sat in an ordinary chair as though it were a throne. The man was broad-faced, wide-shouldered, with short blond hair and a neatly trimmed beard.

Nils hated him more than any other being on earth.

"What is your name?" he asked.

Nils considered not answering, but he knew it would be pointless. "Nils."

"Surname?"

"With all due respect, Lord Dreygard,"—which, as far as Nils was concerned, wasn't much—"your men already questioned me thoroughly."

"Yes, but in the absence of your identification tags—another punishable offense, I might add— I'm not about to assume you gave them your real name. So, give it to me, or you *will* hang when I find out, regardless of my daughter's wishes."

Nils took a moment to read the earnestness on the domiseer's face. "Oakander. I'm Nils Oakander."

The domiseer held aloft a familiar black-stoned piece of jewelry. "And why did you steal this, Nils Oakander?"

"I just needed money," Nils said, shifting a little in the cold room. "I grabbed what I found. I assumed it was valuable."

"There were other pieces far more valuable than this within your reach. Why take this one in particular, and why *only* this one?"

"I just panicked, all right? I heard someone coming, so I grabbed the first thing I saw."

"And you carried no weapons when you broke in to steal from my manor."

"I'm a thief, not an assassin."

"And not a very good one, it seems."

Nils pressed his lips together.

"Now, about your entry into Lady Raeya's chambers…"

"That was an accident, I swear it," Nils said, straightening up. "I was just trying to escape and wound up there. And her claim about the kiss—well, it was true, but it was only to keep her quiet. I didn't want her alerting the guards."

The domiseer raised an eyebrow. "That was a much more fervent reply than your previous ones," he observed. "I wonder then, which was the lie?"

Nils stiffened. The domiseer held him in a level gaze, then rose from his chair and came closer. He pulled one of Nils' shirtsleeves back, turning his arm over to inspect his wrist. His guards had done the same thing the moment they'd taken him in for questioning. The domiseer made no remark on this action, but Nils understood. He wished he could do the same, see what Feren Dreygard was hiding under the leather cuffs he wore.

"You'll live for now, unfortunately," Lord Dreygard said when he was finished. "However, I am far from convinced that you deserve it, let alone that you are fit to marry my daughter."

"I don't even *want* to marry your daughter."

"Good. Let us hope we both get what we want in that regard. Until it's decided one way or another, you are not to set foot outside of the manor for any reason. If I hear of any more attempts at theft, you'll not escape punishment a second time. Any mistreatment of my daughter,"—the domiseer's cold eyes seemed to smolder—"and even death would be merciful. Am I understood?"

"Yes." Nils didn't bother adding *my lord*. What was he going to do now? Stuck in the manor, he could continue his search, at least. With more time he could find what he needed. Then he just had to escape at the first chance and regroup with Taws. Breaking out had to be easier than breaking in, right? And he'd managed that, so...

The domiseer strode toward the door and paused. "It should go without saying," he said, "but you'll be under watch every second, waking or sleeping." He stepped out, and Nils became very aware of the guards surrounding him.

★ ★ ★

It was probably mid-morning when the guards escorted Nils from the outbuilding where he was held overnight onto the manor grounds. There was a chill in the air, lingering from Kirit's season, but birds chirped all the same, knowing Desna had taken the reins and would soon be warming the air and dressing the trees. Nils was nearly deaf to their songs. The manor house loomed before him, and whatever reckless bravado had gotten him through everything so far gave way to panic.

His gaze flicked to the main gate. Six guards there. The doors to the manor house. Four guards. There were several more of them patrolling the grounds. Not to mention the pair right beside him.

More. It was definitely more than before he'd broken in. Were they here to keep other intruders from entering, or to keep him from escaping?

Both, probably.

Of course when they'd asked him if he had any accomplices, he'd said no. He wasn't about to sell out Tawson.

Taws...maybe he'll come. Spring me out. Find some way to help. He glanced at the guards peppering the manor yard again. Gods, he'd never make it in. Would he even try? They'd barely known each other a couple months. What would Nils have done, had their roles been reversed?

Nils swallowed. *Maybe that's why he was so insistent I be the one to enter in the first place. Unholy fives. I'm never going to get out of here.*

"Nils!"

Nils' eyes shot back to the manor house. Someone had just come out of the door, rushing toward him. A smile on her lips. Long, orange hair.

Raeya Dreygard.

"Nils Clayson. How wonderful it is to meet you, *properly* this time."

She did a little curtsy, while her stout attendant caught up to her, huffing and puffing, carrying a cloak that was utterly ignored by her mistress. Lady Raeya was all put together this morning, dressed in a pale blue gown, hair half-up and elegantly styled. Even Nils had to admit she was pretty, but her gray-blue eyes...they were the same color as her father's.

"It's Oakander," he said without so much as a nod.

"Pardon?" Raeya said, blinking.

"Nils Oakander. That's my name."

"But the captain of the guard said..."

"Yes, unfortunately that didn't last long."

Raeya blinked again, then cleared her throat and forced a smile. "Very well, Nils *Oakander*. A pleasure to meet you."

Nils said nothing. Raeya's smile faltered, but eventually she forced it to stretch full again, until she shivered. "Desna's Tresses, it's cold out here," she said, rubbing her arms. "Come, inside. We have *so* much to talk about." She grabbed his hand in both of hers and tugged him forward.

"Whoa, hold on," Nils said. She ignored him just as she had the cloak, turning forward but keeping one of her hands locked on his. Her skin was possibly the softest thing he'd ever felt, but there was too much going on to dwell on that thought. He was swallowed by the house's grand double doors before he'd even had a chance to take in the façade.

"You know, I like Oakander better," Raeya said far too cheerfully. "Has a better ring to it than Clayson, don't you think?"

Nils didn't answer, being too distracted by the sheer opulence of the place. Sure, he'd seen some of the excess of the Dreygards last night, but nothing quite so staggering as this entryway. The rug they were walking on...just how long was it? You could probably feed an entire town for a week with the profits from selling it.

Not that the Dreygards care about feeding the townspeople.

"Here, this is one of my favorite rooms," Raeya said, leading him into some kind of sitting room. The walls were lined with shelves, and their contents made him forget about the rug. They were full of books.

So many. If only we'd had all those for—

"Come, sit," Raeya said, dragging him to a cushioned bench that must've also cost a fortune. She finally stopped tugging his arm, and he massaged his shoulder, sore from the night before. He wasn't built for ramming down doors. If not for his frantic energy at the time, he probably couldn't have managed it.

"Now, tell me more about yourself," Raeya said, sitting upright with her hands clasped and her eyes sparkling.

Nils watched his guards file in behind the bench along with Raeya's attendant, who eyed him like he was the fallen fifth god himself. "You already know all you need," he said. "In fact your father summarized it quite nicely. I'm a lowborn, petty thief."

"Nonsense—I'm certain there's more to you than that. You're my true love. That in itself makes me confident that you are in fact a decent, honorable man."

"Who broke into your room and tried to steal from your family."

Raeya smiled. "It's all rather romantic, don't you think? A cunning thief, stealing onto a young lady's balcony in the dead of night, followed by an unexpected kiss." She sighed, and Nils' eyebrows rose a little higher on his forehead. "Although I'm reasonable enough to know it's never advisable to marry a thief," she added, smoothing her skirt. "We'll need to work on reforming your practices."

Nils wasn't sure how to proceed after that, but something needed to be clarified right away. "Um, listen, Lady Raeya..."

"Please, call me Raeya."

"Fine, Raeya. I don't think—"

"Wait."

"What?"

"You actually did it."

"...Should I not have?"

"No, no, it's fine. It's just that most men would say something like, 'Oh, I could never do such a thing, my lady. It would be far too informal of me after only just making your acquaintance.'"

Probably because they're all stuffy nobles, Nils thought. "Excuse me, then," he said, "but where I'm from, we take people at their word."

"And where are you from?"

She didn't seem to notice the jab, and Nils knew better than to talk about himself. If he accidentally gave too much information, Dreygard could find out where he'd been assigned, and then he may as well have kept his ID tags and dangled them in front of the domiseer's face. If the man found out, would he force Nils to go back? Just the thought of it was enough to send fingers of dread up his spine. The darkness, so deep…

"Nils?"

"Never mind about me," he said. "I'm not worth your interest."

"Of course you are. I want to know everything there is to know about my future husband."

"That," he said, "is what we need to talk about. I am *not* your future husband."

"Yes, you are. You kissed me and—"

"And survived, yes, I got that. But what makes you think this curse or whatever is legitimate? Have any men actually died kissing you?"

Raeya lowered her eyes, her spark guttering out. "Yes."

"Oh. Well, how many? Couldn't it just have been a coincidence? If it was only one—"

"Three."

Nils froze.

"Three have died. Two of them were greedy, and apparently also doubters of my curse's power. When they learned of my secret, they thought they could easily set themselves up to inherit my father's estate and title with a simple kiss, so they forced themselves on me. The third…I…I don't wish to speak about it just now."

Raeya looked like a wilted flower sitting there beside him, and Nils found himself hesitating. He'd never believed in soulmates—still didn't, the whole idea was absurd—but she…

There's no need to feel pity for her, Nils reminded himself. *The Dreygards could use a little more misfortune in their lives. If she really has some kind of a curse, then it must be…*

"A spellweaver," Nils said, "did this to you?"

Raeya kept her eyes down, and nodded.

"Here, in Chanterey? What happened?"

Raeya pressed her lips thin, and before she could answer one of the guards broke the silence.

"My lady, we need to take him back with us now."

"What?" Raeya said. "What is this about? Father gave me permission to meet with Nils."

"Yes, my lady, but his orders were for only a few minutes."

"A few minutes?" Raeya huffed. "That isn't sufficient at all—we've barely spoken! Surely you can give us a little longer."

"The orders are straight from Lord Dreygard, my lady."

"This is ridiculous. I'm going to speak with him right now." She stood from the bench. "Nils, you wait here for me."

"We are to take him back to the guardhouse, my lady," a guard told her.

"The *guardhouse*," Raeya said, flinging up her hands. "That's another thing I shall talk to Father about. I can't believe he has my future husband staying in the *guardhouse*. Nils, I'll see to it you get a proper room, here in the manor house. And some proper clothes, too—not those servant's garments they've given you. Now, stay here, no matter *what* these men say, and I'll be back soon." She gave him a little smile, then her face was all business again as she strutted away. Her attendant followed, sparing Nils one last dirty look on the way. Nils and the guards watched them both until they were gone from sight.

"Get up," a guard ordered. "We're going."

Nils stood. "Fine by me."

3 A MEMORY OF MEETING

Nils stared at the opening to the pit. A great black hole cut into the earth. Every nerve in his body fired a warning signal at the same time, and he never would've moved from that spot had the tasker behind him not held a weapon.

A group of men filed down from the other side of the opening as Nils started to move forward. Grungy, smelly, and coated in black dust, one of them fell into line next to Nils. Through the grime, Nils could still distinguish his tan skin and dark red hair.

He flashed a grim smile at Nils. "New recruit, huh?" he said. "Welcome to Gen Rill. If you ever wanted to know what the darkness of Hearthnight was like, you're about to find out."

4 GUARDHOUSE

Maybe I made a mistake, Nils thought that evening. Whether or not Raeya had succeeded in changing her father's mind, Nils had spent the entire day in the guardhouse, surrounded by Dreygard's men with nothing to do but watch guards come and go and wrestle with his thoughts.

He'd tried again and again to plan his escape, but he couldn't see any openings. How was he supposed to slip away with two watchmen glued to him at every moment? It wasn't like Nils could knock them out and run—they were each a head taller than him, and there was no point comparing the difference in strength. And, in the unlikely event he managed to get away from them *and* escape the guardhouse, he'd have to evade all the guards on the grounds, get over the wall, and do it all without Tawson to keep a lookout and provide information on any weak points in the manor's security.

A persistent knot wound tighter in Nils' stomach. *What am I going to do?*

He sighed and stared down at his fingernails, frowning at the black dust underneath that refused to be washed away no matter how hard he tried. He heard a distant clinking sound, and shook his head. He couldn't pull any stunts like he had back then. Not with his personal sentinels watching him vigilantly the entire day.

Or until their shift change. Nils watched two new guards come to take over watching him with no-doubt equal vigilance, a brown-haired man with square shoulders and a burly, blond man that was tall enough he probably had to duck to fit through doorways half of the time. They chatted briefly with the other watchmen, and Nils listened without enthusiasm until something caught his attention.

"I told you it was three," one of them said. "Heard it straight from those cursed lips of hers."

"Weaver's blood," said the brown-haired man. "She's offed more blokes than most of us."

"Wonder if it was worth it," another said, and they all laughed.

"She must be quite a kisser, if they keep trying it."

They all believe in Raeya's curse, Nils thought. Even Lord Dreygard seemed to believe it. Raeya Dreygard couldn't be trusted any more than her father, but still, it seemed a strange thing to lie about. It was perhaps more likely that Raeya was delusional, or at least highly mistaken—

"Hey, what are you looking at?" one of the guards spat at Nils, and he realized he'd been staring. He looked back down at his hands.

"Nothing."

"Well, it's bedtime for you, Soulmate. Come on, move quick."

Nils grimaced at the nickname, but more at the guard's choice of words. "Quick*ly*," he muttered as he rose from his seat.

"Did you say something?" the guard said gruffly, grabbing Nils by the collar and pulling him forward.

"N-no," Nils replied.

"Good," the guard said, smacking him hard across the face. "Now get moving."

Nils obeyed, not even daring to touch his stinging cheek as he walked. *Fives,* did such a small thing really warrant a hit like that? *Of course,* he thought. *These are Dreygard's men. They'll be as forgiving as the taskers.* In that case, he was lucky he hadn't gotten worse. He squeezed his eyes shut to try to banish the pain, and when he opened them he found someone else about to pass them by. A young man, maybe a few years older than Nils, with a confident bearing and dark brown hair. Uncommonly dark for the region—a visitor from another province, perhaps? His fine clothes painted him a nobleman, or not a guard, at any rate. He was studying Nils in a way that made him uncomfortable, but then he gave a slight smile and an even slighter nod of greeting before walking past.

Odd, Nils thought, but he kept himself from craning his neck to look behind. Instead he said a silent prayer to Desna that his guards were taking him to a small, solitary room with a window to sleep for the night, someplace with much better escape prospects than where he'd been kept all afternoon.

Of course nothing was ever that easy. He was taken straight to where the guards bunked. All of the guards. And there were no windows.

Thanks a lot, Desna.

"There," the heavy-handed guard said, indicating a pile of straw with a sheet thrown over it. Admittedly, Nils had slept in far worse places. He lay down wordlessly, though his face still hurt and his head thrummed with all of the impossible escape plans he'd concocted during the day. *It won't work,* he thought as each one flipped by. *None of them will work. Not tonight. Not tomorrow night. Not as long as I'm here.*

But what if I wasn't here?

He remembered Raeya's promise to get him a room in the manor house. Would her father ever allow that? To be honest he was surprised the domiseer had allowed his daughter to meet with him at all. If Raeya could manage that, maybe she could manage more. She did seem to have a knack for getting her way.

Well, I'm not getting out of here tonight, Nils told his wayward thoughts, *so I may as well sleep.* Generally telling himself that wouldn't have helped at all, but this time, he was exhausted enough that it worked.

★ ★ ★

It was dark when Nils opened his eyes. Too dark. He could hear the sound of hammers clanking, echoes of men shouting. He looked down at the lantern in his hands, its flame barely sufficient to light his way. It flickered, and his heart jumped.

Don't go out, he prayed. The others were too far away. It was the only light. If it went out, there would be nothing but the blackness. Already the shadows fought to close in on him, pushing closer and closer to the lantern, intent on snuffing it out and consuming him. It flickered again, that fragile light, flickered and vanished and the shadows surged into his lungs—

Nils sat up and gasped. One of his hands gripped the front of his shirt while the other supported him and felt the sharp prickle of straw through a bed sheet. The guards on duty raised their heads to look at him.

Not real, he consoled himself, trying to steady his breathing. *Just the same nightmare. It wasn't real.* He shook his head once to clear it, and was about to lie back down when movement caught his eye. A shadow shifting in the barracks. The guards didn't seem to notice, or at least they paid it no mind.

This room is full of men, Nils thought. *One of them probably had to use the latrine. Get a grip, Nils.*

He forced himself to lie down, but his heart was still pounding, and not just because of the nightmare. Something just felt...off.

Of course something feels off, he told himself. *You're stuck in the Dreygards' guardhouse and the daughter of that vile traitor wants to marry you. Now go back to sleep.*

5 THIEF'S EYES

"Why didn't you do as I asked?"

Raeya Dreygard stood before Nils with hands on her hips and a consternated look on her face. An angry glare was provided by her ever-present attendant.

"I told you to wait for me in the library," she went on. "Why did you leave?"

Nils glanced at his watchmen. "The armed guards were very persuasive," he said.

"Well next time, stand your ground and show some courage," she replied. "One day you'll be in charge of every guard in this place, and you'll need to earn their respect."

Nils doubted that. "Your father made it quite clear that he doesn't find me worthy."

"He just needs some time to be convinced. Any man worthy of being my husband is certainly worthy of inheriting his estate. No matter how rough around the edges you may seem at first. Isn't that right, Tilda?" Raeya added with a glance at her still-glaring attendant.

Tilda adopted a look of snobbish indifference instead. "I suppose so, my lady."

"Now, come sit down," Raeya ordered Nils, taking a seat on another plush bench and patting the space beside her. Sitting in the guardhouse for another day suddenly seemed a lot more appealing, but Nils complied. At least in here he could continue looking around the manor house.

This morning they occupied a private drawing room, and while it lacked the shelves of books present in the library, there were still plenty of curios and art pieces to draw Nils' eye. *Could any of these be foreign?* he wondered, surveying a row of porcelain figurines. There was a horse with a black stone adorning its forehead that was of particular interest, but perhaps it was a little too shiny to be—

"Nils, dear, if you keep staring like that the guards will think you're about to make off with our decorations. Money won't be an issue for you anymore, you know, so there's no point in trying to steal anything."

"What? Oh, I wasn't going to steal anything." Not with the guards staring at him every second and a death-threat hanging over his head.

Raeya raised a skeptical eyebrow, then tilted her head to examine the other side of his face. "Is that a bruise on your cheek? Did one of the watchmen strike you?" Her eyes darted to the guards and back to him, sharp as needles.

"Yes," Nils admitted.

"You *have* been trying to steal, haven't you?"

"No, I was just being…smart," he said. There. Leave it up to the guards to figure out if he meant smart-mouthed or intelligent, assuming they were clever enough to notice the double meaning.

Raeya sighed. "Perhaps you've been stealing to provide for the poor."

"No."

"Or, perhaps *lying* is your vice."

"Also no. Look," Nils said. "I wasn't—"

"Regardless," Raeya cut him off, "I won't have *anyone* marring your face for *any* reason. Is that clear?" she said, turning her needle-gaze back on the watchmen.

"As you say, my lady," one of them replied, although the man who'd actually struck him was absent.

Raeya settled back in her seat, and her attendant handed her a book which she opened eagerly, holding it in her hand in a way that looked as natural to her as breathing air. While maintaining her perfect posture, she shifted a little closer to Nils and linked her free arm in his. He looked down at it like she'd spilled something foul on him, but didn't dare scoot away. He wasn't sure what the guards might consider to be "mistreatment of Lord Dreygard's daughter." Resigned to his fate, he skimmed a few lines of Raeya's book, then wrinkled his nose. Fiction.

"My Father lifted our silly time restriction, but we'll have to part ways during lunch, I'm afraid," she said without taking her eyes off the page.

Well, what a bummer.

"Father doesn't think we should eat meals together. Just one more temporary inconvenience, though, don't you worry."

Oh, I'm not worried, Nils thought. *Please, take your time eating. Though, I wonder...* "Did he have anything more to say about me sleeping in the guardhouse?"

Raeya looked unconcerned. "He hasn't changed his mind," she said, "yet. But I'm sure it's only a matter of time. My mother agrees with me that you ought to have a proper room."

So it would be the guardhouse again tonight. For some reason, the thought made Nils shiver.

"Are you cold?" Raeya asked. She leaned her head on his shoulder without waiting for an answer, as though her closeness would warm him. In truth, it was the simmering rage emanating from Tilda that seemed to raise the room temperature a few degrees. Nils quickly forgot about it though, as Raeya's sleeve fell away with her movement, and her bare wrist caught his eye.

Soft, fair skin. Just the faintest hint of blue veins beneath.

Normal. Not that he should've expected much different—if she'd had anything to hide, she would've done a better job of hiding it.

But that wasn't the only thing to be seen. She also wore a silver chain, woven around four gemstones. Emerald, diamond, ruby, sapphire. Nils had never seen one outside of a church, but its purpose was unmistakable. A prayer bracelet. It held a divine stone for each of the four gods, and it was said that by touching the appropriate stone when you prayed, the god was more likely to listen to your request. The jewels were small, but it was still worth a fortune.

If only I'd had that last night, Nils thought. *Maybe Desna would've actually listened.* He tilted his head a little to see more of the chain, see if there was anything else embedded there. *Nothing. No fifth stone. I suppose that would've been too convenient.* He wondered briefly if it could be a sign of her innocence; in spite of what he knew about her father, maybe Raeya was oblivious to it all.

Or maybe she just had common sense. To possess a weaver's stone was to break one of the highest laws of the kingdom, and no one with at least a flea's intelligence would blatantly advertise that on their wrist—

"Nils."

Nils looked up to find Raeya's eyes no longer on her book, but fixed on his. "You're staring again."

Fives. "For the record," Nils said, grimacing at the thought of the guards watching his every move, "I wasn't making any plans to steal your bracelet, either."

* * *

Half an eternity later, Raeya finally departed for lunch. Nils' watchmen took him down to the servants' hall for a small meal, and at last the true state of the kingdom showed itself. Floorboards were broken or missing entirely, giving way to sections of packed earth and straw. There wasn't a chair in the place, nor any item that wasn't entirely necessary to cater to the floors above. Bowls were cracked, cups chipped, cutlery bent and sparse enough that most of the servants ate with their hands. It felt like...well, it felt like being home again.

Nils understood the rift between the rich and poor. Even if it wasn't fair, it was expected. A longstanding feature of society. Some had it better than others, and he could live with that. He didn't even begrudge his own place in the lower end of the spectrum. But what was happening here, and out in the towns...it wasn't that simple. Nils glanced around at the other servants, all of whom avoided his gaze, or perhaps that of his guards. Did they know the extent of their master's corruption? Did they know what he kept within these very walls?

He caught a piece of conversation, a question of the border between Branaden and Galreyva. Still quiet. No news. Words of relief, but tones of fear. Everyone was waiting for it, the day when Galreyva would strike again. Word had it they'd bled themselves nearly as dry as Branaden in their attempt at conquering it, but everyone still expected them to recover first. Branaden wasn't ready. Nearly ten years had passed, and the country was still struggling to find its feet. Nils could only guess how the Galreyvans were faring, but he knew for a fact they had one advantage Branaden didn't.

Two, if you counted their blasphemous magic. Spellweavers were rare even in a land that revered them, but it didn't take many to cause a great deal of damage.

Nils wasn't usually one to engage strangers in conversation, but he wished he could now more than ever, wished he could gain even a hint of a way to escape, or of a potential ally in his midst. Someone who knew, to any extent, what Nils knew. But anyone like that could never talk freely with the domiseer's guards in the room, and he simply wouldn't have any chances to speak to them alone.

*In fact the only servant I have any regular contact with is…*Nils almost could've laughed. *Tilda. Desna's Tresses, I'm really desperate now. The guards themselves would be more likely to help.*

A stupid thought, even if it was true, but…*Fives, why not. I have to try something, and Raeya did order them not to hit me.*

On their way back upstairs, Nils cleared his throat and tried to mimic Tawson's nonchalant way of talking, minus the northern accent. "You two must get paid well for this job, huh? Working for the domiseer himself. What's that like, anyway?"

The guard in front of him paused to give him a quizzical look, but the one behind pushed them forward. "What's it like to work? Guess you wouldn't know, would ya, Soulmate?"

Well, that was about what Nils expected, but even so he felt something inside of him shrink. "Funny," he said, forcing himself to try again. "But really, the domiseer—he has to be strict, right?"

"Are you saying it's anything less than an honor to serve on a domiseer's estate?"

Nils swallowed, ready to flee back into his mind, but the damage was done.

"You ought to be groveling at his feet for keeping you alive, not being a disrespectful little mudhopper," the guard said, raising a hand. "For your lady, I'll try not to leave a mark."

Nils clamped his eyelids shut, waiting for the sting, but it never came.

"I think that's enough," said a new voice, and Nils opened his eyes to see a fourth person standing there with them, holding the guard's wrist. It was the dark-haired man Nils had seen in the guardhouse yesterday.

"A-apologies, sir," said the guard. The man nodded once, then let go of the watchman and held his hand out to Nils.

"Jarik Sowell," he said. Nils put his hand out somewhat lamely, and Jarik shook it with a firm grasp, his eyes searching out every detail of his face. "So you are the one," he said.

"The...one who stole from the manor?" Nils asked.

"Yes, but more importantly, the one who stole a kiss from Lady Raeya. Someday I'd hoped to try it, if she'd allow it, but now...well, maybe I ought to thank you for saving my life." He cracked a small smile. "Sorry for the cold start. You'll forgive me a little disappointment, won't you?"

"Over Raeya?"

"Of course. She has the grace of our warm-weather goddesses, does she not?" He breathed out a small sigh.

"...If you say so," Nils replied. "So you...believe her curse is real?"

Jarik cocked his head. "Do you doubt it?"

"Well, I..." *I think she and everyone else here have lost their minds,* he thought. "I'm still trying to wrap my head around it. I haven't heard anything about how she got this curse, so I guess I do have my doubts."

"I see. Well, I don't know all the details, but I know it happened in Borlund. Lord Dreygard was meeting there with Lord Ashber and took his family along with him to sightsee. Lady Raeya got lost in the woods and encountered a spellweaver. The poor dear was only nine, can you imagine?"

What I can't imagine is taking a nine-year-old to Borlund, Nils thought. *That close to the border? I don't care how nice the sights are.* "Was this before or after the war?"

"Just after, I believe."

So Lord Dreygard met with someone near the border just after the war fizzled out, Nils thought to himself. *Something tells me it wasn't the Ashbers.*

"Well, I won't keep you," Jarik said. "It was an honor to meet you, Nils…"

"Oakander."

"Mr. Oakander." Jarik gave a slight bow and went on his way, leaving Nils in a state of some bewilderment.

Mr. Oakander. An honor to meet you. He looked down at himself just to make sure he still looked like a peasant in servant's clothing. *He's either mudbrained or mocking me.*

Though he had to admit, this was this first time he'd met a noble he didn't immediately dislike.

★ ★ ★

When Nils was brought back to Raeya, she was wearing a shawl and long gloves. "I thought we'd go for a walk," she said, putting on a smile. "Desna's finally taken pity on us and given us some sunshine." After an awkward pause in which Nils declined to speak, she added, "Would that be agreeable?"

He shrugged. "No less agreeable than anything else."

Raeya's smile was noticeably strained. "Fantastic. Let's go then, shall we?"

Nils trudged along, scowling again at the expensive carpet as they exited the manor house. Once outside, Raeya shooed his guards away with a white-gloved hand. "Give us some space, won't you? I want to walk with my betrothed, not his watchmen."

"My lady, we can't—"

"I know, I know. I'm not asking you to abandon your post, only to walk a couple of steps behind us. You can manage that much, can't you?"

The guards looked about as exasperated as Nils felt, but they didn't challenge her further. They let her and Nils walk ahead, if only barely, while Tilda trotted along to the side.

"I'm not your betrothed," Nils reminded her.

"Not yet, my dear."

She blushed a little at her own words. Fives, she was naive. Did she really expect Nils would go along with this? Or her father, for that matter? "Raeya, listen, I don't—"

There was a great gust of wind, and Raeya's cry of dismay cut him off. "Ah, Desna, where is your kindness?" she said, stopping short and employing her fingers in a vain attempt at fixing her hair. "And I'm wearing gloves, of course. Now it will just stick up all over the place."

"Let me, my lady," Tilda said, coming over to smooth her hair back into place.

"Thank you, Tilda. Goodness, it's a cold wind too. I've had quite enough of Kirit's weather. If he doesn't withdraw soon, he'll be the next to lose his season."

Nils lifted a brow. "That's quite a statement over a little wind."

"Yes, you're right," Raeya said, recovering herself and straightening her shawl. "Forgive my outburst. I suppose my hair is as much at fault as the wind. It's always getting in the way like that."

"You could cut it shorter, you know."

"What, like a common scullery maid?" she said, clutching her orange locks and looking at him like he'd suggested murder.

Yes, she was a Dreygard, all right. "Forget I said it, then."

Raeya took in his sour expression. "Wait, could it be…that you prefer short hair?"

Nils looked at her, one hand still grasping her tresses, her blue-gray eyes wide and worried. He was almost tempted to say yes just to see how she'd respond. Maybe she'd actually cut it.

But then she'd probably be upset afterward, and her father would say it was his fault, and he wasn't about to hang for tricking a girl into cutting off her hair. "I don't have any particular preference."

"Oh," Raeya said, while her body language said something more like, "Thank the gods and praise them too." She took a deep breath and let it go with a smile like sunshine. Whatever Jarik had said about her having grace like the goddesses…it was more like dramatic flair.

"That's better," Raeya said.

"Hm?"

"You were staring again, but this time at me," she said, cheeks turning rosy for a second time.

"Oh. I was thinking about Jarik Sowell."

"You were…what?" Her sunshine turned to rainclouds.

"Jarik. I met him earlier. He seems…fond of you."

"A little too fond," Raeya said with an irritated sigh. "He's practically lived here this past year. I wish he would take a hint and leave."

"Who is he, exactly?"

"A relative of the domiseer of Tormeron. His nephew."

"And you don't like him?"

"He *seems* nice and all," she said, "but…he has the same look in his eyes as the other two."

"Other two?"

"You know."

Oh. The ones who'd kissed her and weren't so lucky as Nils. There wasn't a drop of light left in Raeya's visage now. "You think he's just after your father's estate? He didn't seem that way to me."

"Well, he's after something. I'm a good judge of these things."

Nils had his doubts about that, regardless of her experience with the other two men. *She said there was a third man who died…I wonder what—*

"Enough about Jarik; it's ruining our walk," Raeya said, linking her arm in his. "Let's talk about something else. Like weddings. Do you prefer Pria's season, or Raulen's?"

Nils let out a groan that couldn't be contained no matter how uptight he was about the guards, and turned his head to look at the outbuilding they were passing. The door opened and a few men came out, the last of which was Feren Dreygard.

And there was Nils, walking by, arm linked to Raeya Dreygard while she prattled on about weddings. He could've died right then and there, even before Lord Dreygard's eyes fell on him like a searing hot iron.

"Hello, Father," Raeya called to him, clinging tighter to Nils' arm as though it gave her reason to be proud. The domiseer's frown deepened, but he said nothing, going back to his business without another glance in their direction.

But Nils swore he could feel an angry heat on his back for a long while after they passed him.

6 A GIFT OR A CURSE

Nils was almost relieved to go back to the guardhouse that evening. It was cold and full of strangers who hated him, but at least none of them were eager to discuss wedding plans.

When the hour was late enough, the guards took Nils to his straw-bed, and he collapsed onto it without pause. *Ow,* he thought. There was something hard under the sheet. Certainly harder than straw. He began to reach a hand under, but decided to pull the sheet back instead. No need to get scratched up pawing through stiff hay.

When the sheet was withdrawn and the straw pushed aside, Nils squinted in the torch light. Not because he couldn't see what was there, but because he couldn't believe it.

It was a knife.

Nils' heart stuttered. Had someone left it there to help him? An ally he didn't know he had? The guards wouldn't have seen the knife yet; from their angle, they wouldn't know what he'd found. He could grab it, hide it, and use it, when the opportunity presented itself. But what if he didn't get the chance? What if someone found the knife on him before he'd made an escape? The leather sheath looked to be of fine quality. He'd be accused of stealing it, and then killed. Perhaps Lord Dreygard had left it there as bait for that very reason.

But if not…should he pass up the opportunity? He reached trembling fingers toward it, almost touched the handle…

But there was a better question. If he got the chance, would he actually be able to use it on someone? There was a reason he'd carried no weapons when he'd broken in. He hadn't lied to the domiseer about that.

"What're you doing?" a guard drawled, and Nils made up his mind.

"There's a knife here," he said. "S-someone left a knife under my bedding."

"What?" The man came over, peering down past Nils. "What in the—Did you put that there?"

"How could I? I was under guard all day."

"Weaver's blood," the man said, stooping to pick up the knife. "Somebody musta—"

His words cut off the moment his fingers wrapped around the weapon. "Aran?" asked the other on-duty guard, the ridiculously tall one with blond hair. "What is it? Aran?"

Aran tore the sheath off the knife and lunged right at Nils. Nils threw himself to the side and scrambled to his feet, barely in time to dodge another swipe from the watchman.

"Aran, what in Desna's name are ya doing?" the tall guard said, grabbing his wrists and trying to wrestle the knife from him. Aran shrugged him off, his eerily blank eyes fixed on Nils, and flew at him the moment he was free. Nils shuffled backward, crashing into another guard who had come over to help, while several more rushed past. Every guard in the barracks must've heard the commotion, and it took nearly all of them to restrain Aran and force the knife from his hands. It fell to the ground with a *thunk*, and Aran sank to his knees.

"Aran, man, what in Hearthnight came over you?" the tall guard asked. Aran groaned and lifted his head with effort, then seemed to frighten awake the moment his eyes focused on the knife. "Get that thing away," he said, waving an arm wildly. "Get it away!" He stumbled to his feet, trying to move backward, but the other guards held him. "Let me go. That thing is cursed!"

Cursed. Nils' blood chilled in his veins, and if the guard he'd crashed into hadn't been holding his arms, he might've sunk to his knees.

The tall guard approached the knife and nudged it with his foot.

"No, don't touch it—Don't touch it!" Aran shouted.

The watchman deliberated, then looked to his fellow guards. "Be ready to stop me," he said, "if something goes wrong." He looked at Nils next. "And get him away." Nils wished they would've taken him outside—better yet, out of the country—but he had to settle for the far side of the room.

"Don't do it, Bern, you're crazy," Aran said. Indecision dripped from Bern's brow, but he stooped and picked up the knife by the handle.

The whole room held its breath. Nothing happened.

Bern wiped his face with his sleeve. "Well. Guess it's safe now."

"That thing made me attack him, I swear," Aran said. "You know it wasn't me, right? What reason would I have?"

The guards all looked at Aran, then looked around at each other as though trying to guess what the others were thinking. They all seemed like believers to Nils, if the fear in their eyes meant anything. "We'll...we'll have to report it to the captain one way or another," Bern said. Aran appeared most shaken of all, but he nodded. He glanced once at Nils, then down at the floor.

Nils believed him. That knife had been planted there for a reason, by someone who wanted Nils dead. Even now the men were whispering the word amongst themselves. *Spellweaver.* It would be a weaver skilled in cursing inanimate objects, choosing his words so that whoever touched the knife would forget all else except killing his target.

If Nils had picked it up, he would've killed himself. The spell would've vanished after the first use, as it did for Aran. No one would've known there was a curse at all. It would've just been a prisoner's suicide. An untraceable murder.

There was no doubt in Nils' mind who had done it. He could still feel the heat of the man's gaze, hating him, wishing death upon him. He couldn't do it by any direct means, not with the promise he'd made to his daughter. If he couldn't catch Nils stealing, he'd just eliminate him another way. And the fact that the knife was cursed only confirmed one of Nils' greatest suspicions.

Lord Dreygard wasn't only a traitor. He was a spellweaver.

7 A MEMORY OF DISCOVERY

"Nils, man, you're shaking. What is it?"

Nils slumped down against the wall of rock where Tawson was sitting, a lantern at his feet and a water flask in his hand. "The tasker's logbook," he said. "He was just standing there with it open."

"You read it?"

"Yes."

"Fives. Mudbrained bloke probably figured nobody here could read, so he didn't bother hiding it. Well, what did it say?"

"It was mostly lists and numbers, and some of it was in code, but there was enough for me to figure it out. I mean, I already knew our economy made no sense. If we're the richest province in the kingdom, where is all the wealth? For a long time I figured it was just being hoarded by the upper classes, or funneled toward the military, but that can only account for so much."

"So…"

"So Dreygard's even worse than we thought. Everything we're working to death to accomplish? It isn't helping our country at all. He's giving it straight to our fiving enemies. The ones who ravaged our land in the first place."

Tawson's eyes flashed. "The Galreyvans?"

"Yes. He's trading with them. The man's a filthy traitor."

"Weaver's blood."

"To make matters worse, I…I think he's receiving weaver's stone in return."

"Weaver's—are you kidding? You think Dreygard's using it himself?"

"It seems fitting. Regardless, I can't stand this, Taws. I can't just let this go."

"I agree. But what are we gonna do?"

"I don't know, but I won't stay here and fill Emperor Ri'sen's purse. Not one second longer than I have to."

Tawson grinned, firelight glinting on his teeth. "Count me in—and after we escape, I say we find a way to visit ol' Dreygard and show him just how we feel about this."

Nils dropped his voice lower. "What, an assassination?" Tawson nodded, and Nils shook his head. "I won't kill him. Even if he deserves it, I won't…" Nils glanced down the tunnel where a whip cracked in the darkness, a distorted shadow disrupting the flickers of lanterns. The scream that followed was agony just to hear. Nils swallowed. "I wouldn't have the stomach for it."

"Fine. I'll do it. Or, if you'd rather, we find a way to reveal the traitorous cur for what he is, and let the king give him the punishment he deserves."

Nils mulled it over. The whip was cracking again, more screams. "I like that plan, but…"

"What?"

"I don't know, Taws. I'm just not made for this sort of thing, and I—" Nils took a breath. "I need to check on something back home."

"Suit yourself," Tawson said. "But we're getting out of here, yeah?"

"Yes," Nils said, tightening his hand into a fist, feeling the grit of earth digging into his palm. "I have an idea."

Tawson grinned again. "Let's hear it. We have about three seconds left of our break, and then we'll be the ones getting the flesh whipped off our bones."

8 DARK STONE, DARK ROOM

Chrysolin. A black stone, nearly as hard as diamond, but with a more subdued luster. The gem of the fallen god Lyare, and the substance necessary for spellweaving.

Nils thought he'd found a weaver's stone the night he'd broken in, embedded in that necklace. What better way to smuggle a forbidden material into the country than to hide it in a common item? But chrysolin never would've broken so easily. Only weaving a spell would manifest any fragility in the gem, disintegrating it into a vanishing dust.

There had to have been chrysolin in that chest, or if not that, at least some proof of where it had come from. Taws had received word that a small but well-guarded shipment was on its way to the domiseer, its origin unknown, and nothing could've smelled more strongly of suspicious conduct. Nils was certain he'd found the right chest, right where he'd been told he'd find it, so everything should've lined up.

He just hadn't had time. Hadn't been able to look thoroughly enough. Yes, there must've been some proof in that box, it just wasn't the necklace.

But now…did it even matter? If Dreygard was a spellweaver, seeing his wrists was all the confirmation Nils would need.

Today, the domiseer once again wore leather cuffs.

"I'm done with him," Lord Dreygard said, waving one of those cuffed wrists as though Nils were a dog to be taken away by its handlers. The domiseer had questioned all of the guards before hearing Nils' version of what had happened the previous night. It was ironic, being questioned about an attempted murder by the would-be murderer himself. The domiseer hadn't let on to any involvement, but Nils wasn't fooled. If he could serve the king for this long without his treachery being known, he no doubt had a well-practiced poker face.

Nils was given a bowl of gruel at the guardhouse, which he ate without tasting, spoon shaking just enough to betray the nerves he tried to suppress. On one hand, this was all a good thing. He'd all but confirmed that Dreygard was a spellweaver, something he could use against him. On the other hand, this meant his enemy possessed an inhuman power that he would almost certainly employ again and again until he actually succeeded in killing Nils.

And here he thought unwanted betrothal might be the worst of his problems.

When Nils was cleared to leave the guardhouse, his watchmen took him back to the manor. The moment he stepped through the front doors, something soft and warm latched itself onto him.

"Nils!" a female voice cried uncomfortably close to his ear. "Oh, darling, I was so worried. Are you all right?"

"I'd be better if you let go," Nils said after a failed attempt at breathing.

Raeya backed up enough to search his face. "You look even paler than usual," she observed, putting a hand on his forehead. "What a horrid thing to happen. I would've come to see you right away, but Father forbade me from leaving the house until this is all cleared up."

Her hand wandered to his cheek, and Nils pushed it away when it didn't seem she'd be removing it herself. "I doubt you have anything to worry about," he said. "The curse was targeted at me."

"The what?" Raeya said, eyes widening.

"On the knife," Nils said. "Didn't you hear...?" He trailed off, looking to the watchmen on either side of him. They both seemed determined not to meet his eyes.

"Hear what?" Raeya asked. "Father said one of his guards lost his temper and attacked you. Did something else happen?"

"I..."

Could he say so? Dreygard had covered it up—unsurprisingly—and had probably ordered his guards to keep silent. So what would they do with Nils if he spouted off about it?

"Never mind," Nils said. "I'm just...overwhelmed at the moment. Can we sit somewhere?" He was reeling a bit, either from lack of sleep or the residual shock of the previous night. Or perhaps bad gruel.

"Of course," Raeya said, still looking concerned. "Come, we'll go to the parlor. I have good news to help cheer you up," she said, taking him by the arm again. "After what happened, Father's finally come around to my request. You'll be staying in the manor house from now on."

"Really?" Nils said. That *was* good news. The domiseer must've felt he had no choice but to allow it if he wasn't going to look suspicious.

"He hasn't told me which room, so that probably means it isn't a guest suite, as it ought to be," Raeya drawled, "but at least it will be better than the guardhouse."

Nils didn't care if it was a storage room, as long as it was private and had a window. Maybe there was hope for an escape yet. He needed one now more than ever if he didn't want to risk contact with any more cursed items.

Gods, it could be anything, he realized. *Lord Dreygard will be smart enough not to use the same thing twice. The next time I pick up a fork, I could end up stabbing myself with it until I've bled to death. I doubt the guards would even try to stop me.*

With that thought, he resolved to avoid contact with sharp objects at all costs.

* * *

The rest of the day dragged by. All Nils could think about was getting to his room that night. *Will the watchmen stand right in the room with me?* he wondered, feeling an unpleasant tug in his stomach. He couldn't very well break out of a window with two armed guards staring at him, and they probably weren't unprofessional enough to fall asleep on the job. There was nothing for it but to wait and see, and yet Nils couldn't stop his mind from poring over every detail of every way the scenario might play out. By the end of the day, he was exhausted.

"I still don't understand why that guard would just attack you like that," Raeya said. "You truly don't know what you did to anger him?"

"No," Nils groaned, wishing she would drop it. This was at least the fourth time she'd asked him that.

"Perhaps it's your history as a thief, and he was once your victim? Or perhaps the guard was *in league* with someone. Yes, someone else could've hired him because they knew he could reach you. Someone with a personal vendetta, some grievance with the thief who stole his most valuable family heirloom…"

Nils raised a brow. Where did she come up with this stuff?

"No, I just can't picture it," Raeya said. "Why should anyone be trying to kill you?"

"I can't imagine," Nils droned.

Raeya looked at him hard. "You aren't implying my father had something to do with this, are you?"

Nils tensed. *Fives.* "Well—"

"You think he ordered his guard to kill you in secret!"

"Um…" What should he say? At least she hadn't said anything about spellweaving or curses; if she brought that up to Dreygard, Nils would be slaughtered immediately. "He does…have quite a strong reason to hate me," Nils finally squeaked out.

"No," Raeya said, "it was *not* him, I guarantee it. He promised me you wouldn't be harmed, as long as you behave yourself. I trust him completely."

"If you say so," Nils said. Better to let Raeya be the victor in this argument, even if she was wrong.

"Although, on that note, why hasn't my father issued you more guards? Screening them for reliability, of course," Raeya said, eyeing the watchmen behind her. "If your life is in danger, you should be thoroughly protected."

"They aren't here to protect me," Nils reminded her, "they're here to protect you *from* me. It's not as though they're my bodyguards."

Raeya looked especially irked by this, but she couldn't deny the truth. She sighed, then looked back at him.

"You seem tired," she observed, trying to check the temperature of his forehead again. He shrugged her off a little less gently this time.

"I didn't exactly sleep last night," he said.

"Of course," Raeya said, holding her hand like he'd wounded it, though he hadn't even touched it. "I…suppose you'd like to leave my company and get some rest, then."

"That would be nice."

"Nils, do you…dislike being with me?"

"Huh?" Nils glanced from Raeya to Tilda, to the guards, and back to Raeya. Everyone seemed to be waiting for an answer. "I'm…tired," he reiterated. "That's all."

"But, it's just, you don't seem to enjoy yourself when we're together."

Nils blinked at her. "You do know I'm being held here against my will, right?"

"Yes, but I'm your true love! Aren't you excited to have found me? Doesn't your heart beat faster when we're together?"

Admittedly it was beating faster right now. Gods, what a time to have an audience. "Raeya, I don't believe in true love, or soulmates," he said. "That *fate* somehow places two people together. It's just a fantasy for romantics."

"The *gods*, not fate," Raeya said. "And how can you not believe? My curse—"

"I know what you think about your curse, but, well…maybe there's some other reason I'm immune to the spell."

"Impossible," Raeya insisted. "And can't you feel our connection? Every time we touch, it's like a shock races through my skin, and like a…like a *fire* surges up inside."

"Sounds painful," Nils said.

"Stop playing around—you must feel it too, right?" She placed her hand on top of his, letting their fingers mesh together. Her thumb gently brushed against his skin, and she looked up at him with a pink-tinted face. "Well?"

Her skin was soft as ever, and not unpleasant to touch, but it didn't exactly light a fire in his soul. Nils looked from their hands to Raeya's eyes and shook his head. "I don't feel anything."

Raeya's brow creased. "I...I see." She took her hand away, folding it in her lap. "Maybe...maybe it's different for men," she said. "Or perhaps it just takes a little longer for some people to feel it."

Or maybe you're out of your mind, Nils thought. His skepticism must've shown on his face, because she looked as though he'd said the words out loud.

"I'll go now, shall I?" Raeya said in a light voice that sounded a little too forced. "You can go and get some sleep. I hope you'll enjoy your room."

She left in a hurry without so much as a second look in his direction. Tilda bustled along after her, but stopped and turned back to Nils. "That's some way to treat a lady," she said, face matching her wine-colored blouse. "Do you have any idea how worried she was when she heard you'd been attacked?" She thrust a finger at his chest in a way reminiscent of Aran with the knife. "You don't deserve her," she said. She spun back around and hurried out of the room after her mistress.

Nils stared at the empty doorway when she'd gone. *Maybe not,* he thought, *but whoever said I wanted to?*

* * *

Finally, Nils was on his way to his new room in the manor house, and a potential way to escape. Now more than ever he should've been thinking about his plans, taking note of where he was in the manor, memorizing the hallways.

Instead his mind was stuck on his fiving conversation with Raeya Dreygard.

But I'm your true love! Aren't you excited to have found me? Those words kept repeating themselves. It was stupid, and Nils knew that, but…

But three men had died so far at the power of Raeya's curse. He believed that much was true, so then…did it really give validity to the idea of soulmates? And could Raeya possibly be *his?* Was there any escaping it, or was that in itself a curse, an unavoidable fate that left you bound to someone against your will?

If the gods really do tie people to one another, Nils thought, *then they have a terrible sense of humor, and I'm not playing along with their joke.*

They passed another hallway, and Nils looked down it, but didn't retain any information. *Blast it all,* he thought. *I can't focus. Why should I even care if I have a soulmate? There are more important things to worry about. Like getting out of this fiving manor tonight and seeing if any of this plan can be salvaged.*

He made a last great effort to take note of his surroundings. It seemed Raeya was right; this didn't look like a guest wing. It was still too nice to be servants' quarters, though. Maybe a place for the more important staff members, or visitors who weren't nobles. *Lesser* guests, as deemed by the Dreygards.

"Your fancy private room, Soulmate," one of the guards said, stopping in front of a door and opening it for him. Nils stepped in eagerly, looking around. It was dark, but the hallway's torches revealed a simple bed—on an actual frame, which was something— a small dresser, an unlit hearth, and…

No windows.

The door shut and locked behind Nils, and he was plunged into darkness. "Wait!" he said, spinning around. The guards had stayed outside. He was alone, no light, not even a lantern. "Hey!" He banged on the door, and the next three seconds felt like years before one of the watchmen opened it.

"What?" he said, looking at Nils like he was a madman.

"You...you haven't given me any light. Light the hearth, or give me a candle. Something."

"What, so you can start a fire? Your eyes will adjust."

"Not if there's no light at all. It doesn't work like that."

The guard smirked. "Afraid of the dark, eh, Soulmate?" He shared a glance with the other watchman—Bern from the barracks—who chuckled. "Guess you shoulda stayed in the guardhouse."

He shut the door again, the lock clicking as loud as an axe-fall, and Nils' heart pounded in his ears. He wanted to shout again, to bang on the wood, but he knew what kind of men wore smirks like those. They wouldn't have any pity. And neither would the darkness. He stood as still as possible, pretending the room was dark because his eyes were closed, but he knew his lids were wide open. He could feel the air on his unsheltered eyes. Slowly, slowly, a faint crack of light appeared. The gap under the door was small, the light outside dim, but it was something, and with time the darkness was a little less complete.

He stood there for several more minutes, breathing carefully, before he dared to turn around and shuffle toward where the bed ought to be. Yes, there was a vague shape there. He could manage this. As long as he could see something, he'd be all right. He climbed onto the bed and kept his eyes wide open, staring at the crack under the door until he fell asleep.

9 A MEMORY OF DARKNESS

For Nils' escape plan to work, he and Taws had to wait for a cave-in. They didn't have to wait long.

Nils knew the signs. He was hyper-aware of every rumble, every tremor in the rock. He just never imagined he'd find himself running toward the destruction. He and Taws moved quickly against the flow of frightened miners, toward the darkness ahead of them—deeper than the darkness behind them only because any pitiful light had been extinguished by falling rubble.

It was a bad one. Even though that served their purposes well, Nils felt queasy at the thought of the poor souls who'd actually been crushed. He and Taws were here on pretense; it was the only way he could think of to get out of this pit without being watched too closely to make an escape. No one got out of the mine without being hauled up by overseers, but overseers didn't pay much attention to the dead.

Nils and Taws crouched in the darkness near the rubble, waiting for the cart to come. As the bodies were piled, they watched for their opening, then, fighting every instinct, forcing down his revulsion, Nils sprinted for the cart, Taws right behind. He jumped on it while the workers were busy, falling still, shutting his eyes and trying to shut down his mind, to forget what lay around him, beneath him. His jaw groaned in protest at how tightly he clenched it, forcing himself to lie soundlessly in that pile of death.

The cart began moving, and Nils opened his eyes a crack. A mistake. The lantern at the front of the cart threw bouncing light over its macabre occupants, and Nils was face to face with a man who could no longer clench his jaw. Below his upper teeth, just a cavity of glistening darkness...

Nils snapped his eyes shut again, but he still had work to do. He had to remove himself not only from the mine, but from the tasker's record-books. He felt with his hands, trembling, jerking back at every touch of wetness, until he finally found the tags on the corpse in front of him, pulling them off over what remained of his head, unable to suppress a sob that would blessedly be covered up by the rattling cart.

The tags were off. Now to replace them with his own.

The cart hit a bump, and Nils' tags fell from his hand, down into the bodies beneath him. He tried to reach down and find them, sobbing, gasping. He couldn't do it. They were lost. But maybe it was enough. A body with no tags, and tags with no body. They could be matched together. Nils threw the dead man's tags off the moving cart, and prayed it was enough.

10 HOPE

Every night in that room passed as slowly as the first.

Nils doubted the guards truly feared him starting a fire. Rather, they were probably entertained by seeing him squirm. The mornings never came soon enough, and each one found him stiff and sore from being curled tightly in the same position all night. He could've sworn the gap under the door was narrower every time he sought it out in the darkness.

The days were nearly as unbearable as the nights. Nils had upset Raeya, even if she pretended otherwise. She'd spent nearly every moment of their time together reading in silence, and Nils wondered why she'd bothered to summon him at all. He'd gotten so bored he'd even started reading her books over her shoulder, as much as he hated fairy tales. But he wasn't about to apologize. He didn't even want Raeya to like him, and yet...

He didn't want her to hate him, either. More like, he couldn't *afford* for her to hate him. If she got to that point, she might just let her father carry out Nils' punishment after all. So he had to play nice. It was a fine line to walk, trying to keep Raeya from losing interest in him without encouraging her affections further. He was stalling, and yet there was no goal, no end point to try to reach.

Help wasn't coming—he'd resigned himself to that—and so this situation was either going to end with a noose or a wedding. He wasn't sure which would be worse.

After another long day, Nils' guards led him on the dreary march back to his room. The tall, bear-armed watchman was there again. Bern. He'd been right beside them when Aran had attacked Nils, seen the whole thing. He knew there was a curse, right? Or had Dreygard managed to convince everyone that Aran was to blame?

Notably, Nils had *not* seen Aran since the incident.

As they neared Nils' room, his skin prickled just thinking of the darkness. *It'll be all right,* he told himself. There was a crack under the door, and torches outside. If he waited long enough, there would be light. He just had to wait. To breathe, and wait.

When they got to his room, the door was already open.

"What in the—" Bern said, peering inside. "Hey, what are you doing in there?"

A maid with wavy, shoulder-length brown hair popped into view. "I was told to bring supper to the prisoner…guest? Anyway, am I early?"

"Don't matter," the guard said with a sigh. "Now's fine. In you get, Soulmate."

Nils cringed. *Desna help these men learn to speak.*

The maid bustled back into the room ahead of him to grab the dinner tray, and Nils noticed that the hearth was lit, *and* there was a candelabrum on the dresser. He could've cried for joy. He was still reveling over this discovery when the maid bumped into him and the tray crashed to the floor.

"Oh, Desna's Tresses, I'm so sorry," the maid said, stooping to pick up the larger shards of a broken dish.

"What happened?" a guard demanded from the doorway.

"Just a little collision. Your prisoner-guest dozed off in the middle of the room. I'll clean it up faster than you can whittle a spoon."

Wouldn't it take a while to whittle a spoon? Nils pondered. The guards didn't seem to give it a second thought.

"Fine, just move it along, but we've gotta keep the door closed."

"No worries, sirs," the maid called back. "If he tries to attack, I'll whack him good with this tray, yes sirree."

When the door was closed, the maid continued cleaning for a few seconds, then suddenly grabbed Nils' hand and shook it with enthusiasm.

"Nils! Here you are, just as he described you," she whispered, practically sparkling with excitement.

"Um…do I know you?" Nils said.

"Keep the voice low, honey. Nice and low. My name's Sandri. Tawsey sent me."

"Tawsey? Wait, Taws? Tawson sent you?"

"Of course! Didn't he ever mention me?"

Nils' pulse was suddenly thrumming. Tawson had come through after all. He'd sent help. "Uh, well, I remember him saying an awful lot about a woman who left him and broke his heart."

"That was me," Sandri said, beaming with what could've only been pride. "We had a big fight, you see, but not so big to break us. No, I knew we'd be back together within a few days, a week tops. But that was when the taskers moved him from the warehouse to that pit of death, of course! I thought I'd never see him again. So, when he showed up a few weeks ago, we wasted no time patching things up. We're meant for each other, him and me."

"He and I. Wait," Nils said, "Taws sent you to infiltrate the manor as a maid instead of coming himself? Isn't this extremely dangerous?"

"I can take care of myself, thank you," Sandri said, holding her head high. "Who do you think snagged the info about that shipment you came here to find? Tawsey knows I can hold my own, and besides, it would've been near impossible for him to get hired here. Men don't *apply* for work, work finds them."

Like a hunter finds his prey, Nils agreed.

"What's taking so long in there?" a voice called from outside the door.

"Boy oh boy, you wouldn't believe how stew can stick to a floor," Sandri called back, taking a moment to loudly scrub at the mess. "Almost done, good Sir Watchman."

Sandri pulled Nils down to floor level to continue cleaning while they talked. "All right, so what's going on, anyway? Why are you still here, and not on the domiseer's chopping block?"

"I was caught."

"Obviously."

"And, well, the domiseer's daughter thinks I'm her true love, so her father's agreed not to kill me for the moment."

Sandri stopped scrubbing. "Excuse me, what?"

"Look, is there some plan to get me out of here?" Nils said, glancing nervously at the door. "We don't have much time."

"Right, sorry. Box, screwed into the bottom of your bed frame. I did it earlier. There's parchment and a pencil in there, plus a letter from Tawsey. Leave your reply in the box, and I'll get it in the morning. After you've read his letter, burn it, so we don't take any chances, yeah?"

Nils nodded. "All right. Anything else?"

"Mm, yeah." Sandri fished into her apron pocket and pulled out something wrapped in a towel.

"What's this?" Nils said, accepting it from her.

"Dinner rolls, since I sabotaged your supper." She winked at him.

"All right, time's up," the guard said, opening the door just as Sandri and Nils stood up. Nils hid the rolls behind his back and looked down at the floor, his heart jumping, but found it completely clean.

"Perfect timing," Sandri said with a little curtsy. "Sorry for the trouble, gents. I'll get out of your way, quick as a spooked rabbit."

"Wait," the guard said. "Put out the fire and candles before you go."

Nils gave Sandri a pleading look that he hoped the watchman wouldn't see.

"What, and let the poor man freeze to death in the dark?" she said. "Kirit's still ruling the nights, you know."

"Fine, whatever. Just hurry and go."

Sandri saluted and fled the room with her tray, looking back to give Nils one last furtive smile.

"You set your room on fire," the guard said to Nils, "and I'm letting you burn to death in here."

* * *

It was hard to wait.

Nils forced himself to sit on the bed for at least a half hour after Sandri left, just to make sure the guards weren't going to come in again. He ate the rolls, stared at the Desna-blessed flames in the hearth, studied the wax dripping down his room's new candelabrum. All while impatiently tapping his fingers on whatever he was touching until he couldn't stand it anymore.

Then, carefully, quietly, he knelt down in front of the bed and reached underneath, feeling around for the box Sandri had attached under the frame.

There.

The box slid out from its lid into his hands, and he clutched it to himself before he could drop anything. He sat back on the bed with it and snatched out the letter, devouring it with his eyes.

Nils, brother, whats hapening in that maner?

Gods, Nils had never been so happy to read messy handwriting and bad spelling. He could even ignore his urge to strike out mistakes as he mentally corrected the rest of the letter.

I thought you were a goner when you didn't come back out. Can't tell you how glad I was when I caught sight of you on the grounds the next day. I don't know what went wrong, but the gods are with us yet! Dreygard was in need of some new maids, and my gal Sandri impressed the daylights out of the old housekeeper. (She's a real beauty, isn't she? But hands off, or I'll let you stay in that big house!)

Anyway, she'll be able to get notes from me to you and back again, so don't go worrying. (I mean it, you worry like an old mother hen.) We'll get you out of there, but first let me know what's going on. Did you find the shipment? Were there stones? Or manifests? Does Dreygard know?

Hang in there—

Taws didn't sign his name, but he didn't have to. Nils could tell it was him just from how he wrote. It was good fortune that the man *could* write; that skill was getting increasingly rarer among townsmen these days.

Nils let his eyes retrace a certain line several times. *We'll get you out of there.* It actually said *Well get you out of there*, but Nils focused on the sentiment. He swallowed, feeling something like hope filling a hole in his chest he hadn't realized was there. He wasn't alone. Someone had come to help.

Please hurry, Nils thought. *Also, Taws, when we meet again, I'm going to teach you about apostrophes.*

Nils took the pencil from the box next, and thought about his reply. Where should he even start? The last week was unbelievable even to him, and he'd lived it. Raeya's curse, Dreygard's threat, the knife in the guardhouse…He summarized it all as best he could, careful to emphasize the direness of the situation and how important it was that he was removed from it promptly.

Lastly, he answered Taws' question. *I wish I could say with confidence that Dreygard doesn't know what I was after,* he wrote, *but he seems very*—what was the right word—*perceptive. He's anxious to get rid of me, if that knife incident tells us anything. I don't think he suspects our goal though. At least I hope not. On that note…*

I don't think we'll need the stones anymore, or the trade manifests. If I'm right about Dreygard, then all the proof we need is right on his wrists. The king won't tolerate a spellweaver any more than he would a traitor or a chrysolin smuggler, and all his crimes will likely come to light in the end. We just need the right person to see those black veins he's hiding, but if I make any noise about it before I've seen them myself, I'll only build my own coffin.

Nils finished writing his message, reread it a few times, then folded it neatly and put it in the box. He scanned Taws' letter once more, then fed it into the hearth and watched the fire consume it.

With any luck, Lord Dreygard still thought Nils a petty thief— or even an ambitious thief, should he have guessed that Nils was after chrysolin when he'd taken that necklace. If he knew why Nils was *really* here, well, he might not care to be so round-about in his attempts to kill him. Nils didn't care about money, not even the fortune one would get from selling weaver's stone on the black market. He just wanted to see the domiseer deposed, and then given the just punishment for his crimes.

II A MEMORY OF MOM

"So," Nils' mother said, an alarming amount of mischief coating the word.

"What?"

"I was talking with Mrs. Silvy, and she said she saw you speaking with a young lady at the market today."

"Oh. She was asking how to get to the mill."

"And?"

"And she said, 'Could you tell me where the mill's at?' so I corrected her grammar and she stormed off saying she'd ask someone else."

His mother's head drooped. "Ah, such a pity. Mrs. Silvy said she was a pretty lass, too. You know, my dear, correcting people isn't generally a good way to make friends."

"I'm aware, but I can't help it. I grew up hearing these corrections all my life, and now it's part of my job to make them. It just slips out by habit."

"Well," his mother said, "I guess we'll know you've found your soulmate when you correct a girl's grammar and she says thank you."

"Nobody thanks you for that. And I don't believe in soulmates."

"No?"

"Of course not."

His mother shrugged, about to say something, but her breath caught and she coughed raggedly into her hand. Nils dropped his book, looking to her, but she waved it off. "I'm fine," she rasped. "The air's just dry."

Nils grabbed a chipped mug and filled it with water. "That's what you said last time. I'm taking you to see the doctor."

"It's too expensive, Nils. I'm fine, honestly."

"He owes us a favor. I'm sure he'll look you over. Now here, sit down for a minute. I'll finish grading these."

12 GARDEN

The candles snuffed themselves out overnight. Nils found only waxy stubs in the morning, but he was grateful for the first decent night's sleep he'd had in a long time. He hadn't even opened his eyes yet when the maid arrived, bringing clean clothes and breakfast.

It wasn't Sandri.

She's probably planning to come later, when the room's unoccupied, Nils told himself. He had to tell himself a few more times to quell the nagging fear that something had already happened to her. Maybe Taws wasn't far off in calling him a worrying mother hen.

After the maid left, Nils regarded the clothes she'd brought him. *Another victory on Raeya's part, apparently,* he thought. He held up a fine shirt, neckband, and a pair of leather cuffs, then glanced down at the servants' clothes he was still wearing from the previous day. *I don't care to let her dress me up as a noble,* he thought, nearly tossing the new garments aside, but his hands were wiser than his stubborn brain. It just wasn't worth the risk of upsetting her further. He donned the nobles' clothes with a grimace, but left the cuffs on the bed. He didn't have anything to hide, and he didn't have to cater to anyone's fashion sense.

Nils was a little surprised when his guards—Bern again, and the brown-haired man who'd struck his cheek, named Marks—didn't lead him back to some room with too many cushions, but rather outside. Apparently Raeya wanted another walk. Nils ground his teeth at the thought. *Another pointless waste of time. If only I could at least do something* useful *while I'm stuck here.* Then he noticed Lord Dreygard on the grounds, talking with Jarik Sowell.

His wrists. Is he wearing—

Of course he was. Leather cuffs on both arms. Whatever the two men were talking about, they'd apparently finished, and Dreygard walked right in his direction.

"Good morning, my lord," Marks said, and he and Bern both bowed their heads. Funny how different the guards sounded, speaking to their master. The domiseer barely regarded them, but stopped in front of Nils, looking down his nose at him.

"Staying out of trouble, are we?" Lord Dreygard said in a tone cold as Kirit's breath.

Unfortunately for you, Nils thought. The domiseer would no doubt love an excuse to end his life here and now, and Nils had no plans to give it to him. He nodded.

Dreygard's eyes narrowed the slightest bit as he held Nils' gaze, then looked him over, apparently noting the change of clothes. "The lowborn ought to stay in their burrows," he said, almost as if to himself, then continued on his way toward the main house. Nils shivered in spite of the sunshine. It was even worse to face the domiseer with the knowledge that he was a spellweaver, able to speak death into objects with nothing more than words. Some spellweavers didn't even require an intermediary object, but could pass their black magic straight through their hands to their targets. No spell could kill you instantly, but one touch and you might just carry out your own murder.

"Good morning, Mr. Oakander."

Nils started. He'd been so focused on the domiseer, he hadn't noticed Jarik approaching.

"Steady on, man," Jarik said. "I didn't realize I was so frightening to behold."

"S-sorry," Nils said. "I was…distracted."

"Not to worry. I think many people lose their stream of thought when Lord Dreygard stares them in the face. Where are you off to?"

Nils didn't actually know, and looked to his guards. "The flower garden, sir," Marks supplied.

"To see Lady Raeya, no doubt," Jarik said. "Mind if I walk with you?"

"I don't mind," Nils said, "but Raeya won't be happy to see you."

The nobleman winced. "The truth stings a bit, sometimes."

"Sorry. I've never been good at being…nice," Nils confessed.

"Well, you make up for it with your honesty, my friend. Gentlemen, could we have some space?" Jarik asked the guards, and with respectful nods they both hung back out of earshot while Jarik took over leading the way.

That was…curious.

"I've been away for a few days, but I heard about what happened," Jarik said. "Terrible business. Are you all right?"

"Fine," Nils said, sparing a glance back at Bern and Marks.

"I spoke briefly with Lord Dreygard about it. He's furious that one of his own watchmen behaved so impulsively."

I'm sure he is, Nils thought.

"It scared poor Lady Raeya to death, from the sounds. If I'm being honest, I have ulterior motives for tagging along with you. This is the best chance I have of speaking with her. I've been stationed here much of this past year to manage trade between my uncle and her father, and I'm afraid she's tolerating me less and less."

"Your uncle is the domiseer of Tormeron?"

"That's right. Must be Lady Raeya has spoken about me. Anything good?"

"Not really," Nils admitted. "She thinks you're only interested in her father's estate."

"Ah. I know why she thinks that."

"Why?"

"Because she was right, at the beginning. The nobility of this province are flourishing, and any aspiring lord would love to claim it as his own. I'll admit I had such aspirations when I first came, however since then, Lady Raeya has captured my heart in earnest. I'd gladly forfeit the inheritance if I could have her. Unfortunately, it's a little too late for that." He looked over at Nils. "Sorry. This is probably all strange for me to say. You're nearly her betrothed, aren't you?"

"I wish I wasn't," Nils said. "I'd gladly let you have her *and* this estate if it was up to me."

Jarik blinked a couple times. "I'll admit, that is not the response I expected. Do you find Lady Raeya disagreeable in some way?"

"She's childish," Nils said with a shrug. "Spoiled. A hopeless romantic."

Jarik chuckled. "I'm afraid you'll find me just as hopeless. Not only do I find those things endearing, but even now when she's found her true love, I can't help wishing she'd cast fate aside and choose me instead."

Nils got the feeling this man read as much poetry as Raeya read fiction. "You're awfully kind, considering."

"Thank you?"

64

"I mean, I'd think you ought to hate me, since Raeya believes I'm her soulmate," Nils said.

Jarik smiled, this time with something of an edge to it. "I do, a little bit," he admitted. "But I also know this wasn't your choice. The gods are more at fault than you are, and if I won't shake my fist at them, I can't take it out on you. And, between you and me..." He lowered his voice. "I mean no disrespect toward the domiseer, but anyone who has the nerve to steal from Feren Dreygard is someone I'd like to know."

Nils choked on what was either astonishment or a laugh. "Doesn't stealing from him indirectly hurt you and your uncle?"

"Yes," Jarik conceded, "but I'm still more impressed than angry. Also, you didn't succeed, so no harm done, right?"

Nils couldn't argue with him there.

Their path took them past a couple more outbuildings, through a grove of trees, then over a flawlessly groomed patch of lawn. "The grounds here are beautiful, aren't they?" Jarik said.

Nils snorted. "Too beautiful."

Jarik turned to him with a question in his eyes.

"There's no mud," Nils explained.

"You...are a fan of mud?"

"No, but that's the point."

Jarik shook his head. "You'll have to help me out here."

"This time of year, the towns are absolute mud pits. The fact that they keep this place so immaculate by comparison, it just..." Nils trailed off, remembering who he was talking to. A nobleman, *and* an associate of Lord Dreygard.

"What?" Jarik prompted.

"Nothing. I guess I'm just a little bitter."

"I see. It's sad, isn't it? That the nobility should flourish while the townspeople suffer."

Nils looked at him. That wasn't what he'd expected to hear.

"It seems especially true in Chanterey. Some speculate that Dreygard has more wealth in his home than even the king."

"Why do you think that is?" Nils found himself asking. *Stupid, stupid, I should not have said that. I can't give any hint as to why I came here—*

"I can't say I know the reason," Jarik answered, calming Nils' thoughts. He laughed a little. "My uncle would sure like to know his secret."

I know his secret, Nils wanted to say, but thankfully he didn't spit *that* out. This nobleman…he was a bit odd, but not in a bad way. Nils didn't think there *were* any noblemen who would actually lament the hardships of the poor.

They came around a row of neatly trimmed hedges, passed over a completely unnecessary bridge that spanned no water, and the flower garden came into view. They passed under trellises of hanging vines and a few more rows of shrubs before Nils could get a good look at the place.

In the center was a small man-made pond with a stone statue at its middle, a narrow path connecting its island to the rest of the garden. From there the path split and wove between bushes and trees that were all far too green for this early in Desna's season. Somewhere nearby, a familiar voice gave orders.

"No, no, plant these over *there*. And not too close to the crocuses. They'll clash terribly. Ah, Nils!" Raeya said, spotting him. Surprisingly, she carried a trowel—which she handed off to Tilda—gardening gloves—that even had soil on them—and a dirt-flecked sun hat.

"Good day, my lady," Jarik said to her with a bow. "You look lovely as always, beautiful as the jewels of morning dew, fashioned by Desna herself."

"Thank you, Jarik," Raeya said, though her tone was decidedly aloof. "Nils, I'm glad you're here. I was going to wait to show you this place until more of the flowers had opened, but I didn't want to have to choose between a planting day and spending time with you. You'll have to trust me; the garden will look absolutely *magnificent* once everything is in bloom."

"I have no doubt," Jarik said. "And yet its beauty shall still fail to trump that of the one who cares for it."

"How kind of you to say, Jarik. Nils, dear," Raeya said, coming alongside him and taking his arm, "let me show you around." She paused a bit unnaturally, and Nils noticed she bit her lower lip before smiling again, then she leaned up to kiss him on the mouth. It was brief, but it caught him off guard. Why would she suddenly—

Oh. Jarik. Standing right behind them.

Raeya was sending a message, something along the lines of *I found my soulmate, and it isn't you.*

Gods, women could be cold. Though, to his credit, Jarik barely missed a beat. "Perhaps you and I could have a walk another time, my lady," he said. "Seems I'd best return to my work."

"Of course," Raeya said, leaving it unclear to which of his clauses she was responding. She didn't even meet his gaze, so the nobleman nodded farewell to Nils instead and made his retreat, somehow managing to keep any signs of disappointment out of his posture.

Nils, however, let his shoulders slump as Raeya began to talk excitedly about flowers.

* * *

Sometime later, a bee buzzed past Nils' ear. He noticed the drone of its wings, a constant, steady hum that would never let up so long as the creature was moving.

It was just like Raeya, except far less annoying.

"Oh, these were just planted last week. They're lovely, aren't they? The flowers look like tiny white bells. I was thinking of adding more of them, over there, perhaps." She pointed to a spot where a couple servants were working, removing a cover from a nearby bush.

"What's that about?" Nils asked.

"Hm? Oh, we have to keep some of the plants covered at night. This early in the season, the frost could kill them."

"You have blankets for your flowers?"

"I guess you could call them that. Is that odd?"

"You do realize many of your townspeople don't even have blankets to get them through Kirit's season."

"What? Of course they do. Everyone has *blankets.*"

Nils let his stare give answer to that statement.

"No. Truly?"

"Yes," Nils replied. "Why do you think Kirit is considered such a harsh god throughout the towns? We don't have the luxury of thinking him *majestic* like some do when we're freezing to death in his ice storms."

Raeya's brow furrowed. "Are you saying people really *die* for want of *blankets?*"

"Yes!"

"Dearest Desna," she said, looking down in thought. "For such a simple thing...I wish I'd known sooner." She leveled herself and resumed walking. "Right, then. I'll speak to Mother and Father. We'll distribute blankets to anyone in need throughout the towns before Kirit takes power again."

"Really?" Nils said, not hiding the skepticism in his voice.

"Yes, really."

"That's going to be a lot of blankets. Probably an impossible amount of blankets."

"Well, we'll do our best."

"Would you sacrifice your precious flower beds to do it?"

Raeya paused and looked back at the bushes they'd left behind. "I...would," she said, "if I had to."

It was a better answer than Nils expected, assuming she really meant it. She looked awfully sad at the prospect of surrendering her plants, though. As if they mattered beyond looking pretty.

They'd circled back around to where they started, and Raeya retrieved her trowel from Tilda. "Well, back to work, I suppose," she said cheerily. "Nils, perhaps you could rake out that patch over there. Would you mind? The rake should be around here somewhere...Tilda, did someone move it?"

"I didn't see, my lady," Tilda answered, looking around. "Ah, there it is, by the wagon. Geff," she called to a servant working nearby. "Could you bring over that rake?"

"Of course, ma'am," the man said, reaching for it. As soon as he touched it, he paused. Nils' eyes traveled down the wooden handle to the sharp metal points at the end, then back to Geff's eyes, which had gone blank.

Just like Aran's when he'd grabbed the knife in the guardhouse.

Nils stumbled backward into Bern, who cursed. Nils had gotten careless. He should've thought about the garden tools all around them, should've known Dreygard was due to try again to end his life. Now it was too late. The guards wouldn't risk their own lives to save him when their master didn't even want him alive.

Nils braced himself as the servant charged for him, expecting the others to scatter, but after a cry of alarm Raeya latched herself onto him instead of running away. What was she thinking? She was going to—

A strong arm shoved both of them out of the way, and Bern grabbed the haft of the rake, yanking it from the servant's hand, then knocked him to the ground. "Snap out of it!" he shouted at the man.

Geff blinked, then held up his hands in front of his face, trembling. "What…what was I doing? Oh, gods."

"Dearest Desna," Tilda said. "Graham!" she called. "Somebody find Captain Clerrit, and tell him to alert the domiseer immediately."

A couple servants hurried off to follow her orders, then Tilda rushed to Raeya, who'd been knocked to the ground with Nils. "My lady," she said. "Oh, dear Raeya, are you all right?"

Raeya was still staring at Geff, a hand to her mouth. "Tilda, what just happened?" she said. "What was that?" Tilda tugged at her arm, trying to help Raeya to her feet, but she ignored it. "Nils," she said, looking right at him. "Why…why did he attack you?"

Nils looked back at her and couldn't process that question. All he could do was ask one of his own. "Why didn't you run?"

"Because I knew the guards would protect me," she said, "but not you."

Nils took in a sharp breath, and Tilda finally succeeded in hauling Raeya to her feet, brushing her off. "Oh, my lady, that was…oh that was just awful. Are you hurt?"

"I'm fine, Tilda. Where is my father? He needs to know about this."

Nils was still staring when someone grabbed his arm and yanked him up from the ground. Bern. "Unholy fives," the guard muttered, then left to aid Marks in apprehending Geff. The servant was sobbing.

Nils looked back to the rake, lying harmlessly in the grass. The domiseer was on his way. He wouldn't be happy to see he'd failed again.

13 A NEW PLAN

Nils was sent back to his room almost the moment Lord Dreygard arrived. He sat on his bed, numb.

She saved my life.

In truth, it was the second time Raeya had saved his life, but this time she did it at significant personal risk.

And afterward, she asked for her father. If she knew he was a spellweaver, why would she do that? Nils already doubted she had any awareness of her father's treason, but this seemed to solidify it in his mind. She was innocent.

Not that that changes anything, Nils thought, *except...maybe I can afford her a little pity after all.*

Nils found himself holding a hand over his heart, taking the repetitive *thump-thump* as a comfort. The metals rake-spikes hadn't run him through, and as long as he lived, he still had the chance of escape.

Weaver's blood, Taws' letter!

Nils leapt from his bed and thrust his hands underneath, cursing at the splinter he received from the crude wood of the hidden box. He'd been so distracted by everything else, he'd nearly forgotten to check for Taws' reply. Would Sandri have had time to deliver it?

72

Yes, it was there. A simple, folded piece of paper. He nearly ripped it in half he opened it so fast.

Nils, this is amazing, it read. Technically, it said *amazeing*, but Nils couldn't be bothered with errors at the moment.

You're little Lady Dreygard's soulmate! Or as good as, if she truly believes it. Why on earth are you so keen to escape? Just marry the girl and all our problems will be solved! We'll take care of ol' Feren, and you'll be the new domiseer. It's perfect!

No it is not perfect! Nils wanted to scream back, instead letting his grip crinkle the paper. The thought of marrying Raeya and becoming domiseer had come to mind early on, but he'd immediately dismissed it because it was a *fiving terrible idea.* He'd almost rather have died in the blackness of Gen Rill than appoint himself the new head of the province with a Dreygard at his side.

He read on.

I knew Dreygard would turn out to be a weaver. It makes perfect sense, and it's all the more reason to see him buried. At any rate, I'm not pulling you out of there when you're perfectly positioned to keep the plan going. Just be careful. You can outsmart him, I'm sure.

Weaver's blood, Taws, Nils inwardly swore. *Be careful? Are you kidding? I have to get out of here, now!* He fought hard to stifle a growl of frustration, remaining aware of the guards outside the door. If not for that, he might've thrown something, especially after reading the next line.

So, do a proper job of romancing that lady, young man, for the good of our kingdom. Even if we get Dreygard sacked, there's no telling who would take his place otherwise. They could be even worse.

The letter ended there. *Worse than a traitor and a spellweaver?* Nils thought. *I doubt it.* Though admittedly no one would understand the plight of the peasants better than a fellow peasant. Nils could already think of so many things that would help—

No. That was a path he wasn't willing to tread. He was *not* a leader, he just knew how to spot an inept one. Even without his treachery, Lord Dreygard had failed his people utterly, using them for his own gain instead of seeing to their care. Maybe his successor would have the same failings in that arena, but Nils would have to take the chance. After all, not *all* nobles were that corrupt. Jarik sure seemed a decent type. In fact he—

Nils paused, his thoughts slowing, then suddenly racing off ahead of him.

Jarik wanted to marry Raeya.

Jarik wanted to be the domiseer.

Jarik noticed the townspeople and their plight. He listened to Nils. He treated him like an equal.

But Raeya hated Jarik.

Fives. It was all lining up for a second there. Still, this was something he could work with. He hadn't known him long, but Jarik already seemed a prime candidate for the position, and Desna's Tresses, he might even listen to some of Nils' ideas for improving life for the people of the province. If the taskers were disbanded, if wages were improved, if *all the fiving money wasn't being funneled to our enemies…*

Yes, it was a solid plan: set Jarik up to inherit the province once Lord Dreygard took the fall. As a citizen of Tormeron, he'd never be selected by the king to govern Chanterey, but if he married into the line of the house, it was guaranteed.

Right, then. All Nils had to do, besides secure proof of Feren Dreygard's treachery or villainous spellweaving, was convince Raeya Dreygard to forget about him and marry Jarik Sowell. A man she believed wholeheartedly was not her true love, and was only interested in her for the inheritance she carried.

Nils sighed, wadded up Taws' letter, and tossed it into the hearth. Something told him this new mission might just be more difficult than the first.

14 A MEMORY OF DUCKS

"Don't forget to sprinkle that on your food. Twice a day, the apothecary said."

"Yes, dear."

"What?"

"What do you mean, what?" Nils' mother asked, an innocent look on her face.

"You were laughing."

"Because I heard a duck," she said, "keeping its ducklings in line."

"Funny, Mom."

"Indeed, which is why I was laughing."

Nils rolled his eyes, but the edges of his mouth tugged upward anyway. As long as she still had her sense of humor, he knew she'd be all right. They'd both be all right. Even with the chill in the air announcing the change in power amongst the gods. Another of Kirit's seasons was about to begin, and there were whispers it was going to be a bad one.

Nils glanced down at the threadbare blanket draped around him. His mother's looked worse, holes already losing their most recent patches. He'd swap them tonight. If she was asleep when he did it, she at least wouldn't tease him until morning.

15 ALLY

"First the guard, and now a *gardener*," Raeya said, clinging tightly to Nils' arm the morning after the rake incident. "You're certain you've never met either of them before?"

"Yes," Nils sighed. It was too early for this. Raeya hadn't even waited until breakfast to summon him from his room.

"Well, it wasn't my *father* behind this, before you try and tell me that again. But why should these men..." She trailed off, seeming reluctant to voice her thoughts for once. "Nils, last time, you said something about a curse..."

Nils could feel the guards standing behind him, watching him. "I was just frightened," he said. "I don't have a clue what's going on." *Not good enough*, Nils thought. *I need to get her off this trail.* "Maybe these men are lashing out because they've gotten jealous. You know, because you've found your...true love."

Nils wanted to slap himself for uttering those words, even more for lying to cover up Dreygard's sins. He didn't want to look at Raeya, but—

Fives. Just as he feared, she was staring at him with a look of sheer amazement, her cheeks tinted pink. "Anyway," he said, blazing onward, "I don't know a thing about any of this, and I'd rather think about something else. What book did you bring today?"

"Hm? Since when have you been interested in my books?" Raeya asked. She hadn't been reading this morning, but she'd still brought a book with her, and Nils plucked it from the table.

"The Passions of Roses," Nils read from the cover. "Sounds inappropriate."

"It is not *inappropriate*," Raeya said, grabbing the book from him and clutching it to her chest.

"May I see it, then?"

Raeya hesitated, staring at him for a long moment before finally handing it over. Nils opened it and flipped through the pages, skimming the paragraphs. "He trailed kisses down her back," he read, "and her skin blossomed with heat at every touch of his lips. Romin's hands were rough and rugged, but they were gentle as rose petals sliding down her neck, caressing her—"

"That's enough," Raeya said, snatching the book back from him and gripping it protectively. Her face had turned red as the book's cover. "It's not as though the whole book is that way. I mean, every story has a scene like that, doesn't it? Nils?"

Nils was shaking from holding in his laughter, and finally he let go and bellowed out a laugh. "I wouldn't know," he said. "I don't read inappropriate novels."

"I said it's not inappropriate, it was clearly just that one—Nils, are you listening?"

He was laughing again, he couldn't help it. "Her skin blossomed," he said. "I'm sorry, it's just so...so terrible."

Eventually Raeya let out a little huff and slumped back into her seat. "Well," she said, "it's good to know you're capable of mirth, at least. I was afraid I'd never see you smile."

Nils regained control of himself and looked over at her. When was the last time he'd smiled? It had been a while.

"You're very handsome when you do," Raeya said, retaining a little of her blush.

"As handsome as Romin?"

"Stop," Raeya said, hitting him lightly on the arm with the book. "You know, you're awfully good at reading, for a common thief."

Nils froze.

"You speak well for one, too," Raeya added.

"Who says thieves can't do those things?" Nils said, forcing himself to sit back. "They can be educated."

"One would think an educated person would have better choices to make than thievery."

"We would, if your father would allow it," Nils muttered.

"What?"

Nils glanced back at the guards. "Nothing. Perhaps I'm just...a higher class of thief."

Raeya's eyes widened a little, and her cheeks got pink again.

"That should *not* excite you," Nils said.

"But just think of it," Raeya said, clutching her book once more. "A thief of the highest rank who turns out to have a heart of gold after a chance encounter with a domiseer's daughter. Oh, what a thrilling story we have!"

"Thieves don't have ranks, and you've been reading too many of those," Nils said, nodding at her book. "Not to mention, you have an awful lot of faith in your curse to think I have a heart of gold."

"No, I have faith in *you*," she said, giving Nils pause. "An indecent person would've pressed his advantage long ago if put in your situation."

Huh, Nils thought. Perhaps she wasn't quite as naive as he assumed.

Raeya looked down at her hands. "I know I've probably seemed…disappointed that you haven't felt the way I do thus far, but I've realized something."

"That I'm not actually your true love?"

"No, rather that it takes *time* to fall in love with someone, even if they *are* your true love. So, I will be patient, my dear, until you can feel it as I do. I know the gods have destined us to be together." She held his arm and leaned her head on his shoulder, and Nils did his best to contain his annoyance.

Never mind, he thought. *She's hopeless.*

* * *

When Raeya left for breakfast, Nils refocused himself.

Stick to the plan. Find Jarik. Say your piece. And pray to Desna that it works.

There. Partway through the great hall, Nils spotted the nobleman, practically in their path. *I might be half-crazy for doing this,* he thought, *but if Taws won't get me out of here, then I have to find another way to save myself. Jarik's the best bet I have.*

Unfortunately, Jarik looked to be entirely lost in thought, and Nils failed to catch his eye. He glanced sideways at his guards, then decided to chance it. "Mister Sowell," he called. His guards looked surprised, but it wasn't like they could stop Jarik from answering.

The nobleman looked up, eyes still narrowed and unfocused as though whatever was troubling him was taking a moment to release his brain. "You, sir," he finally said, "are one lucky son of the gods, you know that? Desna's Tresses, you must have nerves of diamond to look so calm after another narrow escape like that."

"If only," Nils said. Fives, Jarik had just reminded him to be nervous. He'd been so preoccupied with his new plan, he'd forgotten about the threat to his life for a few hours.

"How's Lady Raeya?" Jarik asked. "Were you with her just now?"

Nils nodded. "She's fine. Shaken, but fine."

"Ah, poor thing," Jarik said, running a hand through his hair. Judging by the state of it, he'd done that quite a few times recently. "I've been trying to see her since yesterday, to make sure she's all right after such a shock, but she wouldn't take any visitors. Well, not me, at least." He offered a wan smile. "She doesn't like me at all, does she?"

"Actually, I wondered if I could talk to you about that."

"Hm? Has she said something?"

"Well, no, but…" Nils glanced at his guards again. How was he supposed to broach the topic with them standing there?

Thankfully, he didn't have to; Jarik was quick to read the situation. "Gentleman," he said to the watchmen, "will Lady Raeya be likely to request Nils' presence anytime soon?"

"Not for at least an hour, sir," one of them answered. "She's dining with her parents."

"Splendid. Nils, my friend, care for a walk?"

* * *

Already, siding with the nobleman had its benefits. Nils' guards hadn't been this far away since they were assigned to him. He found himself repeatedly looking over his shoulder just to marvel at the distance.

"So, what is it you wanted to say?" Jarik asked.

Right. Unholy fives, I was up all night coming up with the perfect way of wording this, and now I'm too nervous to remember it.

"Nils?"

Nils took a breath. "About Raeya," he said, staring down at the grass. They'd gone off the formal path and were walking about the grounds, and even here the grass was kept neatly trimmed. "Do you…do you remember when I said I'd gladly let you have her, if it was up to me?"

"Yes. The most foolish thing I've ever heard anybody say, probably, but it was nice all the same."

"Well, what if we could arrange something?"

Jarik tipped his head. "I'm listening."

"I don't want any of this," Nils said. "All I've wanted since getting caught is to leave, but as long as Raeya wants me, that won't happen, and if she stops wanting me, Lord Dreygard will kill me."

"…I see your predicament."

"Yes, so I…I wondered if you might be able to convince Lord Dreygard not to kill me. I don't want to marry his daughter, and I'm not stupid enough to try to steal from his household again. I'm no threat to him, just a nobody eager to return to obscurity."

"Hm," Jarik said. "I'm not opposed to helping you out, but what makes you think I could influence Lord Dreygard?"

"You're a close associate of his, right? You must be, if he lets you order his guards around."

"If you must know," Jarik said, leaning in, "he allows me control over your guards because he knows I could handle the situation myself, should you try to make a run for it."

Oh. Oh, gods. Didn't that make Jarik one of Nils' watchmen in his own right? Would he also report everything Nils said to Lord Dreygard?

Darkness of Hearthnight, I've made a terrible mistake.

Nils stared blankly ahead until he was distracted from his disastrous realization by the sound of Jarik laughing.

"Honestly, you make the greatest expressions," Jarik said. "Don't worry, Mr. Oakander. I'm not about to sell you out to the domiseer. I don't know what drove you to steal from him, but I get the feeling you're a more decent fellow than he assumes."

"Now you sound like Raeya," Nils muttered, trying to rub the tension out of his arms.

"I do wonder one thing, though," Jarik said. "If you're a nobody, why have two men tried to kill you?"

Nils' legs tried to freeze up, but he forced them to keep moving forward with a jerk. He knew this might come up, and still he struggled with himself to spit it out. "That's why this is so urgent," Nils said, voice low and tight. "I don't believe either of those men wanted to kill me, but their master does."

Jarik looked at him. "You think...Lord Dreygard..."

"Ordered those men to attack me, yes," Nils said. A lie, but close enough to the truth without throwing the word *spellweaver* into the air and letting it wreak its havoc. "He promised Raeya he'd spare me for now, so he's trying to get rid of me without her knowing he was involved. He'll do anything to keep her from marrying me."

"Hm."

There wasn't a single clue in that sound to tell Nils what the nobleman might be thinking. No special inflection, no distinguishing tone. Nils could go mad analyzing that solitary hum. But he could do that later. *Right now,* he thought, *I have to see this through.*

"So, what do you say?" he asked, clearing his throat when his voice came out like a croak. "See if you can get Lord Dreygard to spare my life, and I'll do everything I can to get Raeya out of love with me, and in love with you. Does that sound reasonable?"

Jarik paused long enough to let Nils' heart wear itself out, then said, "I believe it does." He turned to him, and offered a hand. "In fact, protecting your life just became my top priority."

16 ACCOMPLISHMENTS

I don't like this plan of yours. That noble is a partner to Dreygard. He's just going to use you to get what he wants, then hold you down while Feren swings the axe. You can't trust him.

Nils scanned the fresh letter in his hands, a reply to the last one he sent to Taws. *Too late,* he thought in response to the words, scrawled in thick graphite. He probably should've waited to hear Taws' thoughts on the plan to ally with Jarik before moving forward with it, but he'd been too angry at the man for refusing to get him out of the manor. And he was *still* refusing, as the next paragraph spelled out.

I'm sorry to hear of the second curse, but Desna has your back if Dreygard's plan was thwarted by his own daughter. Don't give up! And yes, you made it clear that you are in danger. Grave, grievous, horrible danger. I understand. But pulling you out now just isn't an option. You're in the sweet spot, my friend. Prime territory. And don't you dare give up on your cursed sweetheart! If you ask me, you'd be a mudbrain to pass her off to that noble. You'll do a better job as domiseer than he would.

Nils chanced an audible groan. It was all easy for him to say from the outside. He didn't seem to understand that Nils couldn't carry out their plan if he was killed by a spellweaver first. That, and he didn't see *Taws* volunteering to lead the province.

On a different note, Taws inscribed, *one of my contacts got wind of something. Weaver's stone being sold on the black market. I wonder if some of it has leaked from Dreygard's stores. I'm looking into it to see if I can trace it back to the manor, but you can't just ask about the fifth godjewel. Even in the black market, that can get you killed. I'll keep you posted.*

The letter ended there.

The black market. One of his contacts.

How much did Nils know about Tawson, anyway? He was a refugee—that much was obvious just from looking at him. Dark red hair, tan skin. He was displaced from Thrinia, a small country to the north that had been overrun by Emperor Ri'sen's troops. Commoners and nobility alike had been either killed, captured, or forced to flee into surrounding countries. Any former status would have been lost to him when he became a citizen of Branaden, so it was hard to say what kind of life Taws had led before. Regardless, he hated the Galreyvans for what they'd done, and Nils couldn't blame him for that. He hated them too. But just what sort of person was he to be able to track their shipments, and to successfully help Nils break into a domiseer's well-guarded manor?

Nils had trusted Tawson because he'd helped him survive his weeks at Gen Rill. They'd formed a bond during their forced servitude, perhaps even a friendship. But the more he learned about the man…well, Nils wasn't sure if he should be impressed or worried.

★ ★ ★

"Nils? You seem distracted."

"Hm? Oh, sorry."

Nils sat beside Raeya in the parlor the next morning and yes, he was distracted. Had Jarik spoken with the domiseer yet? Would Tawson be furious when he found out Nils had made a deal with him? He wished he could re-write his reply, giving Taws more reassurance that Jarik was a worthwhile ally, but Sandri would almost certainly take it before he got back to his room.

And really, could he give more reassurance? If Jarik had been an acting watchman all along, maybe he *couldn't* be trusted.

Why did he have to think about all these things when it was too late to fix them?

"Nils."

Nils turned again, finding Raeya's gray-blue eyes staring at him under raised brows.

"What?" he asked.

Raeya sighed, looking down into the book in her lap. "I guess I can't blame you," she said. "I've been distracted too, reliving that awful experience from the garden over and over." She shook herself. "It was a nightmare."

The garden. Nils latched onto that. He hadn't heard anything more from Jarik, but that didn't mean he couldn't start putting his plan into motion. "Have you seen Jarik since then?" he asked, hoping he sounded casual enough.

Raeya let her book rest on her skirt and looked back at Nils. "No. Why?"

"He asked about you yesterday, worried sick about you. I thought he might start losing hair over it."

"Really."

"Yes."

Raeya said nothing more, and continued reading. Gods, this was harder than it should've been. "You know, I don't think he's as bad as you say. You should make good on your promise and at least take a walk with him."

"Did I promise?"

Well, no. No she hadn't. Blast it all. "Almost," Nils said. "Look, would it hurt? He was really concerned."

Raeya locked eyes with him again. "Why does this matter so much to you?"

Darkness of Hearthnight, I am bad at this. "It doesn't. You just…seem awfully cold toward him. I mean, if you hate him so much, you could just kiss him and be rid of him."

Raeya's eyes widened. "*Nils,* what a *horrible* thing to say. You don't honestly think I would kill someone simply because I dislike them, do you?"

Nils didn't, but given the circumstances, he just shrugged.

Raeya looked beside herself. "You…you have no idea what it feels like to have someone die on the other side of your lips. I would never, *never,* do that to another living person on purpose, no matter what I thought of them. In fact, I would rather die than endure that again. Do you understand?"

Wow. Nils hadn't expected such ferocity in her reply. He was actually afraid to say more, so he just nodded.

Raeya didn't look much assuaged by this response, but after staring him down another several seconds, she settled back in her seat and took up her book again. "Fine," she said a moment later.

"Fine?"

"I'll go for a walk with Jarik. If I've really given you such a hideous impression of myself, I have to do something to correct it."

Huh. Somehow Nils had actually succeeded, even if the sloppiness of his methods was a disappointment even to himself.

"But," Raeya continued, "I'll only do it if you come along with us."

"…What?"

"I won't trot about with a man who isn't my betrothed."

"*I'm* not your betrothed," Nils countered.

"Close enough," Raeya maintained.

"It's not like you'd be alone with him," Nils said, scrambling. "Tilda would be there with you." He spared a glance at the attendant, who looked offended that he'd dared to speak her name with his own mouth. "If you're worried about wronging me in some way, you needn't be."

"I appreciate your faith in me," Raeya said, "but I insist on your presence. I won't have it any other way."

Nils sighed, knowing he was defeated. It would take three times the energy he had and probably a couple years to change her mind. "Fine. This afternoon, then?"

"I suppose. Father hasn't restricted me from leaving the house this time, though I'm a little surprised."

Nils wasn't. The domiseer probably didn't feel the need to put on so much of a show the second time around.

Raeya rubbed her arms. "Ugh, what a horrid feeling I get at the thought of returning after what happened. If this has ruined Keden's garden for me—" she cut off, and seemed to remind herself that such an outburst wasn't befitting someone of her station. "Never mind," she said, straightening herself and lifting her book again. "I'll just see to it that every garden tool and gardener are off the premises when you go near."

* * *

Nils was dismissed while Raeya went for lunch. He'd hardly made it two steps out of the parlor when he felt a hand on his shoulder and nearly jumped through the ceiling.

It was Bern. Nils' eyes shot to the guard's hand, looking for a weapon, but—no, his hands were empty, and his sword remained strapped at his side. Nils looked up, searching for blank eyes, but they were normal. Normal, except that they stared down at him like he was a head case.

Bern took in Nils' expression, then glanced off to the side. "Back this way, Soulmate," he said, turning around. "You've been summoned."

"By who?" Nils asked, following with a slight shake in his step, still flanked by his other two guards.

"Guess."

Well, he'd just left Raeya, who was usually the one demanding his presence throughout the day. So that left Jarik, who perhaps had some news to share, or...

Or Lord Dreygard, who perhaps was sick of this ridiculous game and intent on killing him. *Gods, please be Jarik.*

It was, thank Desna, waiting in some kind of a small meeting room. "There you are. Gentlemen, you may wait outside," he said to the guards. Bern lingered a moment, but then left with the others, shutting the door behind him.

"What's happened?" Nils asked. "Did you speak with Lord Dreygard?"

"Yes, at the first chance. He's agreed to reconsider your death sentence."

Nils let his head drop back, feeling like half a mountain had been lifted off his shoulders. "Thank the gods," he said. "How did you do it?"

"I told him about our deal."

Nils' head snapped back up. "You what?"

"Relax," Jarik said, waving his hand. "I simply told him that you were eager to quell Lady Raeya's affections for you—something the

90

domiseer also desires—and that you'd be happy to do so once you no longer had to fear for your life. It wasn't too difficult to convince him; at this point, he just wants to be rid of you, and he knows Lady Raeya won't relinquish you easily."

"So, let me see if I understand this correctly," Nils said. "Lord Dreygard will let me live if I can get Raeya to hate me and love you instead?"

"There are some obvious conditions," Jarik said. "You still have to abide by the rules the domiseer laid out for you."

"No thieving, no trying to escape, and no harming anyone," Nils recited. "But aside from that...I'm free to offend his daughter without fear of consequences?"

"Offend away," Jarik said. "No harm will come to you for that."

"Great," Nils said. "So then, if I succeed...he'll let me go?"

"That's right," Jarik said, and the other half of the mountain started to lift—"But you'll have to resume whatever work you were assigned to before you arrived."

Nils' heart thudded, and the mountain came crashing back down.

"Which does present a slight problem," Jarik went on, "as Lord Dreygard said you refused to tell him what that was, and your registration tags have gone missing. But with a little cooperation, you can be on your way."

"A-all right," Nils said, trying to contain his panic. He would *not* go back to Gen Rill, no matter what, so he'd still have to find a way to escape, but at least for now...he'd focus on his victories. He was significantly less likely to be impaled in the near future, and that meant a lot.

"Well, I have news too," Nils said, trying to move on. "Raeya's going to invite you on a walk this afternoon."

Jarik's eyes widened. "Are you serious?"

Nils almost smiled. You'd think achieving a walk with a lady was just as important as finding out your life had been spared. "Yes, though sadly she insisted I come too."

"Hm. That is somewhat disappointing. No offense."

"Oh, don't worry. I'm disappointed too."

"It could be a good thing," Jarik proffered. "If you're there, you can help smooth things over between us."

"I'm not sure I'll be much help," Nils said, remembering how well he'd done in just convincing Raeya to take this walk. Which was to say, it was a complete miracle he'd succeeded at all.

"Nonsense. She listens to you. That immediately gives me an advantage I've never had before."

"I'll try," Nils said, "but it's probably best if I just stay out of the way as much as possible."

* * *

Nils should've felt better after the meeting, but his uneasiness persisted.

Dreygard knows, he thought. *He knows that I know he was behind the attempts on my life. At least the spellweaving part of it remains a secret, but…fives, can I trust him to make good on his word?*

"Hey," Bern said, and Nils looked up at the tall guard, realizing for the first time he was the only one there.

"I thought I was supposed to have two of you," Nils said.

"New rules," was all Bern said by way of explanation. Maybe it was a perk of Jarik's intervention. "What were you and Sowell talking about back there?"

"Um…" Nils said. Was he required to answer that? "I…believe that is a private matter." He braced himself to get punched, but Bern just scowled.

"Private matter," he mumbled. "Of course it is."

17 NOBLE PROBLEMS

Nils managed to fall in line with Jarik on their way to the garden for the second time. He did his best not to think about what happened last time, but silently prayed that Raeya had followed through on having all the garden tools removed.

I shouldn't have to worry about that anymore, Nils reminded himself. *Right now I have to focus on getting Raeya to care about Jarik.*

He turned to the nobleman, who looked a little sick.

"Are you…all right?" Nils ventured.

Jarik straightened up. "Fine," he said a little too eagerly, then he slumped again. "Fine, yes. I'm just…nervous, I suppose. I mean, this is the first time Lady Raeya has agreed to see me in quite some time, and it will likely be my only chance to make a good impression, so…" He trailed off, looking a bit hopeless. "She just…never responds very well to anything I say."

Nils thought for a moment. Jarik's problem was *his* problem now, so he had to find some way to help. "Maybe it's because you sound like a drunken poet when you talk to her."

Jarik turned to him. "I…sound like what?"

"You're too flowery," Nils went on. "It comes across like flattery. Try speaking like you normally would, instead of—what's so funny?"

Jarik was nearly doubled over in laughter. "Sorry," he gasped, "you just...a drunken poet? Don't hold anything back next time, all right? Tell it like it is, I can take it."

Nils stared while Jarik continued laughing. "Thank you," he said, wiping at his eyes. "I needed that."

"If you say so," Nils replied.

"So, less flowery," Jarik said, sounding and looking much more like himself. "Any more advice you can impart?"

Nils frowned. "Not really. Honestly, I'm the last person you should ask for romantic advice."

"Well, *Raeya* advice is what I need right now, and you've spent more time with her than anyone else lately. Save Miss Tilda, of course."

"All right. Well, she reads constantly, so books would be a good topic of conversation. She likes fiction and fantasies, unfortunately. Um...she really seems to like talking in general, but gets annoyed when I don't respond, so make sure you seem interested in everything she says, but, you know, not in a creepy way. Just be engaged."

"Engaged, not creepy," Jarik repeated. "Solid advice."

"And...I don't know. It's difficult, considering I don't even like her. She just seems so frivolous most of the time."

Jarik gave a wan smile. "I suppose you got to know her under different circumstances than I did. She's more grounded than you think."

"How do you mean?"

"Well, when I got to know her, she was in mourning."

Nils cocked his head. "Mourning?"

"It wasn't long after I met her that her betrothed died."

Nils nearly stopped on the path. "Raeya was *betrothed?*"

Jarik nodded. "I'm surprised she hasn't mentioned it. Too painful a subject, I suppose."

Nils thought back to what Raeya had said to him that first day in the library. She'd kissed—and killed—three men. Two were greedy, and the third…

I don't wish to talk about it, she'd said.

Nils swallowed. "How did he die?" He already knew the answer, but for some reason he asked anyway.

"He kissed her. The night before their wedding."

Nils felt a chill in spite of Desna's warmth in the air. It lingered with them even as they reached the garden, and Raeya greeted them with a smile.

"Hello, my lady," Jarik said with a bow. A perfectly normal greeting, as per Nils' advice. Raeya, no doubt eager to correct Nils' opinion of her, willingly engaged Jarik in conversation as they walked. Nils purposefully fell a step behind them once they were sufficiently distracted by their discourse about plants and gardening techniques.

The second time around, he was struck by what a young garden it was. In fact, as he listened to Raeya and Jarik talking, he learned that many of the flowers were planted recently, and the oldest only last year. He began to wonder about the statue he glimpsed from time to time. A young man, older than Nils but still in his prime, of noble stature.

He also found himself constantly glancing at Raeya. If she'd been mourning recently, he couldn't see it in her countenance. She was well-kept and practically glowing, as always. Glowing even while talking to Jarik.

Huh. When had that happened?

"Ah, Nils," she said, turning back to him. "I spoke with my father about the lack of blankets in the towns. He said he doesn't have the funds to spare to give aid—"

No surprise there, Nils thought.

"—*but* he'll let me work on getting some made and distributed if I can raise the funds myself."

Nils raised a brow.

"What's this?" Jarik chimed in.

"Ah. Nils informed me that people in the towns suffer terribly during Kirit's season and many don't even have blankets to keep them warm. I thought I might be able to help."

Jarik smiled. "Dear Lady Raeya, your heart is generous and kind as—"

Nils gave the nobleman a pointed look, and Jarik cut himself off. "What I mean to say is, that is very kind of you, and I would love to help your efforts."

"Really?" Raeya said.

"Of course. I'd gladly make a donation, and with my trade connections I can help with obtaining blankets and perhaps some other supplies as well."

"That would be wonderful!" Raeya said. She seemed to catch her own excitement, and glanced back at Nils. "Wouldn't it?" she said, banishing a bit of guilt from her face.

Yes, it would. Nils never expected he'd be able to help his countrymen from the strange hostage position in which he found himself. He might've genuinely thanked Raeya for her efforts, but he remembered he was supposed to be falling decidedly out of favor with her, and simply nodded.

Raeya's smile flattened a little at his lack of enthusiasm. Still, she forged on, though it seemed to take a little more effort each time she tried to include him in the conversation.

18 RISKS AND REWARDS

The next day was more of the same.

A meeting with Raeya. She was chatty, Nils was distracted. This time he was distracted by a different problem, though.

There had been no reply from Tawson last night.

He's just busy, one side of Nils' mind told him. The other told him that Taws was furious with him for trusting Jarik and had decided to withdraw his support. That side was louder.

Nils was so preoccupied he almost missed what Raeya was saying, but a particular name jumped out at him. "What was that?" he said.

Raeya looked uncertain of herself. "I said I was thinking of inviting Jarik to spend some time with us again. Maybe tomorrow—he said he'd be gone today on business."

Wow. Nils really hadn't imagined it.

"Don't look at me like that," Raeya said, turning indignantly back to the book she held. "I just want to talk with him more about our plans for providing supplies for the townspeople. He seems like he'll be a big help."

Raeya stared at her book a moment longer, though Nils could tell she wasn't reading it. Finally she turned back to him expectantly. "Well?"

"Are you asking my permission?"

"Of course."

"You don't have to, you know."

"Yes, I do."

"You also don't have to bring me along."

"Yes, I do."

Nils sighed, but it was progress. Jarik was going to be thrilled.

"You...were right about him," Raeya said softly, ducking her head down a little at the words. "Not that he's anything for you to be worried about," she added in quite the opposite tone. "It's just that...he doesn't have that look in his eyes anymore. That's all. But I never would've noticed if you hadn't insisted that I spend some time with him. I...misjudged him."

Jarik is going to be so thrilled he might die, Nils amended. And not just Jarik; this was already going much better than Nils would've expected. Maybe he could push a little farther, work on getting himself out of the picture...

Raeya resumed talking about something uninteresting, and a maid slipped through the other side of the room, bringing something to one of the other people in the library. It wasn't Sandri, but she wore the same uniform. Her hair was a similar tone of red to Raeya's, but it wasn't even long enough to brush her shoulders.

Like a common scullery maid, Raeya had said.

The domiseer's daughter seemed to notice Nils' attention on the maid, and he realized he could use that to his advantage.

"Nils?" Raeya said with an eyebrow raised.

"Nothing," he said. "I was just thinking about when you asked me if I preferred longer or shorter hair." He fought back the reflex to glance at Tilda. She was going to skewer him in her mind for this. Hopefully *only* her mind. "I guess I do prefer it shorter."

* * *

"Good morning, hon," a more familiar maid greeted Nils the next morning.

"Don't talk to the prisoner," the guard by the door scolded.

"Ah, pardon me, sir. I still hadn't sorted out if he's a prisoner or a guest." Sandri winked at Nils when the guard couldn't see and handed him a breakfast tray. He started to smile back, then frowned. He still hadn't gotten a reply from Taws. He would've done anything to ask Sandri about it, and she was *right in front of him*, but with a guard standing nearby he couldn't—

Sandri turned suddenly and knocked the tray from his hands, sending dishes and their contents crashing to the floor.

"Ah, not again! Me and you are bad luck for each other, dear," the false maid said, gathering what she could of the dishes.

"You and I," Nils muttered, looking down from the edge of his bed in shock. It seemed he was going to get his wish after all, but he didn't envy her having to clean that colossal mess.

"It'll be tidied up before you can look twice and twice again," Sandri called to the guard outside, who just sighed loudly. He left the door open a crack but didn't seem to care enough to watch, and Sandri kept a steady noise going as she shuffled broken dishes to cover their voices.

"Why hasn't Taws sent a reply to my last letter?" Nils whispered.

"Because he hasn't even read it yet," Sandri whispered back, still focused on the floor.

"What? Is he all right?"

"Of course he is," Sandri said. "He's out looking for leads on the stones, but I needed to talk to you."

"Why didn't you just leave your own message in the box?" Nils asked. "It's risky to meet this way."

Sandri laughed a little and wrinkled her nose. "Tawsey's started teaching me some words and things, but I haven't gotten the hang of it yet."

"Oh," Nils said. "I'm sorry, I should've known."

"That's all right. Hey, Tawsey told me you're a schoolteacher! I bet you could teach a girl to write some letters." She spared him a smile and a wink.

"Uh," Nils said, "I was, yes. Anyway, has something happened?"

"Yes," Sandri said. "I caught wind of a secret, that an investigator is coming next week."

"Investigator?"

"Yeah, the king's sending somebody to look into that attack that nearly killed you in the guardhouse. A rumor got out that there may have been a curse involved, and apparently Dreygard's not too happy about it. Us though? Sounds like the perfect chance to get him caught, doesn't it?"

Nils' heart thudded. "Yes, it does. Except I haven't found anything to incriminate him yet."

Sandri glanced toward the door to make sure the guard was still oblivious. "You know Raeya's attendant? Tilda?"

"Yes," Nils said slowly, not sure where this was going.

"Try her. I hear she's not too fond of her lady's old man, *and* she's close friends with the captain of the guard. She might be able to help."

"You've got to be kidding me," Nils said. "Tilda? Of all people? She hates the very thought of me. She'd probably burn this bed just because I've slept in it."

"Well, I never cross paths with her, and you do every day. See what you can do."

"I can't—"

"I hear you've recruited a nobleman to your side," Sandri interrupted. "If you can do that, I'm sure you can manage a servant."

"Wait, you've heard about Jarik?"

"The servants' hall is a great place for gossip, and he's practically all the other maids talk about," Sandri said, rolling her eyes. "Not that I blame them. Have you seen that fella? Gods, but *wow*. Don't get me wrong—I'm Tawsey's through and through, but it's no wonder all the other women in the manor are swooning over him."

"All the women except the one that matters," Nils sighed.

There was a shuffle by the door, signifying that their time was up.

"Talk to Tilda," Sandri whispered in their last moment. "This chance won't last long, and I'm getting tired of cleaning!"

"You done in here yet?" the guard said, poking his head in.

"Yes, sir. Done as dinner. Or...breakfast?" Sandri said, wiping up the last of the mess with her towel. "Thank you."

She hurried off in a swish of skirts, and Nils could only stare after her.

★ ★ ★

As predicted, Jarik was in a fine mood once Nils told him about Raeya, even in spite of the steady rain falling outside.

The two of them walked together—trailed by a single guard—passing by gloomy windows as they went to meet Raeya in the library. This was the kind of weather that stirred up the mud in the towns and made everyone miserable, and Nils had a hard time shaking his not-so-fine mood even though he was in the home of comfort itself. He empathized too well with those who weren't.

"How do you think she's feeling about you?" Jarik asked when they'd almost reached their destination. "Any progress in that area?"

"It's hard to tell," Nils said, "but I think so? It helps that I don't have to worry about hurting her feelings anymore."

When they walked into the library, Nils didn't notice Raeya immediately, but then a figure stood up from a bench across the room, and both Jarik and Nils stopped short.

"Nils," the nobleman said to him quietly, "was this your doing, by any chance?"

It took Nils a moment to answer. Raeya was blushing red, clasping her hands before her and looking terribly nervous. Tilda's glare was sharper and angrier than usual, if that were possible. Most notably, Raeya's long, orange hair now stopped quite suddenly a few inches above her shoulders.

And it was cute. Extremely, ridiculously, cute.

Fives. I didn't think I actually had a preference. "Um," Nils finally said, "yes, that may have been due to my influence."

"Desna's Tresses," Jarik said. "Well, at least hair grows back." The nobleman cleared his throat, replaced his full smile, and strode toward Raeya.

"Good afternoon, my lady," he said. "This is quite the surprise, but I must say you look beautiful."

"Thank you," Raeya said, though her attention was focused on Nils. "What do you think?" she asked him.

"It's, um, fine," Nils said. He should've said something derogatory, but he was too focused on trying to banish the heat from his face. Why was his face so hot? If he didn't get it under control, Raeya was going to notice—

She smiled a great, big smile of relief, and Nils knew he'd failed. He must've been blushing brighter than she was. Even Jarik cast him a look, eyebrows raised.

"I'm so glad you like it," Raeya said, beaming like the sun.

Nils didn't know what to say that wouldn't get him in worse trouble, so he waited for Jarik to come to his rescue and continued trying to return his face to a normal temperature.

"My lady," Jarik blessedly said, "I wondered if this would be of interest to you." He produced a book from under his arm and held it out to her.

Gods, thank you, Nils thought when Raeya's gaze was finally off of him.

"Oh, what's this?" Raeya said, taking the book. "I've never heard of this author."

"He's foreign," Jarik explained, "but he's very good. This is a recent translation. I thought it quite an exciting story myself."

"I'll be glad to read it," Raeya said, already flipping through the first pages. "Thank you." She gave him a smile, then handed the book to Tilda. "I wondered if we could discuss more options for gathering supplies. You said you knew of some people who might be willing to donate?"

"Yes, of course," Jarik replied. "We could send out a few letters right now, even." He gestured to a writing desk on the other side of the room. "Shall we?"

Raeya nodded and went with him, then noticed Nils wasn't following. "Nils?" she said.

"I'll stay here, if you don't mind," Nils said, sitting down. "I'm not feeling so good." Maybe if she thought he was sick he could blame his redness on a fever.

"Oh," Raeya said, looking concerned. "Do you need anything? Something to drink, maybe?"

"No, I'm fine," Nils said, waving her off.

Raeya frowned. "I'll have Tilda stay with you then, in case you need something."

"My lady?" Tilda said, eyes begging her mistress to say she'd misspoken.

"Please, Tilda," Raeya said. "I'll be back in a few minutes."

Raeya left, and a crushing force of tension took her place. Nils could feel it, those murderous intentions and hateful thoughts swarming around him, the angry attendant at their epicenter.

Weaver's blood, Nils thought. He glanced around and found his guard hadn't bothered standing too close—they'd all seemed to realize that Nils was no threat whatsoever, especially with Jarik around—so he didn't even have to worry about being overheard. He had the perfect opportunity to talk to Tilda.

But he almost would've rather dropped dead.

He cleared his throat, then did it a second time. He was feeling ill in earnest now. "So, Miss Tilda," he managed.

"It's *Matilda* to you," she spat at him, "or better yet, Ms. Fraim."

"Oh," Nils said, voice as weak as his resolve. "Ms. Fraim. Sorry."

Tilda said nothing more.

"H-how do you like serving Lady Raeya?"

"Oh, *now* you use her title, huh? You disrespectful insect. I cannot fathom why my lady allows you in her presence for even a moment. That blasted curse is going to break her heart a second time, due to your..." She sneered down at him, looking for the right word. "...inadequacy."

Ouch. Well, he'd known this was a doomed effort. All he was going to get out of this lady was a torrent of insults. He may as well just—

"She's a joy to serve, I'll have you know."

Nils looked up. All right, he'd keep trying. "What about the rest of her family? Do they treat you well?"

Tilda's mouth was a tight line. "Well enough."

"Even the domiseer?" Nils pushed. "His delegates in the towns are cruel. I kind of assumed working for the man himself would be equally unpleasant."

Tilda's answer took longer to come this time. "Lady Dreygard has only ever treated me fairly," she said. "Lord Dreygard, he...well, he cares for his daughter. That is commendable."

Nils waited.

"But he isn't so different from his delegates otherwise. In fact...I daresay he has no care for the people in his province whatsoever."

There it was. *Desna bless you, Sandri.*

"Do you...know anything about Lord Dreygard?" Nils chanced. Gods, he was walking on thin ice here.

"Know anything?" Tilda said, looking at him.

Nils lowered his voice. "I heard something. An investigator's coming, from the king himself, to look into the attacks that have happened here. Some people believe there was spellweaving involved. I'd think Lord Dreygard would be glad to get to the bottom of it, but apparently he's quite the opposite. Why wouldn't he want the king to look into this?"

For the first time Tilda looked at him without hate in her eyes. In fact, she didn't seem to be seeing him at all. He'd completely drawn her in with this information. "I..." she said. "I hadn't heard."

"The investigator will be here next week."

Nils let that statement fill the air for a moment. Tilda seemed to be thinking hard about what he'd said. "Why are you telling me about this?" she finally asked.

"Because I feel the same way about him that you do," Nils said, "and I firmly believe he has something to hide."

"Something like...?"

Gods, should he say it? He hadn't even told Jarik the truth about Lord Dreygard. He could get himself killed for making such an accusation, and yet...when would he ever get the chance to talk to Tilda like this again?

"I'll put it like this," Nils said, forcing his voice to stay steady and quiet. "As a front-row witness, I *know* the men who attacked me were cursed, and both those weaver's spells were designed specifically to kill me. I can't think of anyone who wants me dead more than he does."

Tilda's eyes widened and the book she'd been holding for Raeya fell from her hands with a thud. He'd done it now; there was no taking it back.

The attendant tried to say something, but it seemed like words had abandoned her. She closed her mouth, then tried again, but Raeya's voice broke through first.

"Tilda?" she said. "Is everything all right?"

Tilda's eyes finally tore away from Nils, and she realized with a start she'd dropped the book. "Oh, Dearest Desna," she said, stooping to pick it up. "I'm sorry, my lady."

"I'm not worried about the book," Raeya said. "You look all shaken up."

"I..." Tilda started, glancing at Nils. He tried to shake his head, but he couldn't let Raeya and Jarik see. Gods, what he wouldn't give to grab the prayer bracelet on Raeya's wrist and beg Desna to keep the attendant's mouth shut.

"I'm fine," Tilda said. "I was dizzy for just a moment, but it's passed now. No need to worry yourself, my lady."

"Are you sure? First Nils, and now you. Maybe there's something in the air today. Why don't we move to the parlor? We'll have more space to ourselves there."

"Very well, my lady."

Raeya led the way, but Tilda gave one last, long look at Nils before they filed out of the library. He had no idea what she was thinking, and that made his insides twist into knots.

Great, he thought. *Now I've spilled a massive secret to about the riskiest person I could've told, and I can't even find out what she intends to do with this information. What if she goes straight to Lord Dreygard? He'll have me killed immediately, no question.*

And while Feren Dreygard might want me dead more than anyone else, Tilda probably isn't far behind.

* * *

"My lady, I wondered if I could ask you a question."

Nils, Raeya, Jarik, and Tilda now occupied the parlor, along with a lone guard standing off by the door. "Of course," Raeya said, tidying her stack of envelopes to be sent to potential patrons.

"There's a ball at Governor Labrink's estate at the end of the week. I wondered if you'd consider attending with me."

Raeya's hands stilled. "Jarik, you know I can't—"

Jarik raised a placating hand. "I know that you've found your true love, and if you refuse to come, I will understand completely. However, it could be a good chance to find more support for your cause, and since Nils is unable to leave the manor at this time, I thought you and I might enjoy the occasion, as friends." He nodded to Nils. "Assuming, of course, that your true love has no objections."

"None whatsoever," Nils said. "Have a ball. Literally."

Raeya looked between the two of them. "I couldn't," she maintained. "I mean…it's been a very long time since I last danced, and, well…I found I could never go to these things. It was too great a risk for me to dance with the men, and none of the women cared to socialize with me. Even though the nature of my curse remains a secret to most, there are plenty of rumors. I've been touched by a spellweaver." Raeya folded her hands in her lap, looking down at them. "That makes me someone to avoid."

"That's why I was hoping you would come with me," Jarik said softly. "I *do* know the nature of your curse. I'll know better than to get too close, and I also know there is no reason to avoid you. You can just have fun, and be yourself. What do you say?"

Raeya looked up at him, and, surprisingly, she didn't say no. "I…I don't know," she said. She turned to Nils, then shook her head.

Well, she didn't say no right away. Nils decided to preempt her rejection before she could speak it aloud. "I really don't mind," he said. "You should go and enjoy yourself."

"No, it wouldn't be right," Raeya said. "I'm yours, Nils. I won't go out with another man and leave you behind, friend or not."

Nils felt a little of that heat return to his face, with her saying it so bluntly like that. Plus the haircut, which made it hard to ignore how pretty she was.

Her eyes, Nils thought. *Focus on her eyes. Dreygard's eyes.*

"You're not mine," Nils said. "You can do whatever you want."

"That's kind, Nils, but I've made up my mind."

It wasn't supposed to be kind. Nils glanced at Jarik, who was watching him expectantly. *I need to be harsher,* Nils thought. *I want* *to be harsher, but…*He looked to the other side, where Tilda stood. She hadn't once made eye contact with him since they'd left the library. If Nils was cruel to Raeya now, if he made Tilda angry…

She had the power to get him killed.

Weaver's blood, I'm an idiot.

Jarik seemed to realize Nils wasn't going to say more, even if he didn't know the reason. "Well, my offer stands, my lady," he said to Raeya. "I won't push you into anything, but I'd love the chance to be your escort just once, should you change your mind."

Raeya looked at him and nodded, and the subject wasn't brought up again.

* * *

Nils ended up leaving the parlor at the same time as Jarik. While the nobleman didn't say anything, Nils got the impression his mood had dampened somewhat. Maybe it was just the persistent rain that still darkened the windows, but Nils figured otherwise.

"Sorry," he said.

Jarik looked over at him.

"I, uh…didn't do a very good job today," Nils confessed.

Jarik remained quiet, and Nils felt his already substantial sense of unease creeping higher, like tiny insects crawling up his frame. It was hard not to rub at his skin to try to banish the imaginary creatures.

"You were…gentler with her than I expected," Jarik finally said. "Except of course for getting her to cut her hair. That was merciless. Were you feeling remorseful?"

Nils shook his head. "I'm just…out of sorts today," he replied, grasping at any sort of explanation. He couldn't very well tell Jarik about the situation with Tilda. "It's the weather, probably."

"Not a fan of rain?"

"No."

"Because it makes mud, right?"

"Yeah," Nils said, glancing out a window they passed in the quiet hallway. "At least anywhere but here it does."

"Hm. It must be a dreary life in the towns."

"It is," Nils said, but a memory flashed through his mind. A small room, sunlight streaming through cracked windows. A figure turning to him. Warm eyes and a warm smile. Nils swallowed a sudden lump in his throat. "Most of the time, anyway."

"Are you all right?"

"Yes," Nils said, but it didn't sound terribly convincing.

"You want to return," Jarik surmised. "Of course you do. Mud or not, that was your life, your home. Well, there's no need to be melancholy. Our plan is off to a good start, don't you think? Lady Raeya has talked more with me in the last few days than she has in months, and even seemed content while doing so. If we can keep this up, you'll soon fulfill your duty to Lord Dreygard and be released to your family."

Nils' heart sunk. "Not my family," he whispered.

"Ah, yes, I suppose it's to wherever the taskers assigned you. You haven't reported that to him yet, have you?"

Nils felt a shiver run through him, a memory completely different from the last one assaulting his mind. Darkness. Fear. Pain.

"Nils?"

"It was horrible," Nils muttered.

"Your assignment?"

"Yes."

"Where was it?"

Nils looked at Jarik, that shiver turning into a spike of terror. Was he trying to get it out of him? Would he—

"Desna's Tresses," Jarik said, observing his face. "Sorry, Nils. Forget I asked, all right? We'll leave that between you and the domiseer. Honestly, I didn't mean to put you in a panic."

Nils looked away, and remembered to breathe. Just an innocent question. Nothing more. "It's all right."

The rain filled the silence long enough for it to become awkward, and Nils cleared his throat. "Sorry," he said.

"For?" Jarik asked.

"For…nearly having a fit there."

"No, no," Jarik said. "You have nothing to apologize for. In fact…I know Lord Dreygard's taskers are keeping things in order, making sure the province and the kingdom stay afloat, but…Gods, it's unfair, isn't it? This whole idea of being *collected*. Being taken from your family, put to work for someone else's agenda. Even if the purposes are good, it's all still…*cruel* in a way." He ran a hand through his dark hair, frowning. "Even I…well, it wouldn't be right to compare my situation with yours. I've wanted for nothing my whole life, but even so…I understand something of this absence of autonomy. I have great respect for my uncle, but his word is law in my life, so a single command from him can…"

There was a distant roll of thunder, and Jarik trailed off. "Oh, well, enough about that," he said, smiling. "This is where our path splits, isn't it? We should part on a happier note. I will expect to see you and Lady Raeya again soon. In the meantime, don't give Lord Dreygard any reasons to execute you, all right?" He smiled wider, clearly intending that as a friendly joke, but as he walked away Nils' stomach dropped lower inside him.

After what I told Tilda in the library, he thought, *I'm afraid I already have.*

19 A MEMORY OF PURPOSE

"*I can do this, Nils,*" *his mother said, collecting a book from the floor. It had lost its cover sometime the previous year, and the pages were curled at the edges. They were all starting to look like that.* "*Why don't you go out and have some fun?*"

"*Fun? I'm not sure there's any of that to be had,*" *Nils replied, dropping a handful of pencils into an old cup. One fell in two pieces, and he cringed.*

"*Nonsense. Young people your age ought to be out and about, getting into trouble—*"

"*—so the street patrols can throw us in prison or break our arms—*"

"*—making memories, falling in love...*"

Nils scoffed.

"*Come now, Nils,*" *his mother said, setting down a small stack of books in a puff of dust.* "*Life in the towns is short. You've got to make the most of it.*"

"*I know it's short,*" *Nils said.* "*That's precisely why I won't be wasting it pursuing love when there are more important things to be done.*"

"*More important? My dear, reclusive child, falling in love, raising a family...these are the things that make life worthwhile.*"

"*They are the things that cause heartache.*"

At last that gave her pause, but he regretted the words as soon as they'd come out. He didn't like to make her think about Dad. As usual, she covered it up with a good-humored smile and went on. "So what do you propose we all spend our time doing?"

"Fixing things," Nils said, straightening the leg of a chair. "Our country's a mess, so our priority ought to be getting it back into shape. We're doing that here by educating kids, giving them opportunities for better work, and equipping them to face society's problems and come up with solutions."

"Such a serious answer," his mother muttered. "Well," she said more openly, "I admire your wishes to better our youth. That's wonderful. But tell me, where will our youth come from if none of us are falling in love and raising families?"

Now Nils paused, but it was brief. Brief enough his mother wouldn't notice, hopefully. "Someone else can do that," Nils said. "I'll stick to what I'm good at, which is teaching, apparently."

"You could make some friends if you tried. The kids love you."

"The kids love to pester me. And they give me more than enough social interaction, thank you."

"Just try it," his mother said. "I know the street patrols are strict, but there must be someplace others your age are meeting to get away from it all. Find a couple girls in the market, ask if they know."

"Oh, that won't sound creepy at all. Hi ladies, do you know of any place we can meet in secret? No patrols around? Maybe have some fun?"

His mother chuckled. "I trust you can have more tact than that."

"It isn't worth my time," Nils maintained, frowning at the books his mother had stacked. "Isn't there one more?"

She nodded. "One's gone missing. More opportunities to teach the kids to share, I suppose."

"We have too few as it is. I'll go out and ask around, see if someone took it home. Maybe I could get some donations to have it replaced. That would be worth my time."

His mother sighed, but smiled. "Whatever gets you out of the house, my dear."

20 VISIT

That night felt dark, even with candles lit and a fire in the hearth.

Nils couldn't sleep, not with the day's events haunting him. Any second now, guards could burst through the door, dragging him before Lord Dreygard where he'd face his final moments. Tilda had so many reasons to turn him in. She wanted to be rid of him, to get him out of Raeya's life, and this was an easy way to do it. It all came down to who she hated more, Lord Dreygard or Nils.

Putting that aside, Nils felt like he'd let Jarik down. The nobleman had been gracious as always, but that almost made it worse. Nils was going to have to figure something out; he couldn't fulfill his end of their deal without angering Tilda at the same time.

As if all that wasn't heavy enough on his mind, there was Raeya.

Nils had never considered what side effects she might deal with, living with a curse. Her limitations in public gatherings, her isolation. Now that he thought about it, she never seemed to meet with anyone besides him. None of the other nobles visiting the estate came to greet her. The only one by her side was Tilda, a hired attendant. No wonder she seemed starved for conversation all the time.

There I go again, Nils thought. *No sympathy; she's a Dreygard, and she doesn't lack anything she needs in life. She can deal with a little solitude.*

And the one she loved dying at her lips the night before their wedding.

Nils shook himself. None of that should matter to him. He just needed to get out of here, to—

There was a sound at the door, and Nils sat bolt upright in his bed. He knew it; Tilda had sold him out. He never should've listened to Sandri, never should've risked such a thing...

The next few seconds were agonizing. The lock clicked on his door. The knob turned, so, so slowly. A faint crack of light appeared as it opened, and a silhouetted figure slipped inside. Then the door shut behind them.

A step forward, and the hearth light revealed who it was. Tilda? Why would she come herself?

Tilda cleared her throat, and Nils scrambled out of bed and stood before her. She watched him levelly, not saying a word until Nils was tensed beyond what he could bear. Finally, she spoke. "Do you truly believe...that Lord Dreygard is..."

She couldn't bring herself to finish, but Nils knew what she was asking. Could he trust her? Did he have a choice?

He nodded. Tilda shifted, looking chilled. "Why are you here?" she asked. "For what purpose did you break into the manor?"

To steal, was Nils' automatic response, but he bit it off. That was just his excuse, his half-truth. This wasn't a time for half-truths; he could feel it in the air. "To find proof," he answered.

"And have you...?"

"No."

Tilda's shoulders settled a little. "So nothing is certain yet."

"...No."

Tilda held his gaze, and for a moment neither of them spoke. "My sister's family starved to death," she said at last. "Her husband died on some tasker's errand, and she had no means to provide for herself and her children. She wrote to me asking for help, and I filed a request to have half of my savings sent to her immediately and half of my monthly allowance after that, as I couldn't travel there myself. Since it concerned the money in his treasury, the request had to cross Lord Dreygard's desk, although I had no reason to suspect it hadn't been approved. It wasn't until it was too late that I learned. Lord Dreygard apparently hadn't considered my request important enough to be worth his time, and had set it aside. All it would've taken was a signature.

"I would have resigned that day," Tilda went on, "if not for Raeya. After what she'd been through at the hands of that curse, even before losing her betrothed—I just couldn't bear to leave her. I wouldn't add to her isolation. So I stayed. But I've never considered myself loyal to her father since, only to Raeya. And now, if he's truly a...a spellweaver..."

"You'll help me?" Nils asked.

Tilda narrowed her eyes. "What is it you hope to do?"

"Reveal him to the king," Nils said. "Have him deposed."

"If he's a weaver, he'll be executed."

"I know."

"If he isn't..."

"Then there's still plenty to take him to the gallows," Nils said. "He's trading with Galreyva. Of *that* I am certain."

"Do you have proof?"

Nils let out a breath. "No. But I almost did. That's why I broke in here in the first place. There was a shipment, supposedly from Emperor Ri'sen. I thought I'd found it, but I was caught before I could look through the chest. I just grabbed the necklace on the top, with a single black stone, but it was nothing. A fake."

Tilda turned her head slightly toward the door. "You hear all that?" she said, and Nils stiffened.

"Yes," replied a gruff voice. The door was still open the tiniest bit, and Nils hadn't noticed. He looked at Tilda, feeling betrayed, staked-through with panic.

"That's Graham," she said. "Captain Clerrit. He's the captain of the guard here. I believe he's questioned you a couple times since you arrived."

She's close friends with the captain of the guard, Sandri had said.

"Does he..." Nils started, but his throat seemed full of dust.

"He has his own reasons for distrusting Lord Dreygard, and for believing the domiseer has been hiding things from him," Tilda went on, "but he hasn't found any solid evidence either. With what you've said...well, it'll give him one more reason."

Nils relaxed, if only a little. "Does all this mean that you'll help me? Help me reveal Lord Dreygard when the investigator comes?"

Tilda shook her head. "Without proof, we cannot act. We'll only get ourselves executed. However, if you find something, get our attention and let us know."

"How am I supposed to find anything without help?" Nils demanded. "I'm kept on a leash here, constantly watched."

"I don't know," Tilda said, "but we've risked enough already. Also, speaking for myself, I...I don't know if I could help you anyway. If Lord Dreygard is caught and condemned, it would have grave implications for Raeya as well. I couldn't move forward without first seeing to her safety and happiness. That is all I have to say." She turned to go.

"Wait," Nils said. "About Raeya..."

That stopped Tilda in her tracks, and she looked back.

"I'm going to be cruel to her," Nils said, "and I apologize in advance. I want you to know it's nothing personal, but to ensure Lord Dreygard doesn't throw another curse at me, I need to make her hate me."

Tilda didn't look too pleased, but she nodded. "It's just as well," she said. "What the gods were thinking when they picked you out for her, I'll never know."

She left, and the lock clicked behind her. Nils sat down on his bed, then let himself fall backward onto the mattress. "Gods," was all he had the strength to say.

21 A MEMORY OF DEPARTURE

"*Mr. Nils?*"

"*It isn't* **Mr. Nils.** *Surely you know how to address me properly by now.*"

"*Yes, but Mr. Nils, could you tell me what this word is?*"

Nils sighed, but peered over the girl's shoulder to look into her book. "*Irrelevant.*"

"*Oh, thank you.*"

"*You're welcome.*"

"*Mr. Nils?*"

"*Yes, Trina?*"

"*What does irrelevant mean?*"

"*Not important,*" *Nils said.*

"*It isn't?*"

"*No, no, it* means *not important. Not pertaining to the information given.*"

"*Oh. Thank you.*"

"*You're welcome.*"

"*Mr. Nils?*"

"*Pertaining means related to.*"

"*Thank you.*"

"You're welcome."

When the girl remained quiet for the next several seconds, Nils finally dared to move toward the back of the room where his mother was resting. "Your patience has grown, dear," she said.

"I'm trying."

"You're doing wonderfully."

"You're better. People even say you're too soft on the children. Not strict enough to keep them in line."

"Bah," his mom said. "Life's hard enough without a mean-spirited teacher breathing down your neck. I prefer the kind approach."

"I'm not saying I don't," Nils said. "I think you're right. I'm just not very good at it myself."

"What? Of course you are. There's more than one way to be kind."

"Whatever that means."

"You care about them, don't you?"

"Probably too much. A more practical person would be glad that we currently have the same number of students as we do chairs."

"But you'd rather see more students sitting on the floor than wonder why they've suddenly stopped attending class."

Nils nodded. "I'm afraid I don't have to wonder. We've offered to teach even those who can't pay, so I doubt it's their parents pulling them out. Those fiving taskers are taking them all. It's only a matter of time before they—"

There was a knock on the door, and Nils frowned as he went to open it. As soon as he saw the uniform on the man standing in the doorway, his stomach dropped.

A tasker.

"Good afternoon," the man said with a slur that made Nils wonder if he might be drunk. He wouldn't be surprised.

"Can I help you with something?" Nils asked.

The man glanced at the logbook in his hand. "You Nils?"

"Yes."

"Let me see your tags."

Nils took his identification tags from around his neck and handed them over. The tasker gave them a cursory inspection, then handed them back. "You're coming with me," he said. "You've been assigned."

"What?" Nils said. "But I'm already employed. I'm the schoolmaster here."

"Schoolmaster?" the tasker said, looking him up and down. "You're a bit young, ain't ya?"

Nils bit his tongue to keep from correcting the man. "I've apprenticed here since childhood and was registered as my father's successor before he died. Once I came of age, I inherited his title. It's all legitimate, I assure you."

"Oh, I believe you, but that doesn't matter. You're needed elsewhere. The coal mines, to be exact."

"Coal mines?" Nils said, feeling a chill wash over him. "Sir, I...I'm not suited to that kind of work at all. I'm fully trained in all areas of education, and even if I'm young, I've already gained ample experience teaching—"

"Leave the teaching to the women," the tasker interrupted. "You can better serve your kingdom doing man's work, putting your arms and back to good use."

"And who says putting one's brain to good use isn't just as much man's work?"

The tasker smiled, put a friendly arm around Nils' shoulder, and led him down the few steps to the street. He leaned in close.

"Talk back again, muddie," the tasker rasped into his ear, "and your brains'll be spilled right here on the street where your mother and the kiddies can see 'em. Got it?"

Nils glanced back at his mother in the doorway, her face frozen in worry. In that moment, he understood perfectly why his father had left *without a fight when the taskers came for him. Some things are worse than watching your loved one walk away.*

"Yes," Nils said, swallowing. "I understand."

"Atta boy," the tasker crooned, swinging Nils away with his arm. "Everything you need will be provided. You can just come along with me."

"Nils!" his mother called after him, rushing down the schoolhouse steps. She stopped at the bottom, and Nils looked back at her, hoping his expression conveyed the apology he couldn't give in words. She looked so frail, one thin arm outstretched to hold the banister, visibly shivering in the cold. How long could she last? Who would be here to care for her if not him?

"I'll be fine," he called back to her, wanting to leave her some words of comfort. "I'll…I'll see you again."

Kirit above, Nils prayed in fury, hating the tasker, hating the domiseer, hating Kirit himself, let those words be true.

22 STATUE

It felt weird to see Tilda the next day.

She acted as if nothing had happened, except...yes, there may have been a little less hatred in her eyes when she looked at him. Even though he'd warned her about his plans for Raeya, he wondered how long that would last. There were only a couple days left before the dance, and Nils had to make them count.

The skies were clear today, and Raeya wanted to check on her flowers. It spite of the driving rain the day before, the ground was only a squishy bed of grass under their feet, not the mire Nils had come to expect. He tried not to glare at it.

"I'm telling you, there's no reason you can't go with him," Nils said, taking his eyes off his feet. He'd wasted no time in bringing up the ball once they'd set out.

"Yes there is," Raeya said, sounding moderately annoyed. "He isn't *you.*"

"No, he's a much better partner than I could ever be," Nils countered. "He'll fit in there. He understands that kind of gathering, knows how to socialize. *And* he's far better looking than I am, if you needed another reason."

"That all depends on one's taste. I don't think he's better looking than you."

"He's much taller."

Raeya took a moment to size him up, then looked forward again. "You're taller than I am," she said. "That's all that matters."

Barely, Nils thought. *Wear the wrong shoes and you'll suddenly feel differently.*

"Ah, just look at all the fallen petals," Raeya said, crouching near a bed of purple flowers. "The rain was too much for them."

Nils didn't want to let her change the subject. "I can tell you want to go."

"I've made up my mind, Nils," Raeya half-shouted, spinning to face him, and Nils blinked in surprise. Raeya's face went pink as she realized what she'd done. "S-sorry, dear," she said. "I just...don't want to talk about it anymore."

Neither did Nils, but he had to keep pushing, so he muttered one more comparison under his breath, just loud enough for her to hear. "He actually *wants* to go with you."

Raeya visibly tensed, but she said nothing. She stalked over to the next plant, inspecting its blossoms roughly enough that a few more petals fell to the ground.

Now what? Nils thought. *She's angry, which is a good start, but I need more...*

He looked around, eyes resting on the back of the statue he'd yet to see up close. Raeya always seemed to avoid that part of the garden when they visited.

"What's that statue?" Nils asked. Raeya froze, and Nils knew he'd guessed correctly.

"He...was my betrothed, before he died," she said without looking at him.

"Can we go see it?"

Raeya finally turned to him, and nodded.

* * *

"I never intended to kiss him."

Raeya's voice was quiet as they looked up at the statue of her first love, a stranger to Nils.

"I thought we should play it safe, even though I believed with all my heart he was my true love. I...I couldn't imagine loving anyone more than him, and he said the same of me. It all made so much sense."

Nils couldn't look at her while she spoke. If he did, he'd lose all his nerve to be harsh with her, he could tell. Even now, that small tremor in her voice while she spoke...it almost hurt just to hear it. So he stared at the man's stone face instead, looking down at them with a faint smile.

"Keden was never afraid of me. When everyone else avoided me, he didn't. That's what started it all. And he...he was the one who wanted to do it. The night before we were supposed to be married, he told me he had no doubts that we were meant for each other. The kiss would simply be proof of that, and then we could live together without worry."

Nils wished she would stop talking. *This is it,* he said to himself. *Don't back down now. Don't think about it, just say it. You* need *her to hate you. Your life depends on it.*

"How could I not believe him?" Raeya said. "There wasn't the slightest hint of fear in his eyes."

"So that's it?" Nils said. "Most men give their lives in a war or something to get a statue made in their honor. All this guy had to do was kiss a pretty girl."

Raeya turned to him, and it took Nils' entire reserve of inner strength to make himself meet her eyes, to keep his face neutral while she looked at him with a gaze hot as flame and cold as ice. He thought she was going to slap him, but instead she grabbed his collar, pulled him in, and kissed him.

There was nothing timid about this kiss. Raeya's mouth pushed against his, and Nils felt something inside, like a spark, or a fire—

No. Definitely not that.

Raeya broke off and shouted at him. "How *dare* you. *I* commissioned that statue, and this garden, in his memory. Because I *loved* him. He was warm, and kind, and so many things that you are not."

She stalked away, and Nils spun around. "Wait," he said. "What—what was the kiss about?"

Raeya whirled back to face him. "That was to convince myself you really are my true love, because right now, I can't believe it."

Once more she thundered away, and Nils felt dizzy. "Wait, so you...were testing to see if...I would survive?"

He asked the question too quietly for Raeya to hear, and he wouldn't have expected her to answer it anyway. Tilda spared him one exasperated look as she hurried after her mistress, and even Nils' guard looked away from him awkwardly.

Nils didn't need anyone to say it. He could tell. He'd gone too far.

23 A MEMORY OF RETURNING

Nils stood in front of the old schoolhouse. Candlelight shone from every window, warmth glowing through the pristine panes of glass that filled each one. All whole. Unbroken. New.

Wrong.

Nils darted away from the building, not daring to look inside. He could be noticed, caught, sent back to the pits of Hearthnight he'd just escaped.

But worse, he could see the truth with his own eyes. The truth he already knew. Someone else lived in that house now. He dashed blindly through an alley, haunted by the glow most would've found inviting, until he ran into someone.

"Nils?" the someone asked, and Nils registered her blearily. Mrs. Tucker, from the bakery. "Kirit's Sapphire Crown, it is you," she said.

"Please, don't," Nils started, finding it hard to speak, "don't tell anyone, Mrs. Tucker. I shouldn't have come here. I knew it would…that she would…"

Nils' voice and face revolted as one, leaving him unable to say another word, strained with an agony far worse than anything he'd endured in Gen Rill.

"Oh, Nils, dear. I'm so sorry."

Nils bit down on his lip, mastering himself enough to swallow, to breathe. "Where is she buried?" he asked, his voice sounding calmer than expected.

"I don't know. The ditches, probably. They just took her on a cart with everyone else."

"The ditches."

"I really am so sorry, dear. None of us could afford—Nils? Where are you going? Nils?"

Nils didn't stop, or even look back. He was going to find Tawson. There was nowhere else to go, and nothing left to lose.

And Dreygard would pay for this.

24 CAUGHT

Raeya didn't call for Nils the next day.

A maid brought breakfast. Then lunch several hours later. Nils ate his food without tasting it and found he couldn't finish either meal. His stomach felt like a disturbed nest of vipers.

I did what I had to do, he told himself. *She's better off with Jarik anyway, and I just want to make it out of this alive. Her feelings don't matter to me.*

His thoughts had never felt so hollow.

Nils could've sworn a full day passed after lunch before someone finally came to bring him supper. He wasn't interested in the food, but his room felt more like a prison today than any day previous, so he sat up straight when his door opened.

Sandri.

She didn't smile this time when she saw him, and that was his first clue that something was wrong.

He wasn't surprised when she "accidentally" knocked the candelabrum over, spilling hot wax on the floor. She gave her usual patter to the guard, managing to keep her tone light, then whispered to Nils the moment they were in the clear.

"Any luck with Tilda?"

"I talked to her," Nils said, "but she won't help."

"What? That investigator's going to be here in four days."

Four days. That meant two days after the ball.

"And we've got another problem," Sandri said. "Taws still hasn't come back. It's been too long now; I have to go look for him."

"You're leaving?" Nils said, a shock of alarm flaring in his chest. "Won't you be dismissed from the staff?"

"I managed to get permission for a couple days," Sandri said. "Told them my mum died."

That shock of alarm turned to something sharper, and Nils flinched. He shook his head, pressing on. "You shouldn't go. It's too dangerous." *And if something happens to you, I'll be left behind.*

"I have to. Taws was in seriously bad territory, looking for those stones. Something's happened, I know it."

"Is there a chance he just left us?" Nils asked. "Cut out because things aren't going well?"

"What? No way."

"I know you love him," Nils said, "but how much do you really know about him? He said he has contacts watching the black market. The more I think about it, the shadier he seems."

"He likes to keep his secrets, sure," Sandri muttered. "That's what most of our fights are about, but even so I'd trust him with my life. As for the *contacts,* well, he has a lot of people on his side. Lots of Thrinians, like him, and some other folks, like me. I'm not sure what started it all, but we've been keeping an eye out for signs of Galreyvan activity, trying to get back at Emperor Ri'sen however we can. Tracking down and taking out spies who've crossed the border, intercepting shipments. That sort of thing."

Unholy fives, I joined a gang, Nils thought. "So why did Taws send *me* in to steal from Dreygard, when he could've sent any of his followers?" he said, letting the anger boil under his skin. "Because I'm his newest recruit? Because I'm *expendable?*"

"Shh," Sandri cautioned. "Nils, I think Tawsey chose you because he trusted you."

"Why should he trust me more than his other comrades?" he said. "His own people?"

"Because he—"

"Hey," said the guard at the door, and Sandri and Nils froze. "What are you doing? You know you aren't supposed to talk to him."

Sandri immediately bowed in apology. "So sorry, Mr. Guard. You know me—just can't resist a good chat, no matter who the company is. I'll scurry off now and find somebody else's ear to assault."

"I don't think so," said the guard, coming into the room. "You're awfully clumsy a maid to still be working here, girly. You'll come with me and answer some questions."

He reached for Sandri's arm, and Nils felt panic setting into both of them. What could he do? What could he possibly—

"Relax, Marks," came a voice from the door.

The guard turned. Bern was there. "You're making something out of nothing. I've seen this girl around, and she's jabbering away every time."

"This was no friendly conversation," Marks replied. "And regardless, she broke the rules."

"What, like you did takin' a few swigs during your last shift? I'm pretty sure that isn't the staff's drink you've got in your flask."

Marks tensed, and Bern waved a hand. "It's no big deal, Marks. Go rest and have a proper drink—I'll take care of this. My shift started five minutes ago anyway."

"Fine," Marks said, giving one last irked glance at Nils and Sandri. He muttered something unintelligible, then walked away.

Bern gave Nils a long look, and Nils feared they were in even worse trouble now, but then the big guard gestured Sandri to the door with his thumb. Was he…letting her go?

Sandri turned to Nils with eyes that must've looked as surprised as his own. She didn't have much choice but to obey, but she risked squeezing his hand once before ducking out of the room. That gesture of solidarity meant more to Nils than he would've expected, but now he had to stare down the guard by himself, and Bern's height alone was enough to threaten Nils' resolve, never mind the sword on his belt.

"Sit," Bern said, shutting the door to the room. Nils sat on the edge of his bed, and Bern sat in front of the door. "Now tell me," he said, "what you and the maid were talking about, and don't try to tell me it's a *private matter.*"

Nils swallowed. "We were just…That is, she's…"

Unholy fives, what could he say? Whether lie or truth, everything he could think of led to trouble.

Bern huffed impatiently. "Spit it out, kid. *Or* tell me what you and that noble have been meeting about. Just do it quick, in case Marks decides to stick his ugly nose in here again."

"Quick*ly.* Um, aren't you on the same side as Marks?"

"Never liked 'im much. But that doesn't matter. I just…I gotta do something here, kid. Answer me."

"What do you *have to* do?"

Bern growled and stood, lumbering closer and causing Nils to scramble backward onto his bed. "I gotta know what you're up to, because I'm in deep water and you might be the only one who can help me, but I don't know, because I don't know what you're up to."

Nils stared. "Huh?"

"Can you help me or not?!"

"I—hold on, why do *you* need help?"

"Because I tipped off one of the king's men about there being a weaver's curse on the knife, and Dreygard said we weren't supposed to do that, and if he finds out it was me, I'm gonna be slaughtered like a hog."

"You...it was *you?*" Nils said.

"Yes!"

"All right," Nils said, raising a hand to quiet the guard. For someone worried about being overheard, he was awfully loud. "Slow down, and tell me exactly what's going on."

Bern sighed, but let his shoulders roll back and relax a little. "I know Aran was innocent," he said. "He and I have worked together for years. He wouldn't make up stuff about a curse, and he never would've gone after you like that without orders. But Dreygard said he was to blame, and there was no curse. You saw the guy yourself, yeah? There was *definitely* a curse."

Nils nodded. "I agree with you."

"So why's Dreygard covering it up?" Bern went on. "It don't sit well with me."

"It doesn't."

"Right? So that's why I told the king's man. I had to. I can't stand the thought of a *weaver* prowling around here, *cursing* people, and...and I had to do it for Aran. He was a good guy, and I...I think Dreygard might've had him offed. He said he was gonna be let go, but...he just disappeared after that. Same with that poor bloke in the garden."

So that was why Aran never showed up again. Gods, Dreygard was vile. "So...what do you want from me, exactly?" Nils asked.

"You keep meeting with people. Sowell, the maid. Don't think I haven't noticed. You were even chatting with Tilda the other day. You're up to something, and since you was stealing from Dreygard in the first place, I figure you're doing something to bring him down, because Dreygard *himself* might just be the weaver, if he's going to such trouble to cover it all up. Am I wrong?"

Nils blinked. He'd never put much confidence in Bern's intellect, but somehow he'd seen through Nils *and* Lord Dreygard better than anyone else.

Nils shook his head. "You're not wrong."

"I knew it! So, we're teaming up, me and you."

"You and I."

"That's right. You're gonna help me show the king's investigator what Dreygard's been hiding."

"One problem," Nils said.

"What?"

"I don't have anything to go on."

"Nothing?"

"Well…Tilda and the captain of the guard are on our side, but they said they won't help unless I have proof, and I'm in no position to get any proof."

"I'll help you get proof," Bern said.

"You…wait, really?"

"Yeah," said the guard. "And if the captain's in on it, I should be able to move you 'round the house pretty easily, too. He can clear out the other guards while we search."

Nils had a hard time finding his next words. He was starting to question if he was even awake at this point.

"So where do we look first?" Bern asked when Nils sat there gaping like a confused trout.

"Um, well...when I broke in, I was looking for a small shipment. A chest of trade goods. Has anything else like that come in?"

"Oh, yeah, Dreygard gets those now and then."

"Do you know what's in them?"

Bern shrugged. "Just stuff from what I've seen. Books, decorations, jewelry. I figured they were gifts from other domiseers or governors or something."

That's about what Nils saw when he got his brief glance in the chest, although his eyes had locked onto that black-stoned necklace. A fake, a...diversion? "What if that's just the top layer?" Nils wondered aloud.

"Hm?"

"That chest didn't come from some domiseer or governor, it came from Galreyva."

"Galrey—you saying that Dreygard's trading with the Galreyvans? I guess that makes sense, if he's already weaving magic from their fiving dark god, but—*Kirit's Sapphire Crown*, I've touched those chests."

"It's Desna's season."

"Oh. *Desna's Emerald Tresses.* What have I gotten myself into?"

"Exactly what I've been asking myself lately," Nils said. "Anyway, can you find out if one of those shipments has come in recently? I have a feeling if we actually have time to look at it thoroughly, we'll find something."

Bern nodded. "Can do. I'll talk to Captain Clerrit when my shift's over."

"Great."

"Great." Bern stood there awkwardly for a few seconds. "Guess I should get back outside now," he said. "If anyone walks by, they'll notice."

Nils nodded, and Bern shuffled toward the door. "Oh, just to clarify," Nils said, "Jarik Sowell's helping protect my life by keeping Dreygard at bay, but he doesn't know about my plans to reveal Dreygard, or that he's a weaver. Sandri—the maid—is in on the plan and knows everything, but Tilda and the captain don't know about her, so we can't reveal her to them. And Raeya's in the dark to everything at this point, and we need to keep it that way."

Bern stared for a moment, then blinked. "All right," he said. "Got it."

25 GOOD NEWS

Nils was surprised when he was summoned the next day. After the wound he'd given Raeya, he wondered if she would even want to see him again. He wouldn't blame her if she didn't.

"Where are we going?" Nils asked when his guard steered them in a different direction than usual. It wasn't Bern this morning, meaning his shift had ended. Had he spoken with the captain yet?

"Detour," was all the guard said. It turned out the detour was Jarik, waiting for him in an empty corner of the great hall.

"Nils!" the nobleman said when he saw him, then he marched forward and gave Nils a hug.

"Um..." Nils said, not sure what to make of this. Could anyone see them? What would this look like, exactly, a noble hugging the peasant-thief who'd broken into the manor?

Thankfully, Jarik let go. "You, sir, are a wonder. A genius," he said, beaming. "I don't know what you said to Raeya, but it worked. She's agreed to come with me to the dance tomorrow."

"Oh," Nils said. It was all he could think to say.

"She and I also spent most of the day together yesterday, and she's really opened up with me. It's a complete turnaround."

"She...spent time with you without me present?" Nils asked.

"Yes. It's great, isn't it?"

"Yeah. Great."

Finally the nobleman's smile faded. "Nils, are you all right?" he asked. "You don't look so well this morning."

"Fine," Nils lied, while inside his thoughts churned like a tempest. They'd churned like that all night, swaying back and forth. First, there was Bern, who may or may not turn out to be a reliable ally. Then Tilda, who wasn't quite the spiteful banshee he'd expected, but still a frightening person to depend upon. Sandri, who certainly wasn't coming back when she didn't know how things had turned out with Bern, and who had taken Nils' best chance at escaping the manor with her. And Raeya.

Mostly Raeya. That blasted kiss, and the look in her eyes before she'd given it.

"I'm just...tired," Nils said.

"I see. Well, you can rest now, my friend. Things are going well. I...really can't say how much I owe you. Even aside from your help with Raeya, I'm glad we crossed paths, Nils."

Jarik's eyes were surprisingly solemn as he said it, and Nils' tired brain cycled that into the maelstrom of thought as well. He found he felt the same, and actually regretted that if all went according to plan, he would never see the nobleman again. Jarik was kind, well-spoken, easy to talk with. He was just the sort of friend Nils would've wanted to find, had he been looking. He was glad to help Jarik, to see him happy and relieved, even while feeling horrid inside about his own actions.

Making friends, Nils thought, *isn't nearly as straightforward as I imagined.*

* * *

No matter how hard Nils tried to brace himself, it still felt like a punch in the gut when he saw Raeya.

She was reading in the parlor, her hair falling around her face in gentle waves of sunset orange. He'd known from the start she was pretty, but for some reason it almost caused him pain to look at her now. Like she was so pretty it hurt. That was stupid, but that was the only way he could think to describe it.

There was also the punch of guilt he felt from what he'd said to her. That hurt more.

Raeya didn't look up when he sat beside her. Ten seconds in, Nils felt like the silence was going to kill him, so he looked at her book and searched for something to say.

It didn't take long. "You've read this before," he said. It was one of the first books he'd seen her reading.

"And I wanted to read it again," she said. "Is that a problem?"

"No," Nils said, and didn't dare say more. Instead he quietly read along with her. The writing told of a place very different from Chanterey, a land with golden skies and white towers reaching to the heavens. It sounded like a paradise…or perhaps a sanctuary.

"You read to escape, don't you?"

Raeya finally looked at Nils, eyes stormy but questioning.

"Your books. You're always reading when you're upset about something. I guess…that is one nice thing about fiction. It gives you a place to find solace when life is…hard."

Raeya put the book down on the table in front of her. "I'm going to the dance with Jarik tomorrow."

"That's good," Nils said. And it *was* good. Great, even. It's exactly what Nils had been working toward. So why did it feel so bad?

"But we're going mostly to work on our supply project for the towns. He'll be my friend and escort, nothing more."

The sour feeling in Nils' stomach started to evaporate. *No, blast it all,* he thought. *That's the* bad *news.*

"That's all I wanted to tell you," Raeya said, picking up her book again. "You can go now, if you want."

"Oh."

Nils didn't budge. Raeya continued reading for half a minute, then put her book back down with a *thwack.*

"It figures I cut my hair off right before going to my first dance in over a year, and one of only a few dances I've attended in my life," she blurted out. "Gods, what is everyone going to think?" She clutched what remained of her locks.

"It…looks fine," Nils said, feeling like he had to say something. *Why am I still here?* he thought. *She dismissed me. If I stay, I might end up undoing some of my progress in getting her to hate me, because right now I can't…I can't stand to be—*

"It doesn't to me," Raeya said, sighing and slouching in her seat.

"It looks nice," Nils maintained, "but…I'm sorry. I never should've steered you to cut it if you didn't want to."

Raeya stared at him.

"And I…I'm sorry for what I said. In the garden. I'm a jerk."

Nils couldn't look at her, but he could feel her stare intensifying as he looked doggedly forward.

"All right," he said, "I'll go now." He got up to leave, but Raeya grabbed his hand, and Nils was frozen by the spark he felt at her touch.

"Stay," Raeya said.

Nils sat back down.

"You *are* a jerk," Raeya said, then resumed reading. She said nothing more, so Nils just read along with her until she had to go.

26 SEND-OFF

Raeya invited Nils to see her off the next day.

She hadn't yet arrived when Nils was brought down, so he talked with Jarik while they waited at the bottom of a staircase. Jarik seemed nervous

"This is it," he said. "Today will be my best chance to win over Lady Raeya. It…it feels like a last chance, in a way."

"You'll do fine," Nils encouraged him. "You are, in every way, a better fit for Raeya than I could ever be. She's going to see that eventually. Honestly, I think she already has."

"She was impressively angry at you the other day."

"Yeah."

"But I don't know if that's enough," Jarik went on, "to make her forsake her true love."

"A true love she doesn't even *like*. You just have to get her to forget about her curse, to choose for herself instead."

"And how do I do that? It feels like leaping an impossible chasm."

Nils thought hard about it as the footmen at the top of the staircase moved aside, making way for someone. "Just…tell her what you told me," he said. "Even though she's found her true love…you can't help wishing she'd cast fate aside and choose you instead. A romantic idea like that…"

Raeya appeared at the top of the stairs, her parents walking behind her.

"…might just be enough to sway her."

Nils' voice barely lasted until the end of his sentence. Raeya looked…

"Beautiful," Jarik whispered. Nils glanced sideways at the nobleman, who was completely enraptured. Nils turned back to Raeya and did everything he could to keep from becoming the same.

Raeya needn't have worried about her hair; Tilda had styled it perfectly, and Nils imagined every woman who saw her would want to cut her hair short afterward. Nils didn't bother noting what color Raeya's dress was, only that it flattered her in every way.

"I really love her, Nils," Jarik said.

Nils swallowed. "I know." He had to move his attention elsewhere, so he looked to Raeya's parents for a moment. Lady Dreygard, orange-haired like her daughter, observed him with open curiosity, while Lord Dreygard supplied open contempt. There was something intentional in his glare, almost a challenge.

Only one of us is going to make it out of this, Nils thought at him, *and there's no way on the king's soil I'm letting you send me back to Gen Rill.*

When Raeya reached them, she approached Nils first, but the air between them felt…thick. Almost as though a buffer had formed itself there, a barrier that was hard to even speak across.

"Thank you for coming, Nils," she said, giving him a polite smile. He just nodded, and so she moved on to Jarik, just like that. How short a time ago was it that she would've kissed his cheek, or latched onto his arm…

"My lady, you are stunning," Jarik said. He'd learned quickly to remove the air of flattery from his words, and his compliment rang genuine. He took her hand and kissed it. Raeya seemed nervous at the gesture, but nothing happened. It was only kissing her lips that sent men to their graves.

"Shall we go?" Jarik said. Raeya nodded, sparing one last look at Nils before taking Jarik's arm and leaving, heading for the carriage that would be waiting for them outside.

Nils didn't turn around to watch them go. He felt ill inside, though there was no reason why he should. Tilda passed him by, and Nils hardly noticed, although he got the impression she was watching him as she followed after her mistress.

Lord and Lady Dreygard turned to head back up the stairs, having seen their daughter off. Nils caught Dreygard's eye once more, then watched the back of his head as he retreated.

Lord Feren Dreygard. Yes, that was his target. That was why he was here. Gods, he'd gotten so caught up in everything else, he felt like he'd lost sight of the only thing that mattered.

His eyes traveled to Lord Dreygard's wrists, hanging down at his sides. Nils would see those cuffs removed, and reveal those black veins beneath.

* * *

Late that afternoon, Nils was sitting on his bed again. His head felt clearer than it had in a long time.

There was a quiet knock on his door, and a tall figure let himself in.

"Hey," said Bern. "Clerrit's got us an opening. You ready to go?"

145

27 SEARCH

"Fives, it would be so easy if we could just get a look at his wrists, yeah?" Bern said as he and Nils scurried down a passageway. Nils rather wished the guard wouldn't talk at all, even if Captain Clerrit had cleared the way for their passing. He felt pinpricks of nervousness all over, just waiting for someone to discover them. "I don't think I've ever seen him take those cuffs off, though, and it's not like we can spy on his bath. Eck. Wish I hadn't brung up that thought."

"Brought up that thought," Nils corrected quietly, wishing the same.

"But your idea was good. Clerrit said another of those shipments just arrived. We can search it out and see what we find."

"Aren't we going the wrong way?" Nils asked. "I was told those shipments were always brought straight into the manor, to the storeroom I broke into last time. I'm pretty sure you're leading me outside."

"Well they ain't gonna hide their goods in the same place twice once a thief has found it, are they?"

Nils cringed at Bern's choice of words, but felt ashamed of his own logic. Yes, that made sense.

"They're putting them in one of the outbuildings now, till they're unpacked. There'll be guards at the front, so we'll have to be careful getting in, but the back should be clear long enough for us to get in and out."

Evening was approaching now, and the sky was losing its light. Nils was grateful for the cover, though he wished he still had his black outfit and hood to wear. The one that Taws had provided for him when he broke in the first time.

Gods, how had he not noticed sooner what a shifty person Taws was? He'd just seemed so genuine in Gen Rill. They had a common enemy, but in the end that didn't measure up to trustworthiness. Now that Nils thought about it...he'd seemed awfully eager for an assassination. Eager even to carry it out himself.

Not that any of that mattered now. Taws was gone, along with Sandri.

"All right, so we're gonna slip around back this way," Bern said as they approached the appropriate outbuilding, gesturing with his arm. They'd skirted the edges of the grounds and come through a grove of trees to hide their advance. Nils nodded, following Bern's lead. The back entry was a pair of cellar doors, and, thanks to the captain, there were no guards in sight.

Bern and Nils darted out of the trees to the doors, glancing about to make sure no one could see them. Bern held open one of the hatches while Nils descended inside, then the guard shut the door behind them.

Darkness. Nils froze, and Bern ran into him.

"Oof. Buddy, you gonna move?"

Nils tried to say something, but it came out more like a whimper. It was so dark. All the lanterns out. He'd be buried under here, suffocating under the earth—

"Oh, right. You have a thing with the dark, don't you," Bern said. "Made a big fuss when we first put you in that room without candles. Sheesh. Wait here."

Nils didn't move while Bern shuffled on ahead. He just listened to his own labored breathing until there was a glow, and Bern returned with a torch.

"Guess we would've needed this anyway," he said, "if we're gonna find anything."

Nils nodded, intending it as a thank you, though Bern probably thought he was just agreeing with him. It would have to do; Nils needed a moment to recover his voice.

Gods, I need to get it together. It's just a cellar.

"Chest should be down here somewhere," Bern said, holding the torch high and looking around. The cellar's dirt floor was crowded with boxes and barrels, but they picked their way through until they found a relatively clear patch, near the stairs that lead up to the main floor.

"There," Nils whispered. "That's it. It looks just like the other one."

Bern brought his light closer. "Hm," he said, illuminating the lock. "Hadn't thought about that."

"I got it," Nils said. He may have lost his original lock picking tools, but Taws had shown him how to do it with a variety of items that were easily found in a storage cellar like this. A few minutes later, the lock was off.

"Huh. You really are a thief," Bern said. "I was starting to doubt it."

Nils rolled his eyes. "Let's see what's in here," he said, reciting a quick prayer to Desna as he hefted open the lid.

Bern leaned forward, and he and Nils stared intently into the chest. "Stuff," Bern said.

"Yep."

That was what Nils expected: figurines, scarves, books. They were probably worth a fair amount of money, but these trinkets were just a cover. At least, that's what Nils hoped. "Help me get everything out of here," he said, grabbing a couple books.

I wonder...is this where all of Raeya's books come from? Gods, she probably has no idea.

When the chest was empty, they'd found nothing resembling chrysolin, but that was no surprise. Nils felt around the edge of the trunk's bottom, trying to find a place he could slip his finger. It was tight, so he grabbed one of the figurines that had been in the chest, a warrior wielding a sword, and used the miniature weapon to try and pry the bottom out.

It shifted, and came loose. Bern and Nils shared a look, then Nils lifted the false bottom out.

There was a small box underneath. *Desna's Tresses, I was right.*

The box was black, unmarked. Nils took it in his hand and popped off the lid. Inside were four smooth, black stones. Not too shiny. A flawless finish.

Bern stood up and stumbled back from the chest. "Weaver's blood," he said. "Dear Goddess Desna, you have got to be kidding me."

Nils just stared at the thing he held in his hand. Any one of those four stones earned you instant execution just for possessing it in Branaden. "If...if we take them all, it'll be too obvious, right?" he said. The cellar was so quiet, his voice felt like an intruder in the air.

"Do we have to take any of them?" Bern asked. "Can't we just tell the investigator where to look?"

Nils shook his head. "They'll unpack this before he comes. The stones will be hidden away where they can't possibly be found."

"Then what do we do? If Dreygard knows someone took one…"

"Maybe he doesn't know how many were being sent," Nils said, although admittedly they couldn't stake their hopes on that. "We'll just have to risk it. We need a stone to give to the investigator, something that will ensure he looks deeper."

"*I* ain't taking that thing to the investigator. He'll probably send me straight to the gallows, and if he doesn't, Dreygard will."

Bern was right. They had to do this without revealing themselves. "We'll plant it somewhere where he'll find it, then," Nils said, "with a note detailing where we found it, and what these chests look like. Even if it's empty, if he finds a chest with a false bottom, that will help corroborate our story."

There was a quiet shifting sound on the floor above, and Bern looked up at the ceiling. "We'll have to figure out the details later," he said. "I'm not gonna risk being found here."

"Right." Nils held the little box up to Bern, but the guard just shook his head. He wouldn't touch it, and Nils found he couldn't blame him.

Well, somebody had to do it.

Nils put his fingers around one of the stones, and nearly dropped it back into the box. His fingertips tingled everywhere the stone touched. Was that normal?

Of course it's not normal, he scolded himself. *This is the living stone of the fallen god himself, and I can't believe I'm actually touching it.*

The shifting upstairs grew louder.

"We gotta go now, Soulmate."

"Agreed," Nils said. He thrust the stone into his sock where it continued to tingle at his skin, then scrambled to put the chest back together exactly as they'd found it. Bern helped him refill it and lock it up, then the two of them hurried through the clutter to their exit.

They made it outside, where Bern extinguished his torch in a bucket by the door. The sun was entirely gone now, but Nils would be all right. The darkness never got to him as much outside. He prepared to break for the trees.

Bern held Nils back with a strong arm just before he bolted. Nils stopped and listened. Voices, around the corner. If they ran now, they'd be seen for sure. Nils gestured to the other end of the building, but Bern shook his head. There must've been guards posted around the other side. They obviously couldn't go back into the cellar, so what else could they do? They had to stay put, and pray with all their might that whoever was speaking wouldn't come around the corner.

The voices came closer, and suddenly they were familiar.

Jarik and Raeya. They must've just gotten back from the dance.

"Are you cold?" Jarik's voice asked.

"A little."

Nils heard shuffling, and imagined Jarik moving closer to Raeya. It was strange that they'd be taking a walk outside after dark, and where was Tilda?

"Thank you again for coming with me today, my lady. I can't tell you how wonderful it was."

"I enjoyed myself," Raeya said, almost like a confession. "It was the most fun I've had in a long time, to be honest. It was nice to be with someone who...understands."

"I would gladly stay beside you always."

"I know that."

"Raeya..."

"Jarik, wait. You shouldn't come so close."

Nils felt something squirm in his stomach.

"Don't worry," Jarik's voice said, soft and low. "I won't try to kiss you. I know better than to do that. If I can say so, your betrothed should've known better, too."

"It...wasn't his fault," came a softer reply. "I didn't stop him."

"I don't wish to speak ill of a man you cherished," Jarik went on, "but you can't blame yourself, not one bit. Sir Keden *never* should've risked breaking your heart like that, whatever his reasons. I've admired you for a long time, my lady, but I've known from the start I would never try to kiss you, even before Nils came along. Such a thing would be too cruel if it went wrong."

Huh, Nils thought, frowning. *That isn't what he said when I met him.*

"Besides," Jarik said, "even if I can't kiss your lips, we can still..."

There was a moment of silence that was more painful than anything spoken so far. Even though it was brief, it felt like salvation when Raeya broke it.

"Jarik, I—I'm sorry, but please...don't do that."

"I apologize, my lady. That was too forward of me. We can take things slower—"

"No, I...I think it's best we not spend too much time together like this."

"Why not?" Jarik questioned. "Are you...still holding out for Nils?"

Nils swallowed.

"I don't know," Raeya said. "He...isn't anything like I expected, but...I need more time to figure it out."

"I wish I had all the time in the world to give," Jarik said. "Listen, the other day, you were *furious* at him."

"Yes. I'm still upset, but, well. He did apologize."

"...He did?"

Nils squeezed his eyes shut. *Fives.*

"Raeya, I—" Jarik started, sounding entirely vulnerable, "I know your curse has revealed Nils to be your true love, but all the same..."

Oh no, Nils thought. *He's going to say it. I don't want to be here to hear this.*

"...I can't help wishing you'd cast fate aside, and—"

Before he even knew what he was doing, Nils had a rock in his hand, and he chucked it off into the trees.

"—choose—"

Jarik cut off at the sound of the rock striking the ground and shuffling the undergrowth.

"What was that?" Raeya asked in a whisper.

"I don't know."

"I need to get back," Raeya said. "We never should've slipped away from Tilda in the first place, and she'll have the whole manor in an uproar soon if I don't show myself."

"Raeya, I..."

"Please, Jarik. I've stayed too long."

Jarik must've relented, and soon their footsteps and voices faded into the night. Nils and Bern waited in silence until they were sure it was safe, then Bern let out a low whistle. Nils shot him a glare.

"Why'd you throw the rock?" Bern asked.

"Because I'm the worst friend in the world," Nils replied, already haunted by his own actions. "On a more positive note, we can run now."

"Right. Let's go."

28 BROKEN RULE

Nils didn't dare take the stone out of his sock, even though it made his sleep restless and miserable most of the night. He wouldn't take the slightest chance that someone might discover it. In truth, Bern should've kept it—if Dreygard noticed a stone was missing, Nils would be the first person searched—but the guard still refused to touch it. You'd think a trained watchman would have more backbone than a schoolteacher.

Bern did promise to orchestrate a meeting with Tilda and Clerrit, so hopefully the stone could be passed to the captain once that took place. It would have to be soon; the investigator was coming tomorrow, and they had precious little time to plan.

After a maid who wasn't Sandri brought breakfast, Nils was called down to see Raeya. Today she read the book Jarik had given her.

"You must be tired of your room by now," she said to him.

"A bit."

"I wanted to tell you that yesterday was very successful," Raeya said, and Nils tensed a little. "Jarik and I were able to find many willing patrons to contribute toward our project."

Oh, right. That.

"We should be able to have a sizable number of blankets distributed before Kirit takes power again. However, we'll have to limit our distribution to two or three towns. I wondered if you might know which towns are in the greatest need, and I would love to supply them to your hometown."

Nils nodded. That would be nice. Maybe even some of the school kids could benefit from this. Trina's family had been suffering greatly before Nils was taken, and Rella could probably use—

"So which town are you from?"

Nils paused. So much for that. "I can't say," he answered, "and I won't be able to help you. Just find out which ones have the most people. They probably have the greatest need."

Raeya clicked her tongue. "A thief's secrets," she said. "Come now, we could get supplies to your family. Wouldn't that be worth trusting me with the tiniest shred of information about yourself?"

"I don't have any family," Nils said, feeling a familiar ache.

Raeya put down her book. "Oh," she said. "No siblings?"

"No."

"And your parents are…"

Nils sighed. "My father died when I was young. My mother…more recently."

"How recently?"

"…Something like a month ago."

"Nils!" Raeya said, putting her hands to her mouth. "That would've been just before you came here."

"Yeah."

"Is that why you were…and now you've been trapped here all this time. Oh, Nils. Where is she buried? Surely my father would at least clear us to go and pay respects."

Nils steadied himself. "She wasn't."

155

"What?"

"She wasn't buried, except perhaps under other bodies. That's what happens when you're poor, and your family's been snatched away by taskers, and you've got no one to give you a proper burial."

Raeya looked devastated. "That's horrible," she said.

"I should've been there," Nils murmured, forgetting his company. Fives. He'd been trying his hardest not to think about it. The most horrible part wasn't even her lack of a proper burial, but that she'd died alone. Nils had always thought he could at least be there beside her when it happened. "I knew she didn't have long. Her health was failing, and she'd lived a full life. It was her time, and I understood that, but...Darkness of Hearthnight, those fiving taskers."

Raeya was quiet for a while, then asked, "How old was she?"

"Thirty-seven."

"Thirty—that isn't a full life, that's only half of one!"

"For a noble, maybe, or someone lucky enough to work under one. Life is short in the towns." That's what his mom had said.

Raeya looked close to tears, and Nils couldn't deny her compassion. Now that he thought about it, the second she'd learned about the townspeople needing blankets, she'd vowed to help them. She'd inherited her father's cold eyes, but not his heart.

It was time to move on from this. Nils was leaving himself too open. "There's no need for pity," he said. "We had a better life than many, just a bad ending. So, what's this stupid book about anyway?"

Raeya's sympathetic gaze rested on him a few seconds longer, then she took a breath, seeming to understand what Nils needed. "Well, for one, it's not stupid. It's actually quite cleverly written, especially considering it's a translation."

"Let's see it, then."

* * *

Nils was feeling anxious when Raeya finally dismissed him. Half the day gone already, and no word from Bern. He'd tried to catch Tilda's eye to glean if she knew anything, but the attendant hadn't given him any signs one way or the other.

Trailing his guard through the manor, Nils kept an eye out, hoping to catch Bern or Captain Clerrit. Neither of them seemed to be around. If only they—

Nils halted his scanning and did a double-take.

No, he hadn't imagined it. There, standing beside some chatting nobles with a tray in hand, was Sandri.

She'd come back. *Desna's Tresses,* she actually hadn't abandoned him. And better yet, she was smiling.

That meant Taws was all right, and whatever sort of man he turned out to be, he hadn't abandoned them either.

Nils smiled back with what was probably a big, stupid grin, but he didn't care. Now, if tomorrow went poorly, he at least had one last lifeline.

* * *

It often surprised Nils where his guards led him. Rather than his room, he ended up outside.

It was a secluded place, somewhere behind the manor house. Jarik was there, and something about the nobleman felt…different.

"Hello, Nils," he said.

Nils gave an apprehensive nod.

"You'll be glad to know things went well with Lady Raeya yesterday."

"That's good," Nils replied.

"Although, she did say something curious. She said you apologized to her."

Nils let out a quick sigh. He'd let Jarik down even more than he knew. "I had to," he said. "I'm sorry, but—I'd gone too far."

"Wasn't that the plan? Upset her so much that she hates you?"

"Yes," Nils admitted. "Look, I'm not trying to win back her favor or anything—she's yours, and I'll continue helping you. It's just...she doesn't deserve to be treated that way. I can't do it anymore. Not to such a level."

Jarik shook his head, looking disappointed. "You're in trouble, Nils," he said, "though you don't seem to realize it."

"What do you mean?"

"You've broken one of Lord Dreygard's rules."

"What are you talking about?" Nils said. "I haven't stolen anything, or hurt anyone."

Except he had stolen something. Fives, did Jarik somehow know about the weaver's stone in his sock? Even now, it tingled...

"No, but you lied to him about your last name."

Nils froze.

"You see, Lord Dreygard sent emissaries to every tasker post in the province after interrogating you, trying to find where you'd been assigned since you refused to tell him. The emissaries have all now returned, and not one of them found a Nils Oakander in any registry. There were a number of men named Nils, however, including one from a certain coal mine."

No. No.

"He was marked 'Assumed deceased after cave-in.' Does that sound familiar, Nils Tenning?"

Nils was white as a sheet. He could feel it, the cold lack of color in his face. All the blood had drained away under his skin.

Jarik came closer, looming over him. "The only reason you haven't been sent back to Gen Rill is thanks to me. I expect you won't forget that."

Nils shook his head. Or maybe he was just shaking.

"Good." Jarik stepped back. "I trust you to be a man of your word, Mr. Tenning. Finish what you started with Lady Raeya." The nobleman turned to go, but looked back one last time, his eyes a little less hard as he surveyed Nils standing there like a specter. He gave a slight nod, and walked away.

29 PROOF

Nils checked the box under his bed with shaking hands the instant he was back in his room. Maybe it wasn't the safest time to do it, but if Tawson was back, he might've sent a message, and right now Nils needed *anything* to get his mind off of what just happened.

Gen Rill. I can't go back, can't, can't, can't—

Yes, there was a note there.

Nils, it read, *forgive my absence. The things that happened when I was looking for stones, well, I'll have to tell you in person sometime. All you need to know is that I failed, and if Sandri hadn't come looking for me when she did, you wouldn't have this letter.*

I hope you've had more success than I have. Sandri tells me you've done well on your own—I knew you would. Send me an update on your situation. I'll do what I can to help from outside.

Tawson's handwriting was recognizable, but noticeably sloppier than usual. He must've written it in a hurry. It was strange, but for all that Nils doubted this man and his character, he didn't waste any time grabbing his pencil to write back.

Before he could touch the lead to the page, there was a faint knock on his door.

Nils panicked. He hadn't burned Taws' letter yet. It was laid out, unobscured, in front of him. How would he talk his way out of this? What could he do?

Bern poked his head inside. "Hey Soulmate, are you—what's that?" he asked, observing the parchment strewn across Nils' bed.

"Nothing important," Nils squeaked, everything besides his mouth utterly paralyzed.

"Oh. Well, I've got a meeting set up. Tonight. I know it's last minute, but it's all that worked. So I'll come get you when Clerrit and Tilda are ready to meet."

"All right," Nils said.

Bern nodded, and shut the door.

Nils felt like all of his joints had been soldered together. If Dreygard didn't kill him, he was going to do himself in at this rate.

* * *

That night, Bern took Nils to a different part of the manor. A place Nils hadn't been since the first night he'd broken in.

It seemed risky, heading to the *noble* section of the house, but apparently it was deemed the best place to meet. Tilda didn't want to wander too far from her mistress if she could help it, and Clerrit had orders to be on watch in this sector, so here they were. They met in what looked to be a small, private dining room, up on the same floor as the Dreygards' bedrooms, connected to a servants' passage ideal for sneaking Nils in.

"Bern says you've found proof," Captain Clerrit said when they were all assembled. He was a weathered man, graying-red hair and mustache, a stubbled chin. "Tell us everything."

Nils was still a disaster of nerves from earlier, and he found it hard to speak with the captain and Tilda staring him down. Well, he was always a disaster of nerves, and when something had to be done, he did it. That was the only way he'd made it this far.

"Bern and I found the latest shipment from Galreyva, in the cellar of one of the outbuildings," he said.

"Building Five," Bern supplied.

"How do you know it was from Galreyva?" Tilda asked.

"Well, it had to be," Nils said. "Where else would Dreygard be getting chrysolin?"

The room felt quieter after that word was spoken. "So you really found it then," Clerrit said.

Nils nodded.

"Show me."

Somehow, this was worse than speaking. All he had to do was take that little black stone out of his sock. And yet, revealing what he possessed to the captain of the guard...a forbidden object, a *stolen* forbidden object...

It's just one more thing that needs to be done. So do it.

Nils reached down, but a sound from the door stopped him. A key scraping in the lock. The door opened.

And Raeya peered inside.

"What...what on the king's soil is going on?" she asked, looking back and forth at everyone gathered. "Tilda?"

Tilda looked like she might faint. "My lady," she said, "what are you doing out of bed?"

"I couldn't sleep and came to find you, but heard you talking with Captain Clerrit. I wouldn't have followed, but...I heard you mention Nils' name."

"Look, this—this is nothing," Tilda said. "Don't trouble yourself. Here, I'll come back with you."

"No, I'll stay right here, thank you," Raeya said, coming in and shutting the door behind her. Just to punctuate her intentions, she locked it.

"Where did you get that key?" the captain asked.

"I...may have stolen Tilda's spare from her room," Raeya said, looking somewhat sheepish. Tilda blanched. "Now then," Raeya went on, "*what* is going on here?"

Fives, Nils thought. It wasn't like they could just shove her out of here, not even Captain Clerrit. If Raeya got her father out of bed...

"We found proof that your father was behind the attempts on my life," Nils said. The others looked at him warily, but didn't try to stop him.

Raeya huffed. "Nils, I told you, he would *never—*"

"There's more," Nils said. "The guard Aran and the servant in the garden weren't acting on his orders. They were cursed."

"You think...a weaver's spell..." Raeya clearly wanted to deny it, but she'd seen that servant's eyes after he picked up the rake. He may as well have been possessed. Raeya processed all this, then closed her eyes and set her jaw. "Are you saying, Nils, that my father is a spellweaver?" Her eyes opened and pierced him with a stare.

Somehow, Nils felt calmer now than he had all day. "Yes," he said, "and Emperor Ri'sen is providing him with chrysolin."

"That is the most ridiculous thing I've ever heard."

"Have you seen his wrists during the last several years?"

"Of course I have," Raeya said. "I...all right, I'll grant you that I don't have any particular memories of seeing them, but surely I have. Anyway, what is this proof you say you have? Show it to me."

Now Nils hesitated. "There's...an investigator coming tomorrow," he said, "from the king. Just wait and see what he finds."

"No," Raeya said. "If you have it now, show me now. In fact, if you can prove it to me beyond doubt, *I'll* talk to the investigator myself and tell him what you've found."

"You'd turn in your own father?"

"No, but that's how confident I am that you are wrong."

Nils once again shared looks with the others to see if anyone would stop him. No one did. Nils sighed, then pulled the stone from his sock.

"We found this, and three others like it, in a chest that was almost certainly sent from Galreyva. Your father has been getting these for some time. That's...what I broke in here to find when this all began."

Raeya's eyes were fixed on the stone. "Is that...?" she said. Surprisingly, she reached out and took the stone from Nils' fingers. She flinched at its touch. Could she feel the tingling too?

"Desna's Tresses," she said, handing the chrysolin back to Nils in a hurry.

"So...?" Nils prompted.

"This proves nothing," Raeya said, although her confidence wavered. "You...you could've gotten this anywhere. Show me these chests he's been receiving, and we'll see where they're really from."

Nils looked to Captain Clerrit. He shook his head. "I don't know if there's still one in the storage cellar or not," he said. "All I know is that's where it was received."

"We'll start there," Raeya said. "Do it, Captain, or I can simply go and ask my father about this right now."

The captain looked strained. "I'll have to clear the guards," he said. "I'll need a little while."

"Fine."

"Bern, with me," he said. Bern nodded, and they left the room. Before they'd even locked the door, the captain stuck his head back inside. "There's a lot of activity out here," he said to Tilda. "Somebody probably saw Lady Raeya wandering the halls, and now they're searching for her. Take her back to her room."

"And what do I do with Nils?" Tilda asked, exasperated.

"I don't know. Put him there too."

"In *my lady's room?*"

"It'll be a half hour tops, Tilda," he said. "Relax. Just be ready to fend off anyone that comes looking for her, or we'll have an awful lot to explain."

Tilda huffed and puffed, but she couldn't argue. Bern and the captain stayed with them long enough to ensure the way to Raeya's room was clear, then she and Nils were deposited there.

"How do I keep anyone from coming in here looking for you?" Tilda worried aloud. "They could just *barge* in."

"Then go and tell someone I've been found," Raeya said. "That will solve the problem."

"And leave you two alone? I don't think so."

"I'm sensible enough to behave myself," Raeya said.

"When one is young, *sensibilities* are often clouded, my lady, especially when left alone with someone of the same unpredictable age." Tilda looked pointedly at Nils.

"Why, Miss Matilda, would you happen to know that from experience?" Raeya asked. "Perhaps with the captain, some years ago…"

Tilda started, sputtered something incoherent, then pointed a finger at Nils and Raeya in turn. "You *will* behave yourselves," she said. "I'll be right back." She gave them each another glare, then left them alone in the hearth-lit bedroom.

That buffer between Nils and Raeya didn't seem to exist anymore. In fact, Nils found that the air between them felt thinner than usual, making it hard to breathe. He looked at her once and decided he shouldn't do it again.

The last time he'd been in this room, he'd broken through the balcony door in the middle of the night, found her in her nightgown, then pinned her to the wall and kissed her. He could hardly believe he was even the same person. That is, if he were to do something like that *now*—

Gods, he couldn't even think about it without feeling lightheaded.

"Nils?"

"What!" Nils said too loudly, tensing at her voice.

"You're serious about all this, right? You really believe my father is a spellweaver?"

Nils calmed a little. "Yes."

"And that's why you came. You were trying to expose him. As a weaver, and a colluder with Galreyva."

"Yes."

Raeya sat down on the edge of her bed, and shook her head. "There's no way it's true," she said, but her eyes were fearful. Seeing the chrysolin had shaken her, and the attempts on Nils' life were convincing evidence when considered in tandem with it. Nils needed her to believe, but he didn't like seeing her scared. Maybe, if they talked about something else for a while…

"Raeya, how did you get your curse?"

In hindsight, that was probably a stupid thing to ask if he wanted her to feel better, but she didn't refuse.

"I never told you, did I?" she said. "It happened in Borlund. My father brought me along on a trip to meet with Lord and Lady Ashber. I went for a walk in the woods while the adults had their discussions, accompanied by Tilda and a couple guards to ensure my safety, but I slipped away from them. I thought everything was a game back then. I thought myself so clever, hearing the echoes of their calls die out behind me. And then I came upon a strange place."

"You didn't wander across the border, did you?" Nils asked, coming over to sit beside Raeya on the bed. Even though it was a sad story, it was nice to hear her talk. Calming to him, somehow.

"No. At least, I don't think so. It was some kind of rock garden, filled with purple flowers, with a little shack beyond that didn't look occupied. I stopped to pick some flowers for my mother beside a tall stone, natural and unmarked like all the others. I thought nothing of it until the spellweaver came."

"A soldier?"

"No, not a soldier. Just a woman. A terrifying woman. She was furious. She grabbed my wrists and pinned me to the stone, shouting words I couldn't understand while I cried, until she spat out at me in Branic something about a grave. How was I to know? I tried to apologize, but she dug her fingernails into my skin and started chanting in Galreyvan. Her hair was like a curtain around me, narrowing my sight onto the string of black stones she wore around her neck while she poured her hateful words over me. One of the stones dissolved before my eyes, and I remember worrying that the dust would get in them. Silly. That was the last thing I needed to worry about.

"She told me afterward in Branic what she'd done. Made sure I understood what punishment she'd given me for my crime. I'd kill any man I ever kissed, except for one, my true love. 'Good luck finding him,' was the last thing she said to me before she threw me away from her garden. I ran and ran until I heard the guards calling my name, then collapsed and cried until they found me."

Gods, Nils thought in the silence that followed. *No wonder she believes so strongly in her curse. If that's what happened, then am I really...*"Sorry," Nils said, unwilling to think about it. "This must all be difficult to take."

Raeya stared down at her hands in her lap. "I know my father is a hard man," she finally said. "Even so, I never imagined..." She squeezed her hands together, and emotion flickered on her face. "He promised me he wouldn't hurt you."

There were noises outside, and Nils and Raeya both looked toward the door. Tilda bustled in, face red.

"Hide," she said.

"What's going on?" Raeya asked, standing.

"I told one of the guards you were safely back in your room, but apparently your *mother's* been out looking for you, and he was going to get her and send her here. I don't know that I can keep her out of the room, my lady, and she could be here any—"

Tilda turned back to the door, then hurried outside, her voice carrying back to them in placating tones as she tried to assure someone that Raeya was all right.

Fives. Lady Dreygard was already here.

Raeya and Nils looked at each other, then sprang into action. "Quick," Raeya said, "under the bed!" Nils flung himself under the frame while Raeya leapt into the bed from the other side. "Stay quiet, and it'll be fine," she whispered.

Nils nodded—Stupid, given that Raeya couldn't see him—then began to wonder...would it? He'd just accused her father of the very worst of crimes and admitted his intentions to expose him, right after spending several days trying his hardest to make Raeya hate him. To make matters worse, he'd revealed that he presently carried the country's most forbidden object on his person, then obligingly put himself in the most vulnerable position he could think of. If Raeya said even one word about this to her mother, it was all over. But what could he do? There was nowhere to run, no way to escape—

The door opened, and Nils held his breath.

There was a creak as Raeya sat up a little in the bed above him. "Mother?" she said, managing to sound surprised.

"Ah, my dear," Lady Dreygard said. "You had me worried."

Nils heard soft footsteps coming closer, then saw slender feet and a sweep of fabric rustle past the gossamer bed skirt, backlit by the hearth. He instinctively pressed his lips shut tighter, but he couldn't hold his breath forever.

Please, don't say anything. Please, please.

Lady Dreygard stopped beside the bed, and Raeya shifted. Her mother must've been giving her a hug, and the tip of a slippered foot poked under the bed skirt right in front of Nils' face, inconveniently right at the moment he ran out of air. He clamped his hand over his mouth.

"I don't see what all the fuss is about," Raeya said. Her voice was so calm. What was she planning? "I was just looking for Tilda. Am I not allowed a simple walk down the hall by myself anymore?"

Lady Dreygard sat on the bed beside Raeya, and Nils rolled onto his back and gasped for air as quietly as he could.

"A lot has happened lately," Lady Dreygard said. "Your father just wants to take extra precautions for the time being."

"Is it Nils?" Raeya asked, and Nils lost his ability to breathe altogether. "He's not dangerous, you know."

Her mother chuckled. "I think you're right, though don't tell your father I said that. All the same, try not to go anywhere without at least having Tilda with you. You can ring for a servant if you need something."

"Very well," Raeya said. "I'll obey, even if it is a silly precaution."

There was another creak above Nils, and he imagined Lady Dreygard leaning in to kiss Raeya's head. "Goodnight, dear one," she said.

"Goodnight."

Lady Dreygard left, catching Tilda on the way out. "I would speak to you for a moment, Miss Matilda."

"Of course, my lady."

Their voices faded as they stepped outside, and the door shut behind them. It was…over? Just like that, she'd left, and Raeya hadn't—

Nils jumped as Raeya dropped to the floor, then slid under the bed right beside him. "My *gods*," she whispered. "I thought I was going to faint."

So did Nils. Not just from holding his breath, or from the tension seizing every muscle in his body, or the sheer, utter amazement that Raeya had protected him instead of revealing him to her mother and alerting the guards.

But because Raeya was suddenly only a few inches from his face in that small, shrouded place under the bed. The memory of their last kiss flared through his mind and fired off a spark that stunned him with its intensity.

"We should be in the clear now," Raeya said, "as long as the captain can get back here without raising suspicion."

Nils could feel her breath when she spoke. It made him want to move closer, to—

Unholy fives, what is wrong with me? This is Raeya Dreygard. *And what about Jarik? This is the direct opposite of what I promised him I'd do. I should roll out from under here right now, but what if Lady Dreygard comes back? Gods, Dearest Desna, dearest everybody up there above the clouds—*

"Nils, are you listening?"

Nils shook himself, eyes focusing in on Raeya's. Did she…feel nothing? After all she'd felt before, she could lie here beside him and feel nothing, while Nils…

Felt everything. He glanced at her mouth, that instinct to move closer wrangling with him still. She noticed, and cocked her head at him. Then the air between them changed again. It was too dark to see the color of her skin, but Nils felt there was a new heat in it, that pink blush she'd shown so many times before. If she didn't want him anymore, wouldn't she pull back? Or push him away?

She did neither. Her eyes searched his face. Glanced at *his* mouth. Her breathing grew faster, matching his.

Nils swallowed. There was no wisdom at all in what he was about to do, but if he stayed here one more second, he wouldn't be able to—

The door opened. Raeya gasped, and Nils sat up and bumped his head.

"Wha—where are you? Just what are you two *doing?*" Tilda demanded when Raeya peeked out from under the bed.

"Hiding!" she said.

"Out of there, at once," Tilda ordered, and Nils and Raeya hurried to obey. "Your mother didn't seem to suspect anything, miraculously," Tilda said, fanning herself. "Desna's Tresses, I nearly lost my nerve."

"You were splendid, Tilda," Raeya said.

Tilda waved off the compliment. "Graham had better get back here soon," she said. "We need to get this over with, or I'll find an early grave."

30 BUILDING FIVE

"We'll need to make this quick," Captain Clerrit said. He and Bern were leading Nils, Raeya, and Tilda to Building Five, being careful to avoid being seen. "I can't leave half the manor unguarded for long."

Nils shivered a little as they traversed the grounds. It was colder tonight, and darker. It hadn't been so late the last time Nils and Bern made this trek. Raeya didn't seem bothered by the cold; her face showed nothing but determination.

Nils feared his was still flushing. *Clouded sensibilities,* he told himself, *just like Tilda said. That's all.*

They arrived at the cellar doors without issue, and Nils remembered what happened last time. *Fives. I'm going to make a scene.* Would Bern bail him out? Gods, he could already feel the darkness waiting for him, like it was some kind of beast—

Captain Clerrit pulled out a set of matches, and Nils relaxed. For once, he wouldn't have to embarrass himself. Still, his fear was a painful reminder of what awaited him if he failed. He wouldn't survive Gen Rill a second time. He'd freeze up at the mouth of the tunnel, and the taskers wouldn't be patient. They'd beat him to death before he saw one piece of coal.

He *had* to succeed.

Once inside the cellar, Bern retrieved a couple torches from wherever they were stored, and the group began searching for the chest, heading toward the base of the stairs to the next level.

"It's not here," Bern said. "This is where it was, yeah?"

Nils nodded, staring at the empty space on the floor where the chest had been.

"They probably moved it after it was unpacked," Clerrit said. "We'll look around some more—"

Shuffling on the floor above. A great amount of shuffling. Everyone stilled and stared at the ceiling.

"What in Desna's..." the captain started. "No one should be up there, at least not on my orders."

"They are there on *my* orders, Captain."

As one, they all spun around. Not that they needed to see the face to know whose voice it was.

Lord Dreygard.

"M-my lord," Clerrit said, dipping his head. "We were just checking on..." The captain trailed off. There was no excuse that could possibly explain the collection of people he had with him at this moment, and he knew it.

They were doomed.

Raeya stepped forward.

"Father," she said, "I made them bring me here. They've said...they've said something terrible about you, and I have to know if it's true or not. Father, are you..." She struggled with the words. "Are you a spellweaver?"

The cellar could've been a grave for the stagnancy of the air after that question left her mouth. Dreygard stared them down, and Nils felt even Raeya might crumble before him. Then, without speaking, the domiseer lifted an arm and began untying the leather laces of his cuff. He tugged it off, then did the same on the other arm. Then he rolled up his sleeves, and held his arms out before him, wrists exposed.

No black veins.

Raeya let out a sigh of relief, while Nils felt a surge of fury.

Wrong. His eyes were wrong. Those wrists were wrong. It couldn't be true.

Nils stepped forward, ahead of Raeya. "I won't believe it!" he said with surprising volume.

Lord Dreygard didn't flinch. "Then continue deluding yourself, in your final moments."

"No," Nils said, "*you* are a traitor, a sell-out to Emperor Ri'sen. You exploit your own people to fuel your trade with him, and you've smuggled chrysolin onto this very estate. Even—even if you aren't a weaver," he said, "you can't deny that."

This time Lord Dreygard said nothing.

"Father?" Raeya asked. "It's not true, is it?"

"Matilda," Dreygard said, "take Raeya upstairs. A few of my guards will escort her back to her room, and you will come back down here."

Tilda didn't move, and Raeya's composure faltered. "Father—"

"Now, Matilda," Dreygard said louder, "or you need not guess at the consequences."

Tilda was wide-eyed and shaking, but she bowed. "Yes, my lord." She tried to take Raeya's arm, but Raeya shook her off.

"Tilda, no. Father, it's not true! Just say it's not true!"

"Help her, Clerrit," Dreygard ordered. The captain obeyed. Raeya kept shouting, but this time she couldn't break free. "Answer me, Father!" she yelled, until she disappeared at the top of the stairs, and her voice grew muffled above the floor. A moment later, Tilda and the captain returned without her, and the absence of Raeya's shouts left the cellar feeling even quieter than before.

Even more like a grave. Dreygard wouldn't hurt his daughter, but he had no such attachment to the rest of them.

"Three of you are a surprise to me," the domiseer said, weighing each of them with his eyes. "Tell me, have you always been disloyal, or did this one win you over?" He looked last at Nils.

The other three did not speak. What could they say?

Dreygard stepped closer to them, a hand on the short sword at his side. The metal pommel glinted in the firelight, and Nils stared at it, clenching his jaw tight.

It wasn't fair. Proof of Dreygard's treachery tingled at his skin. The investigator would arrive in mere hours. They were so close, and now they would all—

There was a sound from the back of the cellar, and Dreygard halted. The hatch, opening and closing. A guard rushed in and bowed to him.

"Yes?" Dreygard said.

"Jarik Sowell has left the manor, my lord."

The domiseer took a deep breath, and shut his eyes. "Very well. Get the others from outside, and have them restrain these three," he said, gesturing toward Bern, the captain, and Tilda. Again, he looked at Nils last. "Take this one with you," he said, "but don't let yourself be seen. You know your orders concerning Sowell."

"Yes, my lord."

Nils looked between the domiseer and the guard. What was he talking about? Was Dreygard going to murder Jarik, too? He must've been aware of their meetings, figured Jarik was in on their plot. Nils couldn't let Jarik fall with them. He knew nothing about this.

Dreygard stepped closer to Nils, fixing his eyes on him. "I can do nothing to interfere," he said, "but you can."

Huh?

Dreygard motioned for the watchman to move on his orders. "Take him."

* * *

Nils didn't feel the cold air anymore as he was dragged along by the guard. Didn't notice the darkness of the night sky. The weaver's stone tingled stronger than ever, but even that was an afterthought.

What in Hearthnight was going on?

The guard stopped them short behind one of the other outbuildings, looking around the corner. "Fives," he said.

Nils peered around too. The ground was cluttered with something that looked like sacks of grain, spilled open on the grass. Something metallic glinted among them, like a weapon…

The sky shifted, letting through the light of a crescent moon. Weaver's blood, they were *bodies,* clothed in the uniforms of Dreygard's watchmen. Had they been the ones escorting Raeya?

"This way," the guard said, grabbing Nils' shoulder and hauling him around the other side of the building where they sidled along the wall. There was a scream in the night that chilled Nils inside and out, its tone frighteningly familiar. Was that—?

The guard peeked around the next corner, then pulled back and pressed himself against the wall. "Go," he said to Nils, pointing for him to go around. "I'm not going any farther."

"Then why should I—"

"Get going!" the guard said, grabbing Nils and practically throwing him around the edge of the building.

Nils staggered to a stop once he was out in the open, then looked around. There were figures ahead of him amongst some sparse trees. Two isolated, and several more standing around them. None of them seemed to have noticed him yet, so Nils hid himself behind one of the trees, pressing his back against the rough bark. He wanted to stay there, hidden, but he couldn't. He'd recognized those two isolated figures.

Raeya and Jarik.

Nils crept closer, staying behind cover as much as possible, but mostly relying on the darkness to hide him. When he got close enough to hear, he peered out from behind a dying tree, its bark flaking away under his hands.

"I won't go with you," Raeya said to Jarik. "It doesn't matter where you intend to take me, I won't!"

"My lady, you have to understand," Jarik plead with her. "If you stay here, I can't guarantee your safety."

"I don't care. After what you did—those guards—"

Raeya couldn't seem to finish her statement, but she backed away when Jarik stepped closer. "You have nothing to fear from me," Jarik assured her. "Please, Raeya."

Nils took a moment to look at the others gathered around them. Men in dark clothing he didn't recognize, and one of Dreygard's watchmen, who had his back to Nils. He knew the man's build: Marks.

"I had hoped you'd soon be ready to come with me willingly," Jarik continued, "but my time was cut short. I did the best I could, dear Raeya."

Raeya tried to back up farther from Jarik, but some of the men stood behind her, penning her in. What were they doing, and who were they? Nils felt an intense desire to get Raeya out of there that went against all of his instincts for self-preservation, but he couldn't ignore it. He took a tiny step forward, and a branch snapped under his foot.

Marks turned around. The motion was so abrupt, it seemed unnatural, and in the moonlight...

Unholy fives, his eyes were blank.

Nils stumbled backward just as Marks charged at him, and all the others took notice of what was happening. Jarik cursed and started chanting something while Marks revealed a knife in his grasp. Nils crashed into the tree behind him, and the spellwoven guard reached him before he could get around it. Marks' hand was raised, the knife poised to plunge downward, right into Nils'—

Jarik stopped chanting, and Marks' eyes cleared. The knife fell harmlessly from his hand, and the guard fell to his knees.

Nils was left staring at nothing, until his eyes focused on the person beyond his immediate range. Jarik.

"It was you," Nils whispered.

Jarik heaved a deep sigh. "Bring him over here," he said. One of the men came and grabbed him while he was frozen in front of that tree, taking him toward Jarik. Another man came and lingered behind.

"What do we do with this one?" he asked. He must've meant Marks.

"He's no use to us anymore."

There was a noise behind Nils that sparked an immediate wave of nausea, but thankfully his brain couldn't linger on that. He was standing in front of Jarik now.

"I don't see why you didn't just let the guard finish him," the man restraining Nils said. "Isn't this the guy you wasted two stones trying to kill?"

Nils jerked his head to look at the man, then back at Jarik. The nobleman pinned his associate with a glare, then looked down at Nils.

"You're the spellweaver," Nils said, his words barely piercing the night air. "All this time, I thought it was Dreygard."

Jarik's face was unreadable. "You shouldn't have come."

"Nils."

Raeya's voice finally broke Nils' trance, and he looked to her as the men surrounding her crept closer. "Don't touch her!" he shouted.

"They won't," Jarik said, "or at any rate they won't hurt her. Raeya is safe. Now get out of here, and leave the manor. That's what you want, isn't it? No one will stop you."

"You're letting him go?" the man holding Nils said, and Nils was finally aware enough to notice the man's accent.

"He can do no harm to us," Jarik said. "Raeya, I'm sorry, but we have to go now, and I will take you by force if necessary. Nils, go on. You have to hurry."

The hands restraining Nils let go, but he didn't move. "Who are you?" he asked.

Jarik gave him a long look, and then a small, strange smile passed his lips. "I'm Lord Dreygard's trade manager, working on behalf of my uncle, just as I told you."

"Your uncle isn't the domiseer of Tormeron."

"No."

"What is your name, and *who are you?*"

The night was so quiet, it filled Nils' ears with a painful pressure that increased every moment that Jarik delayed answering. He could barely stand it, that tension, rising like the tingling of that blasted stone in his sock.

"I am Isek Ri'sen," Jarik said, "and my uncle is Suloron Ri'sen, Emperor of Galreyva."

Raeya gasped, and finally one of the men grabbed her. "We need to go now, my lord," he said.

"Fine," Jarik said, losing his smile. "I won't say it again, Nils: get out of here."

He turned to leave while his associates forced Raeya along with them, one of them clamping her mouth shut with his hand when she tried to shout for Nils. She reached for him, screaming against the man's hand.

Nils would not leave. He charged after them, but Jarik turned, grabbed him, and threw him to the ground *hard*. "Don't make me kill you," he said, pinning Nils down and punctuating each word. His dark eyes gleamed more dangerously than Lord Dreygard's ever had. Nils' head spun from his impact with the ground, and he found he couldn't move when Jarik finally released him and stalked away.

Nils stared up at the sky. The dark clouds, a crescent moon. Cold blue.

Raeya.

He got up, just as somebody grabbed him from behind. Nils shouted, but his voice was muffled by a hand.

"Shh," the man said. It was the domiseer's guard that had brought him here. "We have to go back."

31 COMMISSION

When Nils was brought back to the storage cellar, his mind was lost in fog. He passed Bern, the captain, and Tilda, the last of whom began weeping at the sight of him returning alone.

Alone, without Raeya. She was gone.

Nils' guard brought him to the domiseer, who regarded him levelly. "Do you understand who Jarik is now?" he asked.

Nils nodded.

Dreygard turned. "Come with me."

He walked to the stairs that led to the floor above, and Nils followed. "I couldn't stop him," he said.

"I know. But I needed you to see."

The domiseer took Nils past the guards upstairs to a small, private room, mostly occupied by a table and a few chairs. He lit a couple torch lamps on the wall.

"Sit," he said.

Nils didn't want to, so he remained standing while Dreygard sat down and folded his hands in front of him on the table. Nils didn't wait for him to start. "Tell me what's going on," he said. "If you try to tell me you're innocent in all of this, I won't believe you."

"I am not."

"So you've been harboring Ri'sen's nephew willingly? Letting him court your daughter?"

"No, not willingly. But I couldn't stop it."

"Explain," Nils demanded.

Dreygard sighed. "I am indebted to Emperor Ri'sen. It is a debt I can't repay."

"And what could he possibly have done for you, or given you, that made you loyal to him?"

"He saved Raeya's life."

Nils stiffened.

"Her curse…was a curse for all of us. She fell violently ill after she received it," Dreygard said. "The trauma was too much for her body and mind to handle. I was certain we were going to lose her, but Ri'sen had spies that discovered her ailment. He knew it was a weakness he could use against me, an opportunity to get what he needed. He contacted me and offered to heal her with his spellweaving if I agreed to open trade with him in secret."

"So you betrayed your entire country for the sake of one person?"

"Not one person. My daughter. Would you have done differently?"

Dreygard stared at Nils, and Nils found he couldn't answer. "Why chrysolin?" he asked, eager to move on. "Why would you trade for that, if you aren't a weaver? Do you sell it?"

"I have no need of chrysolin."

"Then why was it being shipped here?"

"For Jarik," Dreygard said.

Oh. That makes sense. That little box that Bern and I found must've been replenishment for the stones Jarik had used up…trying to kill me.

Nils shook his head. "Those little boxes don't account for what I saw in one of your tasker's logbooks. You're moving large amounts of weaver's stones into the country."

"Not into," Dreygard said. "Out of."

"Out of...No, chrysolin doesn't form in Branaden. Everybody knows that."

"That's why it's so easy to get away with it."

"Huh?"

Dreygard sighed impatiently. "The whole country believes the lie that chrysolin doesn't naturally occur beneath our soil. It's an evil substance in their eyes, and therefore it couldn't possibly exist under our noble land. In truth, we just don't want it to, so we don't look for it. We turn a blind eye to it, cover it up whenever a tiny speck of it is found. While it is a rare substance, I unearthed three mines that contain veins of it just within our province, and, because it happens to form near coal, it's an easy job to dig it out without anybody needing to know about it."

The coal mines. Gen Rill...

"Are you telling me," Nils said, "that Gen Rill was a cover-up, and I was unknowingly forced to mine for chrysolin?"

Dreygard nodded, and a memory zapped Nils' brain. Struggling with his pickaxe, pulling a chunk of stone away from the wall with his hand, and a buzzing sensation on his skin that made him drop the rock and jump back...

You all right, man? Taws had said. *Find a cave bee?*

Fine, Nils replied, shaking his hand. *Cave bee? Are those real?* Taws had laughed at him.

Weaver's blood, Nils thought in the present. *It was chrysolin.*

"It's all a temporary arrangement in Ri'sen's eyes," Dreygard explained. "He failed to claim our country in war, so he's reaping our resources however he can until he can try again."

"But Galreyva is full of chrysolin. Why would he need ours?"

"Another misconception," Dreygard said. "They used to have many active mines, but they've also been practicing spellweaving for centuries. They wove carelessly for too long. They've run out."

There's no more chrysolin in Galreyva. That should've been cause for celebration, a victory Branaden didn't know they'd won: their enemies were out of their most sinister weapon. And yet...

"That's why Ri'sen is conquering all the nations around him," Nils said, glancing at Dreygard for confirmation. "That's why he took Thrinia, and Tarvesh, Khunar, and why he tried to take Branaden. He's searching for sources of chrysolin."

The domiseer nodded.

Weaver's blood.

Nils felt the need to start pacing, but couldn't seem to move, so he settled for tapping one of his feet. "So what do we do?" he asked, mostly to himself, then turned his attention to the domiseer again. "How do we stop this? If you're replenishing Galreyva's chrysolin reserve—and more, if I'm not mistaken—they're going to be strong enough to take our country out before we can possibly muster the strength to defend ourselves. We still haven't recovered from the fighting ten years ago."

"There's nothing I can do," Dreygard said.

"You keep saying that," Nils said. "Stop it, and tell me why."

Dreygard gave him a stare that was half disbelief and half anger at his audacity, but Nils didn't care. "The emperor saved Raeya, placing me in his debt," the domiseer said. "If I break our contract, he has more than enough evidence to reveal to our king what I've been doing for the last nine years. Once I'm revealed as the greatest traitor the country has ever known, I'll be executed..."

"So just take the fall for your country and get it over with!"

"...along with my family."

Nils paused. "What? The king won't kill your wife and daughter. They don't even know about this."

"My wife does," Dreygard said, "and you think too innocently of King Perem. He knows he can't afford mercy in a matter like this. He'll see that my entire household faces death in view of the public, and I will not allow that to happen."

Nils' mind protested this revelation, stuttering against the thought until he forced it to process. *He* had been about to reveal Dreygard, which would've had the same result. "No," Nils said. "No, it doesn't have to be that way. Can't you send your family into hiding or something?"

Dreygard shook his head. "Ri'sen watches my every movement, and he will never let Raeya escape. She is the one thing he wanted from me that I have managed to withhold, until now."

Nils' eyebrows tightened together. "What does he want with Raeya?"

"To him, her curse is a gift. Think about it: Raeya has the power to kill anyone with a simple kiss. No weapon, no poison, no spellweaving. Nothing to cover up and no trace left behind. She's a perfect assassin, and he wants her in his arsenal."

Nils' stomach hollowed out. Raeya? An assassin? "She'd never do it," he said, horrified. "She wouldn't kill anyone."

"No, but he'll do everything he can to change that."

Nils swallowed, feeling like he was going to be sick. *Fives. Unholy fives.*

"I knew about Ri'sen's desires, so I refused to let him have Raeya, even when he made offer after offer to take her into his service," Dreygard went on. "He would've demanded it, but our trade had become too profitable for him; he wouldn't risk the end of his chrysolin supply, and he knew I might give it all up if he took her by force. I thought Raeya would be safe, at least until he'd managed to take our whole country as his own and I no longer held any power over him. However, he's been trying to win her from me indirectly this entire past year."

Jarik, Nils thought. "If she had married Jarik…"

"I couldn't have stopped her from leaving with him."

The sickness inside Nils turned to fury. Jarik. *Isek.* Fives, he'd said he loved her, and Nils believed him. Called Nils his *friend,* and he'd believed him.

"So why did he take her by force now?" Nils said. "What changed?" But he knew the answer even as he asked the question.

"There's an investigator coming tomorrow," Dreygard said, "that I believe you know about very well."

He thinks I tipped off the king's man, Nils realized. Well, let him believe that. "So Ri'sen decided it was too great a risk to leave his nephew here, and he was done waiting for Raeya."

"Yes. He decided to take his chances and hope that I'll keep my mouth shut, in the interest of protecting myself and my wife. And, should I not, or should the investigator find enough evidence to condemn me, Ri'sen at least won't lose out on his prized assassin."

Nils couldn't listen to any more of this. "We have to get her back," he said.

Dreygard inclined his head. "We?"

"Well, I just meant…she needs to be gotten back. Gods, that sounded terrible. Don't make me speak like that ever again."

"Then are you willing to do something about it?"

Nils paused, chewing his lip. "Something like what?"

"I can't take Raeya back," Dreygard said. "I can do nothing to interfere."

That's what he said before he sent me after Jarik, Nils realized, and he finished the statement. "But I can."

"Yes. You are not tied to me. In fact, I don't think Ri'sen could even be *convinced* that you are acting on my behalf."

"And I wouldn't be. I'd be acting on Raeya's behalf," Nils said. "And our country's," he hastily added. "But if I somehow brought her back…"

"He'd just take her again. I'm still indebted to him. So we need to get rid of him."

"Whoa," Nils said. "Are you proposing I *kill* Emperor Ri'sen?"

"His death is the only way to ensure Raeya's safety and bring an end to all this."

"No," Nils said. "No. I am *not* a killer, and I absolutely won't do it." He thought for a moment. "Though…I think I know someone who would."

Dreygard raised a brow. "An accomplice?"

"…Yes."

"Do you have means of contacting this accomplice?"

"…Yes."

Dreygard sat back in his chair. "Good. Because I'm not going to let you go. You're going to have to escape."

Nils blinked. *"What?"*

"I told you there can be *no* evidence of my involvement. If you fail, and Ri'sen lives, and he finds out what I tried to do, my wife and I will die horrible deaths. As will Raeya, unless she agrees to serve Ri'sen forever."

"Fives!" Nils said. "So let me get this straight: You want me to break out of *your* manor on my own power, go to *Galreyva*, of all places, rescue *your* daughter, kill *your* master, and in doing so clear all your debts and ensure the safety of your family."

"Yes."

Nils' fury boiled over again. "And what right do you have to make demands of me?" he shouted. "Do you know what kind of life I've lived under your rule? What kind of lives your townspeople live? Compared to many of them, I've had it good. You work them to death, don't see to their needs, let them get *beaten* for the tiniest infraction of your unnecessarily strict laws. Your taskers are the cruelest men to walk our soil. I've seen them destroy people and laugh while they're doing it. Gods, they beat a child to death in front of our schoolhouse and left her body there to bleed on the street. What could a little girl have possibly done to deserve that? And you don't even care."

"No," Dreygard said, not batting an eye, "I don't care. My concern is spent on meeting the heavy demands of both a king and an emperor, each of whom have the power to destroy the two people I actually *do* care about. I have time for nothing else, and as long as my taskers meet their quotas, they can do as they please."

Nils' fury turned into something cold and hard that curled inside him, filling him with a dead weight. All this time, Nils had thought Feren Dreygard a greedy wolf, preying on those beneath him and reveling in the tang of their blood as it filled him. Now he saw the wolf was bound and leashed, growling at all who came near, trying to keep their eyes on his fangs instead of his tethers.

Even if greed wasn't his motivation…he was still a beast.

"You are right that I can't place demands on you," Dreygard said. "Once you escape the grounds, I'll have lost all power to restrain you, and you can do as you will. However, if you fulfill that which I've asked, it won't be without reward. I will consider you worthy of marrying Raeya. That sets you up as my sole heir, and the future domiseer of the province. If you wish to improve the lives of your countrymen, the power to do so will be entirely in your hands. And, it should go without saying, you need not fear setting foot in Gen Rill ever again."

Nils stared at Lord Dreygard. He didn't want to be the domiseer. Didn't want to inherit the province or Dreygard's wealth. He *certainly* didn't want to marry Raeya…

And yet he felt no need to tell the domiseer that. "I will go," Nils said. *Because someone has to get Raeya out of there, and I might be the only one who can do it.*

Nils wouldn't have said Dreygard looked tense at all, and yet something in his posture relaxed at Nils' words. "Jarik and his men will travel by carriage," he said, "and they will hasten back to Ri'sen's castle. I expect you and your chosen comrade will make slower progress. It will likely take you a month to complete the journey."

Nils nodded, already dreading it.

"If you time it well, you'll arrive during the Hearthnight celebration."

Hearthnight. The word left Nils shuddering inside. Even though the season no longer existed, the Galreyvans still celebrated it during the last week of Desna's reign. A festival to celebrate the darkness, and the fallen god, Lyare.

"With luck, the festivities will be a helpful distraction while you complete your work," Dreygard said. "I can give you instructions on crossing the Galreyvan border without being seen and getting into Ri'sen's castle, but once we leave this room, you'll receive nothing more from me."

"What about the investigator?" Nils asked. It had to be almost morning by now. He'd be here soon.

"There will be nothing for him to find," Dreygard said, showing no signs of trepidation.

"He'll want to speak with the captain of the guard," Nils said, "and anyone who witnessed the knife incident."

Dreygard did not reply.

"I have a condition to make, on my trip to Galreyva," Nils said. "You can't harm Captain Clerrit, Tilda, or the guard, Bern."

Dreygard's face didn't change when he replied, "They know enough to cause a problem."

"I'll talk to them," Nils said. "I promise they won't say a thing against you, if you just give me the chance to explain. If you don't, our deal is off."

Dreygard gave a shallow nod. "The investigator will be especially keen to speak with you," he said.

"I know," Nils replied. "And I…will tell him nothing."

32 MEMENTO

It was one of the strangest things Nils had ever done. To sit before the king's investigator, alone in a room where no one could overhear them, finally able to reveal Dreygard's treachery.

And to defend him instead.

Nils walked back from the meeting, Bern at his side, feeling incredibly uncertain of himself. *Hearthnight take that man if everything he said was a ploy to keep me from telling the truth today.*

Well, it didn't matter now, did it? His chance had come and gone. He had to live with it.

When Nils was back in his small, windowless room, he immediately noticed something was different. Before, there had been one small candelabrum on the dresser. Probably iron, not worth much. It was gone now, replaced by two candlesticks.

Polished silver. Worth *a lot.*

Nils huffed a laugh. Dreygard said he wouldn't help, but those candlesticks were no accident. They were the perfect target for a thief, and once sold would provide a full purse. Enough to make a journey to Galreyva, perhaps.

Nils sat down and took off his shoe and sock from his right foot, extracting the weaver's stone. He'd known he might be searched, so he'd put the fiving thing right between his toes, and the tingling was driving him mad. He could've hidden it in his room somewhere, but he didn't dare. The safest place to keep it was with him, even if he hated it.

I don't even need it anymore, Nils thought, holding the black stone between his fingers and glaring at it with disgust. He'd gladly get rid of it, but it wasn't exactly something to dispose of offhandedly, especially with the investigator around. He sighed and tucked it back into his sock.

One more thing to check on. The letterbox. Nils had been out of the room for a fair amount of time, long enough for Sandri to come twice. He'd left a message for her and Taws, so maybe...

Yes. A reply, scrawled on a shred of paper.

Got it, brother. We'll be ready.

Nils went to his door and knocked on it softly. It opened a crack.

"Bern," Nils said. "I'm going to need a little space tonight."

★ ★ ★

Sandri and Nils made their escape from the manor without much resistance, thanks to Bern's cooperation. The false maid smuggled a disguise in to Nils, and they slipped out to meet Taws on the edge of the grounds.

No more noble's clothing, Nils thought, now wearing something akin to servant's clothing again. *Good.*

Taws appeared in the darkness with a salute, then clapped Nils on the back. The three of them didn't risk saying a word, and they slipped off past the outbuildings and into the trees.

This place...

Nils realized where they were, and paused. It was the last place he'd seen Raeya.

"Nils," Sandri whispered, motioning for him to hurry.

Nils took a deep breath and forced himself to keep walking, but a glint of something on the ground caught his eye. He stooped to pick it up.

A delicate bracelet with four small gemstones.

Nils felt a tightening in his chest he didn't quite understand. He held an item worth far more than the candlesticks he'd just pilfered from the manor, but its monetary value didn't even cross his mind. Instead he thought of the soft skin where this bracelet had rested, Raeya's slender hands holding up a book, the way her hair framed her face while she read.

And the desperate way she'd reached out to him before she was stolen away.

Nils shook his head, trying to clear it. He'd get her back. This tight, painful ache in his chest would go away once she was safe. He put the bracelet in his pocket and followed Sandri, nodding to himself.

Yes. He just...

He just had to get her back.

33 A MEMORY OF...?

Nils.

Nils.

Listen to my voice. Can you hear me?

34 THE PATH TO THE TUNNEL

The next morning, Nils got a good look at Tawson. He could tell last night that the man was roughed-up, but the low light hadn't done it justice. Bruises colored his face and circled his eyes, and scabbed-over gashes criss-crossed his skin.

"Fives, Taws. You look terrible."

Taws laughed, sipping a drink. "You haven't even seen the best of it."

He pulled off his gloves, and Nils gawked. Each hand was missing the top half of the index finger.

No wonder his handwriting was sloppier than usual.

Taws waved away any words of concern Nils might've said. "I'm all right. The barkeep here patched me up, gave me a good drink. Four normal fingers still gives you a decent grip on a knife, yeah?"

"If you say so," Nils replied.

He, Taws, and Sandri had spent the night in a hidden attic at a pub in Crede, Chanterey's center-city that encompassed the manor. Taws promised it was safe, and Nils hadn't argued. The man had resources, associates, and street knowledge that far surpassed anything Nils could offer, and yet it all left him uneasy.

Right. If he was going to travel across the country with this man, into enemy territory, he at least wanted to know.

"Taws, I need you to come clean with me. Are you the leader of a gang?"

Taws choked on a laugh, hastily swallowing his drink before he could spit it out. "I prefer *secret organization.*"

"All right, but are you?"

"I don't know," Taws said, waving a hand. "Gangs are villainous, ain't they?"

"Aren't."

"Stop doing that," Taws said, pointing what remained of his finger at Nils. He looked down at it with a dissatisfied squint, but moved on. "Anyway, we're just after the Galreyvans. You know what they did to my people, my country. I have a score to settle, and a lot of others have the same. We're still fighting the war, just...on a smaller scale."

Nils thought it over, and nodded. He could accept that. He was eager to fight that war, too. Just without killing anyone.

"*Gods,* I can't wait to plunge my knife into that fiving murderer," Taws said. "Here we were, ready to have Dreygard hanged, and now he's given us all we need to infiltrate Galreyva and get after the emperor himself. I won't thank the man, but he did turn out to be useful."

Nils stared at Taws.

"Ah, don't look at me like that," Taws said. "I know I'm a little...rough around the edges, but for what it's worth, you *can* trust me."

Maybe, Nils thought, though he'd also thought he could trust Jarik. He just couldn't shake the feeling that Taws wasn't telling him something.

"I think Nils is smart to have his doubts," Sandri piped up.

"Sands, what's this?" Taws said. "Betrayal? From you?"

"You do keep secrets," Sandri said.

"Not this again, love. What secrets?"

"Like your last name."

"I don't have a last name."

"Everybody has a last name. I mean, how's a girl supposed to marry a guy if she doesn't even know his last name?"

"Marry?" Taws said, fanning himself. "Wow, when's the wedding? I do hope I'm invited."

Sandri slapped him lightly. "I was being…what's the word. Nils, help me out."

"Hypothetical?"

"Yes," Sandri said, snapping her fingers. "That."

"Well I wasn't," Taws said, pulling Sandri closer.

"Tawsey," she said, giggling, and Nils cringed. It wasn't like he could just excuse himself and go for a walk; they were kind of in hiding at the moment.

"Shouldn't we, um, make plans for getting out of the province?"

"Right, right," Tawson sighed, keeping an arm around Sandri but blessedly getting back to business. "My buddy Mica is out selling your candlesticks right now, and he'll bring the funds to us. Once we're out of the area we should consider hiring transport for part of the journey, but this close to the manor is too risky. We'll start on foot, and travel at night. Even if Dreygard *wanted* you to escape, he might have men out looking for you just to keep up appearances, so we'll play it safe. We'll want to stick to, er…less reputable sources for supplies and transportation, even in the long run, since neither of us have tags."

"Lovely," Nils said. "Won't we risk running into street patrols at night? They'd beat us even if we *did* have tags, and without them we'll be arrested for sure."

"We can dodge them," Taws said. "Sands and I have lots of practice, although I should have a word with Bartle before we go. He might have some recent info on patrol routes."

Bartle, Mica. Taws had a name for everything. What was it like to know so many people?

"So, basically, we should all get some rest this afternoon," Tawson said, reclining in his chair. "We're going to be nocturnal for at least a few days."

That was almost the worst thought yet. Worse than Dreygard's street patrols. They'd be living in the dark.

Outside, Nils reminded himself. *It's not so bad if it's outside. I wonder if the darkness bothers Taws, too, since...*

Nils looked at the man across the table, eyes drawn to the bandages on the stumps of his forefingers, stark white against his tan skin.

"Taws," Nils said, "you said you'd tell me what happened when you saw me in person. Your fingers..."

"Mm," Taws said, sitting up again and withdrawing his hand. "I did, didn't I."

"And you'd better do it," Sandri said. "I've been waiting to hear this story too, and I *rescued* you from that nasty place."

"Just thought you'd sleep better at night not knowing, love," Taws said. "But if you insist..."

He took a breath, collecting his thoughts. "I never quite found out who the guys were who captured me. They got wind that I was prodding for weaver's stones on the market. Those merchants'll sell out anyone, so it was no surprise, in a way, but what they did...Well, they tested me to see if I was a dormant."

"Dormant?" Nils asked.

"A weaver who hasn't used his power yet. Obviously I got no black veins on my arms—yeah, yeah, Nils, I *don't have any black veins,* better?—so they knew I wasn't a practicer, at least not yet. They had a weaver's stone with them, and they kept touching it to my skin, asking if I could feel anything. What was I *fiving* supposed to feel? It's a rock."

Could he...not feel the tingling? Nils wondered. He shuddered, feeling it right now.

"So, when I kept saying I couldn't feel anything, they tried to force me to attempt weaving a spell. I wouldn't do it, in spite of their torture. Knew they'd kill me if I wasn't any use to them, and it's better to be tortured than dead, right? If not for Sandri, I don't know how I would've gotten out of there, and they'd have tired of me eventually." He put his arm around Sandri again and gave her a squeeze. "My guess is they were looking for weavers to turn in for a bounty, and they wouldn't get no reward without the black veins on my wrists as proof, although I never found that out for sure either. I think you and I both would be surprised what people want weavers for, even in this country."

Nils looked down at the table. Neither Sandri nor Tawson knew he had a weaver's stone in his sock right now. Should he tell them? And could Tawson *really not feel the tingling?* Gods, what did that mean?

"Looks like I made you ill," Tawson said, shoving Nils from across the table. "Ow. All right, finger still hurts." He shook his hand a little as he withdrew it. "I'm gonna get some sleep. Who's with me?"

Nils nodded, needing some time to think. He always got the most thinking done when he was supposed to be sleeping.

* * *

The next couple weeks passed in a strange rhythm. Hurried flights dodging gazes of patrol officers, long, uncomfortable rides hidden in the back of rickety carts, days spent waiting for nightfall, and nights spent running through alleys or forests or whatever sort of landscape they presently navigated. Underneath it all ran a steady current, a pulsing inside of Nils that cut through him like a river through rock.

He had to rescue Raeya. Had to get her back. Had to know that she was safe.

Where was she now? Had she already arrived at Ri'sen's castle? What would he do to her in his attempt to win her cooperation?

And what about Jarik—Isek—the one who'd stolen her away and would be by her side every moment? Nils' brain revolted at the thought of the two of them traveling this path together, day and night. It burned inside him, right alongside a small, nagging shred of uncertainty about the nobleman.

Why didn't he kill me when he had the chance? He had every reason, and the perfect opportunity, unless...

"I'm glad we crossed paths, Nils."

Nils shook his head. Those sentiments were obviously feigned. Jarik was only after Raeya, and Nils had been a convenient go-between at best and an obstacle to be removed at worst.

Nils rubbed his forehead with his fingers. He longed for a rest from this stress flowing through him, but it wouldn't come, especially not today. Not when Raeya was on his mind even more than usual.

He, Taws, and Sandri had arrived in Borlund. Nils sat on a log, staring off into the woods, remembering what Raeya had told him about the day she received her curse. It could have happened near here; they were very close to the Galreyvan border now. Nils couldn't believe Dreygard had actually brought his family here, his young daughter. Yes, it was a scenic place—everything was in bloom now, reveling in Desna's warmth and provision—but so near to enemy territory?

Nils still doubted that Dreygard had come here to meet with Lord Ashber. Even though it had happened before Raeya's curse, and before he'd become indebted to Emperor Ri'sen. But perhaps Nils would never know for certain.

He looked down at his wrist and the bracelet he'd worn there for many days now. It was somewhat embarrassing that it fit, given it was sized for Raeya, but he consoled himself that it was at least a tight fit. The gemstones rested on his skin, and he'd uttered countless prayers to Desna through the emerald on their way here. *Let her be safe. Let us get there in time. Let us succeed. In your name, Desna, let it be done.*

"I still say we should sell that thing," Taws said, standing beside Nils.

"Not a chance," Nils replied. "It's not mine to sell; it's Raeya's."

"Yeah, but what does she need it for? Her family's disgustingly rich."

"I'm...not sure they are," Nils said. "They're as well-off as any noble family, but I have a feeling most of the riches in their house came from Emperor Ri'sen."

"Well it's not like they'll evaporate after we kill the guy."

"I still won't sell it."

"Show some compassion, Taws," Sandri said. "He's missing his sweetheart."

Nils stood up. "She is *not* my sweetheart."

"Right, sorry. He's missing his *true love.*"

Nils groaned. Sandri shoved him playfully, but he wasn't in the mood for jokes.

"You must care about her, Nils. A lot," Taws insisted. "Why else would you be here right now? Me? I'm here for revenge on Ri'sen. Sandri's here 'cause I couldn't convince her to stay home and cherish safety like a normal person."

"And because *somebody's* gotta keep you out of trouble," Sandri said. "You know it's true, Tawsey; both Nils and I have saved your skin now."

Taws chuckled. "Fair enough. But what about you, Nils? Miss Lady Raeya must've made quite an impression to send you on a *highly dangerous* quest to get her back. You wouldn't have volunteered for something like this before your time with her."

"Maybe so, but that doesn't mean I love her," Nils muttered. "She just...clouds my sensibilities."

"She what?" Taws and Sandri said together, laughing.

"She makes me do stupid things!" Nils said. "Like traveling all the way out here and facing near-certain death in the stronghold of our enemies during their blasted festival of darkness."

"Aw, Nilsey," Sandri said, putting a hand over her heart. "That's exactly what love is, hon."

"No, it isn't," Nils said tersely. "And don't ever call me that again."

"I agree, love," Tawson said. "Too affectionate."

"Aw, have I made you jealous?" Sandri teased.

Taws grinned. "Maybe a little."

Nils groaned again. For the most part, he enjoyed Taws and Sandri's company, but when they got like this, it made him feel awkward, and made him think about Raeya, and he *did not want this to make him think about Raeya.*

"Well," Taws said, "as fun as it is to dance on Nils' nerves, shall we find this border crossing? It can't be far now."

"Yes, please," Nils said. "Dreygard said it's overgrown and hard to spot until you get close, but if we follow the tree line, we should find it."

"All right. Let's go."

★ ★ ★

The three of them stayed in the cover of the trees while they walked. It was warm, but Nils kept the gray hood of his traveling cloak over his head. The other two seemed fine, but he'd be sunburned crimson even with the canopy of leaves dappling the light. He wasn't too excited about making the journey home once Pria had taken the reins. Her sun was merciless.

"It's gotta be soon, yeah?" Taws said from up ahead. "We don't want to overshoot and reach the border by accident. Border guards'll see us for sure."

"Yes," Nils said. "We should be nearly there."

He ought to have felt more nervous about their location, and what they were about to do. Even now they were close enough to Ri'sen's empire to be on the lookout for border patrols. But Nils found himself watching Taws and Sandri's backs as they walked ahead of him, thinking about other things.

I should've told them about the reward Dreygard offered me, he thought, and yet in the same moment he found himself defensive. What difference would it make if he told them? He wasn't going to accept the offer, and they would surely be all over him, telling him to stop making excuses and marry Raeya. He didn't need that, but he felt a twinge of guilt at his growing list of secrets. He still hadn't told them about the chrysolin either, which ceaselessly prickled at his skin. He'd had countless opportunities and impulses to get rid of the stone, but somehow he couldn't bring himself to do it. It just seemed like…he might need it for something. *What* he'd need it for was beyond him, but then it was a godjewel. It shouldn't be dropped lightly, just like an emerald, diamond, sapphire, or ruby.

Huh, Nils thought. *I have one of each of the godjewels with me right now. Even Lyare's. That seems…kind of incredible.*

And wrong. Fives, he should've dropped that black rock ages ago.

"Hey, is that it?"

Nils stopped and looked ahead. Covered in ivy and surrounded by trees and shrubbery was a building so decrepit it seemed the plants were holding the stone walls together more than what little remained of the mortar. "Yeah," Nils said. It could be nothing else. There was a faded symbol, just barely visible above the door, of a tree interwoven with five spheres, four amongst the branches and one in the trunk. It marked this building as a church, and a very old church. No other remained in Branaden that still depicted the fifth sphere.

"Grand. Here we go, then," Taws said, picking his way up the root-covered mound that led to the door. He tested the handle, and he and Sandri had to lean on it together before the door finally gave way and opened. A strong scent of moss and dust hurried to greet them.

Taws stepped into the small building first, then motioned for the others to follow. One foot on the floorboards had Nils wondering if it would hold their weight, as it bowed beneath his shoe and groaned in protest. He stepped as lightly as he could, and they made their way toward the altar at the front.

The windows were shrouded with vines, and so most of the light came in through holes in the roof, along with long sprigs of moss that hung down and nearly brushed their heads. There were rows of wooden pews decaying to either side of them, and steps flanking the altar that nobody dared tread upon. Taws skipped them with a long stride, then pulled Sandri up to stand beside him. Nils jumped up to join them, breathing heavily in the earthy air.

"Gods, how old is this place?" Sandri asked, brushing dirt off of the altar. The tree symbol was repeated here, but in place of the spheres there were settings for actual gemstones that had long since been emptied, likely stolen away by thieves. Once again, there were five.

"A prayer altar," Nils said. Visitors at the church would have touched these gems when they said their prayers, much as people now made use of the prayer bracelets worn by priests. When worshipers still attended here, Lyare hadn't yet fallen. There had still been five seasons. This little church could be a thousand years old.

"So, did Dreygard tell you what to do next?" Tawson asked. "You said there's a passage somewhere."

"Yes, back here, must be," Nils said, turning away from the altar and his thoughts of days when all five stones sat beside one another. There was a doorway tucked back behind the altar with stairs leading down to a basement, which they unfortunately couldn't avoid walking on, so Nils lead the way, taking each step with care, while the spongy wood creaked beneath him. It was darker down here, though thankfully some sunlight still managed to filter through the floorboards above, illuminating narrow channels of dust in the stale air.

"Oh, is this a tomb?" Sandri said, sounding disproportionately excited by the thought. "They buried people beneath old churches, didn't they?"

"Probably," Nils said, not lingering on the thought. He was looking for something. A torch bracket, the third from the left...

He went and pulled it, and a slot opened in the floor in front of them.

"Oh!" Sandri gasped, and she and Taws peered down into it, grinning at Nils' discovery.

"Fantastic," Tawson said. "So this leads to the tunnel, yeah? And when we come out the other side...Nils?"

Nils was staring down into that space, feeling like a pit had opened up inside of him. He knew this was coming, but no amount of mental preparation had helped. No light could reach down that far. All that waited beneath was blackness.

"Nils," Taws said, coming around and putting a hand on his shoulder. He and Sandri had traveled with him long enough to witness his embarrassing phobia a few times over, but this was undoubtedly the worst.

"I don't think I can do it, Taws," Nils said. "Underground, it...it's just like Gen Rill. Can't you feel it?"

"It's not Gen Rill," Taws said softly. "And look, here. Matches. You insisted we stock up on these, remember? There are torches here we can use."

"That tunnel goes for miles, Taws. Miles of darkness. We'll suffocate. We'll never make it to the other side."

"Why are you here, Nils?"

"Hm?"

"Tell me why you came."

"You already asked me that."

"You never really answered me."

Nils still stared at that opening in the floor, a yawning chasm eager to swallow him, to trap him in its depths. "Raeya," he said.

"I thought so. Now, brother, you wait here. Sands, throw me a torch, would you? I'm going to go down first, and you just follow my light, all right?"

Nils shut his eyes and tried to replenish his oxygen, but the air was so thick and damp down here, it felt like breathing water. He struggled through a few more breaths, and nodded.

"All right. Here I go. No running away now; who's going to correct my poor grammar if you ain't here?"

"Aren't."

"That's the spirit."

Taws descended a ladder into the pit, down deep enough that he would surely be trapped if something were to happen to that ladder. What if it crumbled once they were all down there, succumbing to its age? What if the same thing had already happened to the one on the other side?

"Ladder looks pretty sturdy," Sandri said, as though reading his thoughts. "Bet whoever uses this passage has kept it in good shape. Do you want to go next? Or me?"

"I...I'll go," Nils said. Better to get it over with. Nils got his hands and feet onto the rungs, hurling mental prayers at the emerald on his wrist. Sandri handed a torch down to him, its light hot in his grasp, and Nils started down. He kept his eyes on the ladder until his feet touched soil.

"Atta boy. Nicely done," Taws said, clapping him on the back and turning him around. The tunnel stretched ahead of them, but there may as well have been a wall of darkness at the edge of their torch light. Nils whimpered.

Sandri slid down the ladder behind them with a whoop of glee, and the others turned to look at her. "Nice and smooth," she said, holding out her hands. "Look, no splinters! So, how do we close that thing?" She pointed to the open hatch above them, and Nils nodded toward the wall. Dreygard had said there was a lever there. "Got it," Sandri said, pulling the lever and sealing them in. Silt trickled down on them, and then all was still.

"No time to waste," Taws said, pushing Nils forward. He walked, unendingly grateful that the two of them were here with him, although he doubted his ability to speak would return until they were above ground again. "Now we just hope that Dreygard doesn't have anyone waiting to meet us on the other side," Taws went on, "and *bam,* we'll have infiltrated Galreyva."

35 NOT A MEMORY...

Nils.
Do not wake. Let your body rest, while your mind hears.
Listen.

36 GALREYVA

Traveling in enemy territory presented some new challenges.

They stuck to wilderness travel as much as possible, but when they entered the first town in need of resupplying, everyone was on edge, and none so much as Taws. He seemed ready to pick a fight with everyone they encountered.

The beneficial thing about Galreyva having absorbed several other nations was that Taws and Nils could travel here without drawing *too* much attention, however blonds were not common, and Thrinians were not confrontational. Most of them were ill-treated servants or even slaves, and they walked with lowered eyes and stooped shoulders.

"Makes me sick," Taws said when they passed a couple of them at a town market.

"Shh," Sandri said. "As wrong as it is, you need to act like them. You're supposed to be my servant, remember? Just keep your cool."

Taws grunted in reply. At least his recent scars and missing fingers helped him fit the part. Sandri was turning out to be a gem of a companion on this quest, since she looked the most like a Galreyvan with her brown hair and eyes. She could purchase food and drink without drawing a second glance, except perhaps from interested men.

Another benefit of Galreyvan conquest was that everyone defaulted to Branic in markets and public places. "Thank you kindly, my dear sir," Sandri said to a merchant with an impressive Galreyvan accent. She returned to Taws and Nils with their lunch. "Taws, you're glaring again."

"Yeah, yeah."

Nils kept his hood up most of the time, finding he drew fewer gazes that way. Even so, it felt like there were eyes all around him, prying at his coverings, guessing at his purposes. They passed a priest while they walked, wearing something akin to the Seasons Symbol on the chest of his garments, and Nils noticed something strange. "They still only have four spheres on their tree," he whispered.

"Yeah, they leave out the diamond," Taws whispered back. "They think of Pria much as we think of Lyare."

"What? Why?"

"They blame her for the time when Hearthnight didn't end."

"That doesn't make sense," Nils said. "She couldn't have been in the wrong; she still has her season."

"She wouldn't if the Galreyvans had anything to say about it."

"Ack," Sandri said, stopping to examine herself in a mirror hanging at one of the market stalls. "All this time in the sun has really brought out my freckles." She rubbed at her cheekbones and the bridge of her nose.

"Good," Taws said, leaning in from behind to look at her reflection. "They're adorable."

Sandri started to smile, but cut it short. "Another comment like that, and I'll put you in your place," she snapped, spinning around and grabbing Taws by the collar, then pushing him away from her.

Nils gaped until he noticed the merchant at the stall watching them closely, then understood. This was a different place indeed.

Sandri strutted away from the stand, Nils and Taws following silently. "I'm going to grab supplies," she murmured when they were clear of listening ears. "Why don't you two wait someplace inconspicuous."

"As you wish, my lady," Taws said, bowing dramatically. Sandri pretended to ignore him, then moved on to the next stall while Nils and Taws found a place to stand out of the way.

"I hate this fiving place," Taws muttered.

"Is it all right for her to go alone?" Nils asked, shifting his weight from one foot to the other.

"She'll be fine. Seems I'd do her more harm than good anyway."

They waited in silence for a couple minutes, and Nils' brain kept prodding him to say something. "I...never properly thanked you for helping me get through the tunnel."

"No need," Taws said. "It was nothing."

"Taws, how is it that you...aren't afraid of places like that? I mean, you went through the same thing I did. You were in Gen Rill for *longer* than I was. It's paralyzing, and it haunts my dreams all the time."

Taws shrugged. "I have the occasional nightmare," he said, "but most the time I just don't think about it."

"But how?"

Taws considered. "I think...it doesn't bother me so much, because I had deeper scars before going in there. Gen Rill was bad, but not the worst thing I've experienced in life."

At first Nils wondered what could be worse, but the answer was obvious. "The fall of your country."

"Yes. That night...well, *that's* what most of my nightmares are about. I may never be rid of them, but I can at least rest easier once Ri'sen's been made to pay for it."

Nils nodded his understanding. They watched Sandri head to another vendor down the street, and waited until she came back in their direction.

"Here you go, boys," she said, giving them each a load of supplies to carry.

"Wow, thank you, my dear generous mistress," Taws said. Sandri gave him a quick wink.

"I managed to confirm the date, and we're on track for our arrival," she said. "Five more days will see us in the capital, and that same day marks the start of the Hearthnight celebration."

"Great," Nils said, though it came out like an exasperated sigh. They were almost there. Less than a week, and they'd be where Raeya was. Right in the heart of Lyare's greatest following.

"We're going to need these," Sandri said, opening the last bag she carried, full of black cloaks.

* * *

Before arriving in the capital, Nils rehearsed what he'd learned, and taught, about Hearthnight.

It was a season of darkness.

The fifth season, the time when the god Lyare held power, was far shorter than the others. Lasting only a week, it was a time when the sun, moon, and stars vanished, during both day and night. The darkness was absolute, almost physical, as it covered the earth in its cloak. No work could be done in this time, save that which could be done by firelight, which is what inspired mankind to give this season its own name. An extended night, spent in the light of a hearth.

Even without tending the fields or feeding the flocks during this time, everything continued to flourish. The animals slept, and the plants still grew, not seeming to notice the absence of the life-giving sunlight. Lyare's power was enough to sustain all things while the heavenly luminaries rested.

And the humans rested also, each family safe in their homes, having stored up food and supplies in anticipation of Lyare's reign. It was said that even the light of candles and fireplaces seemed muted in the darkness of Hearthnight, but they provided a bright enough glow to live by. Unsurprisingly, many children were conceived in this time, and many wrote about it as a season of peace and recuperation.

But it was a season meant to end. Each year, when the week was up, the sun rose again and normal activity resumed. Until it didn't.

One year, the darkness persisted. One day. Then another. And another. For two full months.

No one was prepared for this. Supplies ran out, and no one could farm, or hunt, for the darkness was too deep. Many of the animals died in their sleep, having stayed under too long. In their panic, people began stealing from even their closest neighbors, grasping at what they needed to survive. They learned that darkness made an excellent covering for atrocities, and stolen goods became one of the lesser crimes as the night went on.

Peace turned to chaos, and rest to hunger and fear. Lyare had refused to relinquish his hold on the world, and it wasn't hard to guess why. The other four gods held power for months, and he was given only a week. But some things are meant to have limits. Before the human race could destroy itself, Desna, Pria, Kirit, and Raulen cast Lyare from their midst to restore order to the world and allow the sun to shine again. Lyare would take power no more, and his name and his season would become symbols of shame.

There were some, however, who continued to worship him. They still clung to his godjewel, the black stone called chrysolin, reciting their prayers. And a strange thing happened.

Some of those prayers were answered in a most tangible way. No one understood why some were blessed, or cursed, with this power, but to a small number of people the chrysolin became a source of magic. Objects, or even people, could be directly influenced by the words they wove around them. Those who saw Lyare as the evil force he had become knew to shun this ability, but there were always two sides where light and dark were involved.

And some reveled in the darkness.

* * *

They entered the capital city at noon.

Already the Hearthnight celebration was underway, although it would apparently hit its height at night when the world was truly dark. They couldn't shut out the sunlight during the day, but there were great canopics erected in every square, shrouding citizens under black cloth, and every market stall and entryway was covered with the same. Pinpricks of candlelight glimmered here and there in the shadows, even while the sun shone overhead.

It was fortuitous that Sandri had purchased black cloaks for the three of them; without them they would've stood out like white frogs on a bed of tar. Everyone wore the cloaks—even children— which had deep hoods to cover the face, probably intended to enhance the illusion of darkness in the daytime. To Nils, it all felt a bit silly, but also unsettling. It was like watching a horde of executioners travel between candlelit pavilions, except everyone was far too cheerful to be attending anything like an execution.

Taws, Sandri, and Nils did their best to stay out of the way of the masses. "We're going to need a base of operations," Taws said. "I'll scout one out. You two stay here and watch for anything interesting."

"I should be the one to go," Sandri said.

"Not this time. If I have to stand meekly in the background any longer, I'm gonna lose it. Besides, as long as I'm wearing this, no one will give me a second glance." He tugged on the hood of his cloak.

Sandri sighed. "Off with you, then," she said.

"Do I get a kiss for luck?"

"When you get back."

"Smooth as ever, love."

Taws brushed her cheek with his thumb, gave her and Nils a smile, and took off.

"Somehow I worry more about him being alone than you," Nils said.

"Yeah. It's something like a fifty-fifty chance that he'll get caught and we'll have to bail him out."

"He's never scared, though," Nils said. "I wish I could say the same."

"What scares you?" Sandri asked, and Nils snorted.

"What doesn't? Feels like everything puts me on edge these days."

"You can talk to us about it, you know, if it helps."

Nils looked sideways at her, then looked back out at the street, thinking about that. There was still so much he hadn't told her and Taws, and yet they'd both been extraordinarily kind to him. Maybe...maybe he could try.

"I've been having these weird dreams for a while now."

Sandri's eyes still scanned the crowd. "About Gen Rill?" she asked.

"Well, those too, but no. This is something different."

"What's it like?"

"There's someone speaking to me," Nils said. "It's like they're right there beside me, but just out of my vision, and I can't turn to look at them. It feels so incredibly real, but yet the moment I wake up, I can't remember what the voice sounds like anymore. Not even if it was male or female. It's just...gone."

"Wow. That *is* weird."

"Thanks."

"You remember what they said?"

"Mostly. They keep asking me to...listen."

"And are you?"

Nils shook himself. Had Sandri just asked that question? For a moment, her voice hadn't been right. It had been like...

He turned to look at her, and Sandri looked back, blinking at him. "What's wrong?"

"I'm...not sure," Nils said. The weaver's stone thrummed in his sock so strongly he starting tapping his foot on the ground to try to silence it. He'd thought about bringing the stone up next, but perhaps that was a bad idea.

"Hey, what's this?" Sandri asked, drawing Nils' attention back to the scene in front of them. A crowd was growing in the nearest pavilion, forming up around a single person who stood on a small platform with their hands raised above their head. Between the distance and the shadow of the canopy, it was hard to tell what was going on, but it seemed like the person was holding something, and...chanting. Yes, the crowd was quieting now, and the person was chanting.

"Fives," Sandri whispered, and Nils felt a chill. "That's a spellweaver."

The chanting stopped, and the weaver held the object out in front of them, offering it to the crowd. There were excited murmurs from the people, and then a man stepped forward and held out his hand. The weaver gave him the object, and his feet left the ground.

Nils drew in a sharp breath at the same moment that there was a collective gasp from the crowd. The man hovered there, now half his height off the street, flailing his arms in a panic. He calmed a little the longer he was up there, then finally raised a hand up high, mastering his fear and exulting in his flight. The crowd cheered with him. A minute later, the weaver chanted again, and the man's feet sunk back down to the ground.

"I had no idea weavers could do that," Sandri whispered, sounding both awed and terrified.

"Neither did I," Nils said. That must have been an exceptionally strong weaver, or perhaps this was the first presentation of a newly mastered spell. Whatever it was, the gathered Galreyvans continued their celebrating, and Nils felt sick to his stomach.

A fallen god's twisted magic had been performed out in the open, at high noon, for everyone to see. And it was met with cheers.

Nils wished he'd dropped that weaver's stone a long time ago.

* * *

Taws came back for them a couple hours later. "Found us a place that should do the job," he said. "A manufacturing building not far from the castle, and since no one's allowed to work during the festival, we should have it all to ourselves."

Nils and Sandri followed him to a tall, old building in a section of the city that felt deserted compared to the roaring festival several blocks away. "Part of the building's still in use," Taws said, "but the upper section's all broken windows and empty as can be. Probably isn't needed anymore, so no one's bothered to fix it up." Taws started scaling the wall, and Nils watched him with growing unease.

"I can feel your anxiety from here," Taws called down to him. "Relax, brother. The bricks jut out plenty far enough to make good handholds."

Nils ground his teeth together. Well, better up there than going underground again. He followed, wishing he didn't have to do it in a long cloak, and Sandri came up behind him.

Up top, the city spanned out before them through the glassless windows, and Nils' eyes immediately fixed on Ri'sen's castle. It was a huge fortress of dark gray stone, topped with burgundy banners emblazoned with Ri'sen's family crest. Black flags flew amongst the banners and flowed beneath the windows.

Raeya was there. She was *right there.* Nils wanted to charge over and barge in this very moment, but still he had to wait.

"Not bad," Sandri said, sounding impressed as she looked around their corner of the building. "Might be the most spacious hideout we've ever had."

"I thought it would do nicely," Taws said. "And I believe you owe me a kiss."

Sandri smiled and stood on her tip-toes, kissing him on the lips. Nils looked away, but his brain betrayed him and allowed Raeya's face to flash through his thoughts. He tightened his jaw, trying to shut it out.

She doesn't even want me anymore. Probably. Maybe.

They'd been so close, lying beneath her bed. She'd looked at his mouth…

Fives.

Sandri heaved a sigh, drawing Nils' attention back to the room. "Guess it's my turn to leave now," she said, reluctantly letting go of Taws.

He frowned. "I'm not crazy about this plan, love. I had my reservations about sending you into Dreygard's manor without me, and this is infinitely worse."

"I know, but it's the best option we have."

They'd talked at length on the way here how to go about infiltrating Ri'sen's castle. Dreygard had told Nils how to get in, but they had no idea where Raeya was being held, or how to get to her. Sandri, looking like a passable Galreyvan, intended to go in as a servant. There would be plenty of important visitors to the castle during the festival, many of whom would bring their attendants with them, so she doubted anyone would even question her presence. And, as she'd said before, the servants' hall was the best place for gossip.

"Guess all that's left is to change my clothes," Sandri said. "Make sure I fit the part before heading in. I'll just be a minute."

"I doubt it," Taws called after her as she left for one of the connecting rooms. "I know how you are with clothes."

Sandri poked her head back around the wall to stick her tongue out at him, then disappeared again. Taws put his hands in his pockets when she was gone, looking deflated.

"She's great at this stuff, but I don't like it," he muttered. "It's weird out there."

"Yeah," Nils agreed, once again staring at the castle.

"You seem a bit dazed," Taws said to him. "Something on your mind?"

"I was wondering…do you think Sandri is your soulmate?"

"You are a man of deep thoughts, Nils."

"I know it's stupid," Nils said, "but just answer."

Taws chuckled. "Can't say I've given it much thought, to be honest. A few women have caught my eye in the past, but with Sandri, something just feels *right*. No one gets under my skin the way she does. That sounds like a bad thing, but it isn't, and I couldn't imagine life without her."

"So what if someone told you she wasn't your true love?"

"I'd say to Hearthnight with that, and keep loving her anyway. She's the one I want."

Nils nodded, and fell silent.

"You thinking Miss Dreygard might just be your true love after all?" Taws asked, and Nils regretted having brought up the subject. He wasn't ready to face that question, though it had plagued his mind for what felt like ages. Even back at the manor, he'd wrestled with it more and more.

"I don't know," he said, but he did. How much longer could he stare the truth in the face and deny it? "It doesn't have anything to do with my own feelings," he went on, "but looking at all the evidence, at the reality of Raeya's curse…"

Tawson nodded. "Curses don't lie."

Nils felt cold inside. He'd tried to give his true love to somebody else.

He immediately tried to shake away that feeling, that guilt. Taws wouldn't let himself be bound by some cosmic force, and Nils didn't have to either. He didn't love Raeya. Or at least he didn't *want* to.

Gods. There was a frightening difference between those two statements. He needed to think about something else, but all that kept coming to mind was what Sandri had said to him in Borlund: *That's exactly what love is, hon.*

If only annoying thoughts could be swatted away like flies.

Thankfully, Sandri chose that moment to return from the next room.

Taws whistled. "Sands, I hate to tell ya, but servants have no business looking that good." She laughed, and he pulled her close. "Sorry, Nils. I'm going to have to kiss her again. Probably several times."

"If you must," Nils said wryly. "I'll just be over here, staring out the window, pretending I'm somewhere else."

For a while the sound of them kissing behind him was obvious—and cringe-worthy—but after they had been quiet for a time, Nils dared to glance back. Taws was holding Sandri in his arms, his cheek resting on her head while she held him tight, both their faces hidden from view. Nils quickly turned back to the window, feeling as though he'd witnessed something far more intimate than a kiss.

"If anything happens to you," he heard Tawson whisper, "this whole thing won't be worth it, not even if we succeed in killing that spellweaving murderer."

"Same goes for you," Sandri said back to him, then louder, "both of you."

Nils looked over his shoulder to see Sandri smiling at him. "Be good while I'm gone, yeah?"

Nils smiled back. "It's Taws you'll have to worry about."

"Boy, ain't that the truth."

"Isn't."

"Tawsey, I'll be back before you can teach that one proper street-talk," Sandri said, giving him a last quick kiss before collecting her things and heading to the window. She gave a two-fingered salute. "I'll return when I've learned how to save Nils' sweetheart!"

She didn't give Nils time to protest before slipping out the window and disappearing from view. Taws waited several seconds, then walked over and lay down in the middle of the floor.

"Taws?"

"Wake me when the waiting's over," he said. "It's always the worst part."

37 A DREAM?

Nils.

You can hear me. I know this.

Do not forget my voice, and do not ignore it.

You are so close.

Listen.

38 THE CASTLE

It took Sandri two full days to return.

They knew it might take some time for her to collect all the necessary information, but even so Nils feared he was going to have to physically restrain Tawson to keep him from going after her. The man was taller and stronger than he was, so he was beyond relieved when Sandri's arrival spared him making the attempt.

"Sands, you about did me in," Taws said, taking her in his arms after she'd climbed in through the window.

"Aw, you were worried?" she asked. "That's not like you."

"He was worse than me," Nils told her, "and that's saying something."

Sandri laughed, and Taws scowled. "Enough about that," he said. "What did you find?"

"Well, for starters," Sandri said, "let me tell you how glad I am I wasn't acting as a maid this time. I thought cleaning Dreygard's big ol' manor was a pain, but this place was *huge*. I couldn't even begin to memorize the floor plan, but here, I'll draw out what I can."

Nils gave her paper and a pencil from their supplies, and Sandri sat down on the floor and got to work. "This was *not* easy to find out, but your Miss Lady is up here," Sandri said, starting her drawing with one of the upper floors.

"Did you see her?" Nils asked.

"No, but there are plenty of rumors. Pretty girl with red hair. They don't see too many of those around here, and she's causing quite a stir with the company she keeps, too. All the ladies were going on about her being close with the big man's nephew."

Nils' stomach soured. Jarik.

"*And* she's always got guards following her steps, so everyone thinks she's someone important. Likely Lord Isek's betrothed."

Not if Nils had anything to say about it. "So how can we get to her?"

"Guards outside her door all the time," Sandri went on, "*except* when she's not in there, so that'll be your opening. Get in the room when she's out, and hide. Then, when she's back in, Taws and I will create a great big distraction—you know, like killing the emperor—so you can lead her out of there."

"That sounds extremely risky."

"Yep."

Nils sighed. "So how are you going to go about assassinating Ri'sen? If it was easy, someone would've done it already."

"You can let us worry about that," Taws said. "That's why you brought us, right?"

Nils shook his head. "I want to know. What if something goes wrong?"

Taws shrugged. "All right. How much do you know about Ri'sen's heir?"

"Only that he has one. A son."

"He's a sickly young man," Taws said, "with some kind of disorder that makes him susceptible to illness and injury. As a precaution, Ri'sen weaves a healing spell on him every night to ward off anything infectious he may have encountered during the day."

"Every night?" Nils asked. If the emperor was using chrysolin on a daily basis, it was no wonder he was so eager to find more.

Taws nodded. "Part of Sandri's reconnaissance was finding out where the son's room is, and when Ri'sen performs the healing. We'll take out his guards, and make our move then."

"What about the heir?" Nils asked. "Will you kill him too?"

"Not sure yet," Taws admitted. "I'd love to be rid of the whole lot of them, but we're thinking we'll leave him alive. From what we've heard, he isn't much like his father. People say he isn't ambitious enough to continue the nation's conquest once he's in charge, but whoever's in line after him could be a different story."

"But won't he die before long without his father's healing?"

"Maybe, but my guess is Ri'sen has another healer in his service. Weavers can't cast spells on themselves, and he'll want someone around to patch him up if he needs it."

Nils ached with tension just thinking about what they had to do, but waiting around any longer almost sounded worse. "So when do we leave?"

"Soon as we're ready," Sandri said. "I need to grab some new clothes in the market, but otherwise I think we're good to go."

"More clothes?" Taws asked, smirking.

Sandri grinned. *"Fancy* clothes. I noticed some Thrinian servants in there, so I figure I can go in as a noble this time, and you and Nils can be my attendants."

"Always here to serve, my lady," Taws said, bowing and kissing her hand. Sandri adjusted her posture and made like she was examining Tawson for flaws. "Hm, yes. I suppose you'll do."

"So, just clothes?" Nils said, tapping his foot. Sandri looked to him.

"Yep. And it looks like I'd better get to it."

* * *

Dreygard's knowledge of a small, unguarded point of access into the castle got Nils and the others inside with surprising ease. Ri'sen never would've divulged such a weakness to Lord Dreygard; the man must've found it with his own spies, or bought the information off of someone. He'd been planning for an opportunity like this for some time, it seemed.

Now that they were in, the hard part began.

The main floor was crowded with guests, all wearing black cloaks, but wearing them open—to reveal their rich clothing, no doubt—and with hoods down. Nils felt dreadfully exposed, but reminded himself that no one here would recognize him anyway.

Except for two people, of course, who mattered very much. *Gods, we'd better not run into Jarik while we're here.*

That thought on his mind, Nils lowered his head and tried to hide in the crowd, following Sandri—who strutted like a born noble—and Tawson, who was blessedly tall enough to hide behind. At the same time he kept his eyes scanning in the hopes of catching a glimpse of orange hair. The crowd thinned as Sandri led them up a couple floors, then a couple more.

"Guests aren't supposed to be up here," Sandri whispered as they neared Raeya's holding room, "but I've found that if you look like you know what you're doing, people tend not to question it."

They passed a couple servants, and Sandri arrogantly ignored them while Taws nodded to them politely. Nils followed his lead and nodded too, and gritted his teeth until they were safely beyond them. No alarms were sounded. It seemed Sandri was right.

"Wait here," Sandri whispered, walking ahead of them to peer around the next corner. She motioned them forward. "Perfect. No guards outside her door. She must be out in the castle somewhere."

"Sands and I will watch the hall," Tawson said to Nils. "You get to work on the lock."

Nils nodded, pulling out his tools and crouching in front of the door. "Done," he said a moment later when the latch clicked open.

"Desna's Tresses, that was fast," Taws said. "I taught you how to do that, and you're better than I am."

"I grew up in a schoolhouse," Nils said. "I'm good at learning."

"Yeah, but I don't think they teach anything like that in school."

"Time to go, Tawsey," Sandri said. "I can't imagine they'll keep a prisoner out much later than this."

"Right." Taws put a hand on Nils' shoulder. "You sure I can't convince you to take a weapon?"

"I'm sure," Nils said.

"Remember, if you get stuck, put your signal in the window, and we'll do what we can. Otherwise...good luck."

Nils nodded while his insides twisted into a nervous knot and the weaver's stone thrummed so strongly he could almost hear it. "You too."

"Try not to make your sweetheart scream when you reveal yourself," Sandri said with a wink. She gave him a peck on the cheek, then Nils entered the near-dark bedroom and listened to the door lock behind him.

From here, he was alone.

* * *

Nils only had to wait about half an hour.

Once his eyes had adjusted, he thanked Desna for the room's small window and wasted no time finding a place to hide. The wardrobe seemed the best choice, even if closing himself in that dark little space was about as pleasant as eating a slug. He kept his eyes fixed on the slit between the double-doors, staring out at the room. It was a small but comfortable chamber, far nicer than Nils' accommodations at the manor, which was a relief. At least the emperor hadn't been treating Raeya like an animal during her captivity.

And then he waited. A half hour that felt both long and short as his brain raced through everything that could go wrong, and how insane he was for being here at this very moment.

Then voices. The lock clicking open. Light from the hall.

And Raeya.

He recognized her silhouette instantly, and lost his breath. She was here.

There were two more figures behind her—guards—and one of them said something Nils couldn't hear, then handed her a candle before shutting her inside.

Nils' heart thrummed harder than the chrysolin in his sock as he watched her, lit by the warm glow of the candle. She put it on the nightstand, then removed the black cloak from around her shoulders and threw it on the bed.

She was distressed. She made no sound, but Nils could see it in the way she moved, in the set of her shoulders as she came around and sat on the end of the bed, her face cast in shadow.

Right. Now was the time. How exactly did one announce his presence in a situation like this *without* making the other person scream?

Nils cleared his throat.

Raeya's head immediately turned toward the wardrobe, her posture alert and ready to dash.

"Don't scream," Nils whispered, suddenly reminded of their first meeting. "It's me."

If he'd had his senses about him, Nils would've given his name, but even so Raeya's shoulders relaxed just slightly. She stood up from the bed, and Nils cracked the door open, stepping out into the room.

He could see her properly now. Could see the fear in her eyes turn to surprise, then relief.

"Nils," she breathed, and that was all he let her say. Before he even knew what he was doing, he'd closed the distance between them, pulled her against him, and kissed her.

Raeya tensed, then relaxed, leaning into him. Every pinprick of emotion he'd shoved down for the last two months now fought to express itself all at the same moment, and Nils was overwhelmed. He couldn't kiss her deeply enough, couldn't hold her close enough. He broke the kiss just long enough for her to take a breath and speak his name, then he kissed her again. He never would've stopped, but this time she pushed him away, and when she said his name again, it was with a tone of alarm.

"Nils, someone's coming!"

Fives. How had he not heard the voices outside the door?

He looked Raeya in the eyes for one more second, then squeezed her hand and ran back into the wardrobe, shutting the door and layering himself behind the clothing inside for good measure. He left only a tiny crack to allow him to see through a gap in the panels.

The door to Raeya's room opened. Two guards walked in, one of them carrying...something. It was so hard to see. Nils adjusted himself slightly as the guard reached Raeya.

It was a mask. He bound Raeya's hands and then tied the mask over the lower part of Raeya's face so that it covered her mouth. Why would they—

Oh. So that she couldn't kiss anyone.

She didn't struggle while they did their work, and as soon as they were done, two more figures entered the room, one of them bringing a candelabrum for more light, which he set on the dresser. Nils felt a thrumming of a different kind looking at this man, a hatred—no, a sense of betrayal—that hurt like nails piercing his skin, while an undercurrent of anger swept through his veins.

Jarik.

The other man stepped toward Raeya, and all that hot anger turned at once to ice, shocking Nils so that he nearly gasped.

Dark hair in a short ponytail, a goatee, a robe far more elaborate than anyone else's, and a crown.

Emperor Ri'sen.

Fives. If he was here, then what was happening with Taws and Sandri? They'd expected to find him at his son's room about now.

"Raeya, dear child," he said, his accent strong and crisp, "you've disappointed me again."

He sounded young. He *looked* young. Nils knew this man to be well into his fifties, and yet he looked twenty years younger. *He's a weaver,* Nils remembered. They were said to have excellent health, and they didn't show their age the same way others did. Nils had thought that part a legend, or at least an exaggeration, but Ri'sen proved otherwise.

"I told you I won't do it," Raeya said back to him, voice slightly muffled through the mask, "no matter how many times you try and force me."

"That man deserved to die," Ri'sen went on. "He'd committed atrocities you couldn't imagine."

"I don't care. That still doesn't give me the authority or desire to take his life from him."

"Raeya, *I* have given you the authority—"

"It's not yours to give!"

Ri'sen stiffened, then sneered. "I don't know who endowed you with this lofty set of morals, but it surely wasn't your father. A ruler has full rights to carry out judgment on those deserving of it, and I only endeavor to use the best tools available."

"Then let Isek be your *tool*," Raeya spat, and Isek grimaced. "He's plenty willing and well-practiced."

"He's imperfect," Ri'sen said. "Proficient, highly valuable, yes, but his methods still leave a trace. Yours do not, nor do they cause any pain. Can't you see? The death you give is merciful. The pleasure of a kiss, and then darkness. That is greater kindness than foul men deserve, and yet you despise me for desiring to give it to them."

Raeya shook her head. "I will not be your executioner, and this is not fair judgment. You may be throwing the worst criminals you can find at me right now, but you won't stop there, and we both know it. You seek the end of any who oppose you, and everyone is guilty of one crime or another if you dig deep enough. Your judgment is as twisted as your methods."

The emperor looked ready to lash out, but Isek interjected. "Uncle," he said with a jarring Galreyvan accent he hadn't had before, "Lady Raeya may still need more time to acclimate to her new home and the task you have given her. Please, if I may—"

"Silence," Ri'sen snapped, then addressed Raeya again. "I won't allow Isek to cover for you any longer, or to finish off your targets. If you don't succeed on your next trial, you'll find the consequences to be most unpleasant. In fact, I'm ready to give you a taste now. A disobedient servant is undeserving of such a fine room, wouldn't you agree?"

Raeya said nothing, but Isek shifted on his feet. "Uncle, I don't think this is necessary—"

"Oh, but I do. Some time in our dungeon may help her *acclimate* a little faster."

"Perhaps we could—"

"Away, Isek. Now."

Isek hesitated, then bowed. "Yes, *Ni Sol'emi.*" He looked at Raeya, but Nils couldn't quite make out his expression before he opened the door and left.

Ri'sen came closer to Raeya, too close, and Nils felt his muscles tighten, longing to throw himself out there and stop him. "We'll try again, my dear," he said, "but you'll find that even patient men have limits. Your chances will run out, and I know what kind of woman you are. Threatening you won't do much, but remember that I hold sway over those you love most." At this Raeya showed a hint of fear, but Nils could feel her fighting to contain it. "And, of course," Ri'sen went on, running his fingers through Raeya's hair, making Nils' anger seethe, "a little pain for you won't hurt, either.

"Take her," he commanded the guards. Nils gripped the clothing surrounding him while the guards took Raeya by the arms, hauling her from the room. Ri'sen stepped out behind them, and Nils was frozen, tormented by his inability to do *anything* of use. A servant scurried in, blew out the candles, and then the door was shut.

Darkness again, and the scent of smoke. Like a lantern extinguished.

Nils tore out of the wardrobe. He would not lose Raeya again.

* * *

Nils wasn't even close to careful as he pursued Raeya's guards.

He still wore his cloak, and while he wasn't certain if he looked like he knew what he was doing or not, he at least looked determined as he ran through the halls. Those two things seemed enough for the few people he passed to leave him alone. Nils wracked his brain, trying to remember if Sandri had mentioned the dungeon entrance after her reconnaissance, but that wasn't a place they thought they'd need to go. He didn't know how to get there, and he didn't know which way Raeya's guards had taken her.

So he used common sense, and went down. Down every staircase he found, sticking to the least populated routes, figuring the guards wouldn't be hauling a bound and masked noblewoman through a lively party. He lost track of how many floors he'd descended when suddenly he heard echoes of boot steps around the next corner. He stopped, pressing himself against the wall, and only dared to peek around when he could tell the footsteps had passed.

A glimpse of sunset orange between two tall men in black cloaks, disappearing down another hall. That was them.

Nils progressed more slowly now, and noticed with unease that the air was colder here, and the walls were made of rough, unfinished stone. At some point, he'd descended underground. There were torch lamps at the top of the walls, but these became less and less frequent as he sneaked through the passages.

Noises again. Shuffling and muffled cries of distress. He peeked around the next corner just in time to see the upheld arm of a guard—bearing a torch—disappearing down a hole in the floor.

A hole. In the floor. And they were already underground.

Nils stayed there, frozen in the same position for an unmeasured amount of time, until he heard the guards returning. He quickly found a nook to crouch in and watched them go by, no longer accompanied by Raeya. They took their torches with them.

Nils looked back toward the hatch they'd vacated, then crawled over to it, grasping the lid's catch with shaking hands. It was heavy, and he threw all his meager strength into opening it, cringing at every creak and thud it made in the process.

He waited, and no guards returned. He peered down into the hole. He could make out the top of a ladder, but beyond that…

Nils recoiled, clamping a hand over his mouth, trying to muffle the series of gasping breaths that came out of him. Memories of Gen Rill flooded his mind, seeping into every corner. The heavy air, flickering lights. Explosions. Rumblings above, ceilings of crushing rock ready to fall at any moment. The pale hand jutting out from a mound of rubble that he tripped over his first day. Cracks of whips, cries of children and adults, dust-covered faces and red eyes.

But most of all the darkness. Fire was a danger amongst the fumes, but the only way to see. Clinging to your life and your death, watching the light falter and give out.

He could not do this.

But Raeya was down there.

Nils waited until his breathing quieted a little, then looked again into the pit, forcing his eyes to stay on the top of the ladder.

Just like the tunnel beneath the church, he told himself. He looked up at the nearest torch lamp on the wall, but it was too high for him to reach. He swallowed with a dry throat, and got onto the ladder.

Count the rungs, he told himself. *Don't look anywhere else. Just count.*

One, two, three, four, five…

He kept counting, but soon he couldn't see them anymore. He closed his eyes. Counting. Stepping. Counting.

His feet hit the ground. He looked up at the dim circle of light above him, then turned around.

It was not like the church. If the darkness there was a wall, this was a sea, and Nils had already drowned. Worse yet, he was alone. No one was here to give him a push this time.

But Raeya was down here. Somewhere in this darkness.

Trembling, Nils took a step, and another, arms held out in front of him, sinking deeper into the black sea. He could hear it, the sobbing in the distance, the clanging of hammers—no, the hammers were his imagination. And the sobs were his own.

Not Gen Rill. It's not Gen Rill. It's not—

Nils' knees gave out, and he collapsed there on the hard earth. He tried to look behind, but the sea had swallowed him up. No light in either direction. Just nothing. He would die here. He'd be crushed.

Then a shock.

The weaver's stone had provided a constant thrum against his skin, but this was a sudden jolt that took his mind off the darkness for half a second.

Not alone.

You are not alone.

Why are you here?

Nils' eyes widened in the dark. He was losing his mind, and yet somehow he got to his feet.

Why are you here, Nils? Tell me why you came.

Not Tawson's voice, but his words. And Nils knew the answer.

Raeya.

He took a step. And another.

Raeya.

Nils couldn't see a thing, but he forced his mind to repeat that answer over and over again, taking a step forward each time.

And then he started running.

39 REUNIONS

Nils had been wise to keep his arms outstretched, or he would've run into a wall.

After a while the tunnel took a sharp turn, and then another, and he felt his way forward with his hands, moving as quickly as he could, letting only one thought fill his mind. Another corner, and then...

He might've been imagining it, but the darkness seemed to be thinning. Yes, there was light ahead, a fluctuating orange glow that manifested itself into a torch in a stand when Nils turned yet another corner, and found himself in a passage lined with cells. He was still blinking against the change in light when someone cried out in a muffled voice.

Raeya. Nils ran to her cell where she stood at the bars, unable to grasp them. The guards had left her hands bound behind her back and the mask still covering her mouth.

Those monsters.

"Hang on," Nils said, fumbling with his lock picking tools. "I'll get you out. Just hang on."

Nothing went wrong, but it felt like an eternity before the padlock finally fell open. Nils yanked it off the door and rushed in to Raeya, working to untie her hands. He wished he *had* accepted that knife from Taws, if only to get those fiving bonds off of her wrists faster.

As soon as her hands were free, Raeya tore the mask off her face, and then she was in Nils' arms. He held her tight, and the shaking in his limbs finally found reason to subside.

"Nils," she said, "I can't believe you're here."

"I'm here," he said. "I'm here." Repeating those two words was all he could manage as his breathing began to even out. Raeya drew back to look at him, searching his face with her eyes. Gods, he wanted to kiss her again, but he resisted. He needed to get her out of here.

"Come on," he said, taking her hand. "We should hurry." He grabbed the solitary torch from its stand and started walking back the way he'd come, but there was a tug on his arm.

Raeya had stopped. "Nils, there's somebody else down here," she said. Nils turned, looking back toward one of the other cells. She must've been hidden in shadow before, but now...

There was a woman sitting hunched over on the floor behind the bars, staring at them.

Nils felt like a fish had swum into his stomach. "Leave her," he said, but Raeya let go of his hand. "Raeya—"

"I know her."

"You...what?"

Raeya approached the other cell with caution. "You..." she said to the woman. "Gods...you look exactly the same."

The woman looked up at her with sharp eyes. She was dirty and her long, dark hair was unkempt, but otherwise she seemed healthy. Alert. She smirked. "You think you know me, girly?"

Nils came and stood beside Raeya, fidgeting. He didn't want to get any closer to this person. He wanted to leave.

"I have no doubt," Raeya replied.

The woman looked her up and down. "You're not the sort of company I'd keep, and I haven't left this cell in a long time."

"Raeya, we should go," Nils said, trying again, but she gave him a pointed glance and turned back to the prisoner.

"You don't remember," she said to the woman, "but I'm the girl you cursed, nine years ago."

Nils started, looking back at the woman. A spellweaver. *The* spellweaver who…Unholy fives.

The prisoner cocked her head, studying Raeya again. Then she grinned. "The little grave defiler, all grown up."

"I didn't know it was a grave," Raeya snapped, getting closer to the bars than Nils liked. "I was only a child. And you—"

The woman stood, looking down on them with a dangerous gleam in her eyes. "I gave you what you deserved. Has it treated you well?"

"How dare you ask me that," Raeya said. "Three men died because of your impetuousness, your absolute lack of compassion."

"Only three?" the woman said. "Aren't you a chaste little thing. But tell me—did you love any of them?"

Raeya didn't answer, but her features twitched, tightening against her grief, and the woman could see for herself. "Good," she said.

Raeya forced down her emotions, and stood taller. "You sought my misery for an innocent mistake. But I'll have you know, in spite of your designs, I *did* find my true love."

"This boy?" the woman asked, looking at Nils, and she cackled. "He is not your true love."

"Of course he is. He survived my kiss."

The woman laughed again, a cutting, biting laugh, and Nils' uneasiness turned to nausea at the sound of it. They never should've spoken to her.

"My spell had nothing to do with your *destined lover*, girly," the weaver said. "In fact, there is no such thing. Spellweaving is a precise art, and only tangible bonds can be created. Nothing so vague and fantastical as *true love.*"

Raeya stared. "But, you told me…"

"I told you that you'd kill any man you kissed besides your true love because I *wanted* you to search for him. Wanted you to wait until you'd fallen so entirely for someone that you were confident enough to kiss him. And then you'd lose him, and know the same pain I did, and your punishment for disturbing the grave of my beloved would be complete."

Raeya's face became a wide-eyed mask, frozen in disbelief. "No such thing…" she whispered. "You wove your spell in Galreyvan, and then…you lied."

The woman's cruel smile only lasted long enough for Raeya to grab her clothing and yank her toward the bars. "You lied!" she screamed in her face. "I told Keden my true love would survive, and he never even had a chance! I *killed* him because of your lie!"

No amusement remained in the spellweaver's face, and Nils was keenly aware of her long fingernails as she reached up toward Raeya's hands, still grasping her shirt. "Enough," Nils said, grabbing Raeya and pulling her a safe distance from the bars.

"But Nils—"

"I know," he said. "I heard."

Raeya wasn't his true love. There was no such thing. He'd told himself that so many times at the start, so why, *why* had he let himself believe? And now, after what he'd done upstairs…

Desna's Tresses, I'm an idiot.

Nils had to restrain *himself* from reaching for the woman behind the bars. "If you didn't bind Raeya to her true love," he asked, "then to whom did you bind her?"

The woman smiled again. "That's almost my favorite part," she said, flicking her eyes to Raeya. "In the unlikely event you actually *found* the man on the other side of your curse, I wanted you to pledge yourself to someone you'd loath, and you Branadites are all the same. I tied you to the one closest to your age who was also a spellweaver."

The thrumming in Nils' sock heightened again. "I'm not a spellweaver," he said.

"Oh, I guarantee you are."

Nils stuck the torch back into its stand, yanked up his sleeves, then held out his bare arms. Raeya's bracelet gleamed on his wrist, but aside from that, his skin remained ordinary.

"That means nothing," the woman said, "except that you haven't used your power yet. The curse has shown what you are."

Tawson's words blared through his mind. *Curses don't lie.*

Fives, fives, unholy fives.

Nils swallowed, though his mouth was still dry. "You lied once about your spell," he said. "You're simply lying again."

The woman's dark eyes were nothing short of hypnotic as she stared at him. "You don't even believe your own words, boy."

"Nils," Raeya said, "I've heard enough. We should go now."

"Not yet," Nils replied. "You—what's your name?" he demanded of the weaver.

"Kara'ni."

"Kara'ni, before we go, you will remove your curse from Raeya."

The woman's eyebrows rose, and she cackled again. "Will I, now?"

Nils was aware of Raeya staring at him, but he kept his eyes fixed on the spellweaver. "You said her punishment was complete. She's suffered enough."

"I don't think so."

"I'll consider unlocking your cell, if you do it," Nils added, even though he doubted the wisdom of that offer.

Raeya stepped forward, mastering her temper. "Please," she said, only a slight edge of anger remaining in her voice. "I'm sorry I disturbed the grave of someone you cared about. I never meant any harm."

Kara'ni regarded them. "I won't."

"Why not?" Raeya plead. "What more would you demand of me?"

Kara'ni didn't budge.

"Why are you here?" Nils asked. "If you're a powerful Galreyvan spellweaver, I'd think you'd be at the emperor's right hand, not in his dungeon."

"Because I'd rather be in his dungeon than anywhere near that *bekanthin,* that's why. I'd die before I'd serve him."

"Then unravel Raeya's curse, and strike a sharp blow against him. He's intent on using her for his own purposes."

Kara'ni smiled. "Now *this* one knows how to entice me."

"So you'll do it?"

The woman thought it over. "That's not enough."

Nils could've strangled the air between them with his fingers. "Then what is?"

"I want to kill him."

"You want to kill the emperor?"

"Yes."

"Well what a grand coincidence!" Nils said, throwing up his arms. "That's one of the reasons I'm here. But if you want to do it, you'd better hurry, because I have a friend upstairs who's eager to do it first."

"Then get me out of here, and deliver me safely to the emperor in a place where he will be without defenders."

"How am I supposed to do that?"

"That is your problem."

Nils breathed out heavily, and reached for his tools.

"Nils, are you sure about this?" Raeya asked him. "We can't trust her."

"I know."

"If all you hope to accomplish is releasing me from my curse, well...I've lived with it this long."

"And this is your only chance to live without it. I'm setting her free."

Nils kept his eyes on the lock while he worked, not daring to look at Raeya. If he wasn't her soulmate, then being bound to him was only cruel. She'd never liked him from the start. All her feelings were grounded on the belief that he was meant for her, a life companion chosen by the gods. And he wasn't. He was just a lowborn townsman, and maybe something worse.

Never mind that he'd come to love her. She wouldn't want him now.

The lock fell open, and Nils let the door swing loose. "Let's go."

★ ★ ★

Nils had long since lost track of the time, but it must've been late, or maybe early.

The back hallways of the castle were even quieter now than before, which was fortunate. Nils had Raeya and Kara'ni hang behind while he went in search of cloaks for them. He found a couple hanging outside of a washroom and brought them back. Maybe no one else had the hoods up indoors, but Raeya and the spellweaver needed to be covered. Raeya's hair would give them away in an instant.

"Nils...are you really here to kill the emperor?" Raeya whispered as they tiptoed up a staircase.

"Not me personally," Nils said, "but I brought someone to do it, at your father's request."

"My father?" Raeya asked. "But why would he...Nils, you were entirely right about him. Maybe not about him being a spellweaver, but he's been allied with the emperor for years, trading with him in secret."

"I wasn't entirely right." Nils confessed.

"What do you mean?"

"I mean that yes, your father's a traitor and a generally terrible person, but I thought it would end there. Turns out his one redeeming quality is that he's a good dad. He's been doing all of this for you."

"For me? Are you telling me he's betrayed our king and country on my account?" Raeya looked aghast.

"Yes," Nils said, "but that's why he wants to be rid of the emperor. Once he's gone, it can all stop, and your family can be free."

"Then he wasn't arrested by the king's investigator?"

"As far as I know," Nils said.

"So you didn't..."

"I didn't incriminate him, no."

Raeya was quiet as they reached the top of the stairs and started down the next hallway. Nils would have to fill her in on the details when they had more time.

The hall branched apart at the end. "Wait here," Nils said. "I want to look ahead." He wouldn't go far, lest the women try to gouge each other's eyes out while he was gone, but he was completely lost at the moment and wasn't even sure where to go if he wasn't. Finding Taws and Sandri and avoiding everyone else seemed like the best course of action, but he may as well have been looking for a thimble in a cornfield while dodging crows.

Nils went to the right, and before long the wall split on one side, offering a view down to the floor below and across to an identical hallway on the other side. Nils peered over the edge, seeing the tops of a few heads going by underneath. There was a distant sound of music and conversation. Whatever the hour was, some were still up enjoying the festival. Nils didn't want to get any closer to the party, and he doubted Taws and Sandri would be in this direction. The heir's room would be someplace more private in the castle, wouldn't it?

Nils looked back up just in time to see someone walk into the hallway across the gap, a dark-haired man wearing black and a short cloak. He looked back at Nils, and both of them froze.

Startling, painful recognition blasted through Nils' senses. For a moment, his mind couldn't comprehend if he was looking at a friend or an enemy, just someone blatantly familiar despite his entirely unfamiliar surroundings. And then it fell into place.

Jarik stared back at him as though he was working through the same process. "Nils," he said, then his expression darkened. "What in Lyare's season are you doing here?"

Anger fizzed inside Nils, but he held his composure. "Nothing," he said. "After all, I can do you no harm."

Jarik grabbed the banister in front of him, and Nils spun on his heel and ran back the way he'd come. Jarik wouldn't try to jump that gap, would he? Nils wouldn't wait around to find out.

"What's wrong?" Raeya asked when Nils came charging into view. He grabbed her wrist and pulled her along by way of answer, hoping Kara'ni wouldn't delay in following. They dashed in a billowing train of black cloaks, picking hallways at random until they turned a corner and Nils ran directly into somebody and they fell over in a heap.

"Unholy fives," the somebody said. "What in Hearthnight— Nils!"

Nils sat up, ready to run again, but panic turned to relief when he saw who it was. "Taws!"

"I'm here, too," Sandri said, poking her head up behind Tawson's shoulder and waving. "Oh, Nils, you got her! Way to go!"

"Yeah, congratulate me later," Nils said. "We've got to move. I just ran into Jarik, er, Isek back there"—he really needed to get that straight—"and for all I know he's right behind us."

"Thoughts on a place to hide?" Taws asked Sandri over his shoulder.

"Mm, maybe? Either way, let's go."

* * *

Nils resumed his grip on Raeya's hand as they took off again, unwilling to risk another separation. Sandri led them up to the next floor and into a large chamber with a high ceiling and a raised platform at the front.

"What is this place?" Nils whispered once they were inside, doors shutting behind them with a quiet yet deep *thud*.

"Private theatre," Sandri replied. "Heard somebody talking about it the last time I was here. There's a loft up above the stage that could be a good place, so long as no one's planning a play."

Sandri plucked a few unlit candles from along the aisle as they walked, and Tawson carried a lamp he'd grabbed from outside. The light only carried so far into the chamber, so most of it was lost in deep shadow, the echoes of their quiet movements whispering back at them through the empty air. Nils looked behind to make sure Kara'ni was still with them. She was, and she took in the room through narrowed eyes. Raeya gazed up at the ceiling with open fascination until she noticed Nils' eyes on her, and then she looked at him. Nils looked away.

Sandri led them behind the stage and up a steep, wooden staircase to a rectangular room that held a few large chests and racks of clothing. She lit the candles she'd brought and set them about, making the space a little less eerie.

"So, who's your new friend?" Taws asked, nodding toward Kara'ni.

"It's a long story," Nils replied, not ready to tackle that explanation yet. "What's happened with you? Did you find the emperor?"

Tawson frowned. "No. He must've changed his schedule, or maybe the last two nights weren't an accurate picture of his habits. At any rate, he never showed, and the heir's wing was getting awfully crowded with patrols. We had to bail."

"Well, I saw him."

"You did?"

"He was in Raeya's room." Nils looked back at Raeya, who watched him and Taws with curiosity.

"Fives. That figures," Taws said.

Sandri brushed past them, holding out a hand to Raeya. "Hello, my lady," she said. "I'm Sandri. I saw you loads of times at the manor, but never had the chance to introduce myself."

"You were at the manor?" Raeya asked, hesitantly accepting her handshake.

"Oh yeah. I was impersonating a maid, sneaking secret messages into your sweetie's room."

Raeya blinked. "You were…what?"

Nils cleared his throat. "This is Tawson," he said, gesturing. The Thrinian bowed.

"A pleasure to meet you, m'lady," he said. "And Taws will do just fine."

"Tawson…" Raeya said, scrutinizing him. "You wouldn't happen to be Tawson Rafford, would you?"

Taws gaped, and Sandri looked between them. "Is *that* your last name?" she demanded. "Gods, and I learn it from another woman?"

"Whoa, hold on there, missy. Er, Lady," Taws said to Raeya. "We haven't met before, have we?"

"No, but I learned about all the foreign nobility as a child, and I heard rumors that you and your parents entered our country upon Thrinia's absorption."

"Nobility?" Sandri said. "What does she mean, *nobility?*"

"Rafford," Nils repeated, feeling an energy grow inside his chest as his brain worked. "I…recognize that name."

"All right," Taws said, holding up his hands. "All right, let's stop right there."

"Taws," Nils said, shaking his head in disbelief, "you're a—"

"*Fives,* man, at least let *me* say it. All right, yes. Here goes." He shook himself, then straightened. "If you all must know who I really am, I'm Tawson Rafford, son of Brith and Carmin Rafford." Taws took a deep breath, then spit out his final words in a hurried jumble. "Prince of Thrinia."

"*What?*"

Sandri looked absolutely beside herself, and Taws cringed at her outburst. "Listen, Sands, it's not—"

"All this time," Sandri said, shaking her head from side to side, "you had me believing we were a perfect match. A team. But *you* listen, Taws; I work in a pub in one of the poorest towns in all of Chanterey, and now you tell me you're a *prince?*"

"This is exactly why I never told you," Taws said. "You'd think this somehow means we're not a match for each other. Sands, I was only *Prince Tawson* until I was nine years old. You can't be prince of a country that no longer exists."

"That doesn't change who you were. Who you *are.*"

"Um, guys? Can we keep it down?" Nils interjected.

"That's not me anymore. Don't you get what I'm saying?" Taws continued as though Nils hadn't spoken. "I'm a nobody now, and have been for more than half my life."

"So that's what we poor folks are, huh?" Sandri shouted. "Nobodies?"

"You know that's not what I mean!"

"Guys, is this really the time—"

"Just give us a minute, Nils!" Tawson roared at him.

Nils looked between the two of them, at a complete loss.

"This is my fault, isn't it?" Raeya squeaked by his shoulder.

"Boy," Kara'ni said from behind them. She'd hung back by the door, and stood with her arms crossed. "What are your plans for getting me to the emperor?"

"I don't know," Nils said. "I need to brainstorm with Taws, but it would seem he's busy at the moment." He flung a hand back toward the still-arguing couple, and Kara'ni snorted.

"You could pitch in some ideas too, you know," Nils went on, walking over to her. Raeya followed. "Do you have any insight on

Ri'sen that might be useful? None of us have faced down a weaver."

"You won't have to worry about his weaving."

"Why not?"

Kara'ni sighed. "Because most weavers have something particular they're good at, and all he's good at is repairing people. Why do you think he's trying so hard to enlist cursers and killers in his service?"

"I didn't know he was, besides Raeya."

"Well, he is," Kara'ni went on. "I used to be one of his favorites."

"You worked for him?"

"Until he sentenced Anseph to death."

"Who is Anseph?" Raeya asked.

Kara'ni shot her a dangerous glare. "Speak his name again, and I'll hurt you."

"Fine. But who is he?"

"You ought to know," the spellweaver said. "You pranced all over his grave."

Raeya's hands formed into fists at her sides. "I did not *prance—*"

Nils put a hand in front of Raeya, but she glowered at him and ignored it. "So he was the one you loved," Raeya went on in clipped tones. "What did he do to deserve a death sentence, I wonder? Curse a child? Kill an innocent man?"

Kara'ni uncrossed her arms, and Nils wanted to die. Raeya just *had* to poke at the viper's nest.

"Anseph was a priest," Kara'ni said, her temper barely contained beneath her words, "and a weaver, but not a killer. He claimed to hear the voice of a god, then started preaching Pria's innocence. A Branadite might not understand, but when a Galreyvan priest starts wearing a diamond and praying publicly to Pria, people don't like that."

The voice of a god…

The tingling of the weaver's stone pulsed harder, and Nils shook off a chill. "Which god?" he found himself asking.

"Lyare."

Another pulse. He couldn't shake the chill this time.

"He was probably mad," Kara'ni said, "but I didn't care. I'd have loved that man no matter what he believed. After Ri'sen's sentence, I broke him out of prison and we fled the country. Branaden was the only option available to us, so we intended to live quietly there near the border, but Anseph's madness got the better of him. He started reaching out to the people in the closest town, trying to convince them that Lyare wasn't evil. It wasn't long before a patrolman checked his wrists, and attacked him on the spot.

"Don't pretend to look shocked," Kara'ni said to them. "Either of you would've done the same. You all think people like us deserve death merely for having a power that you don't. Or," she added with a wicked grin, "one that you *do*, but don't have the courage to use."

Nils tried to shut his ears to the words, tried to keep them out as they squirmed into any space they could find, burrowing deeper.

"Well, Galreyvans have no fear of the dark," Kara'ni continued, "and I cursed that vile blood-spiller so thoroughly he died of his wounds even before Anseph did."

Blessedly, Raeya seemed to have run out of retorts at this point, and she was as speechless as Nils. In fact, the whole room had gone silent until there was a quiet whistle behind them.

"You've been making interesting friends lately, brother," Taws said. He and Sandri must've been distracted from their argument when Raeya and Kara'ni started one of their own.

"Taws," Nils said. "We need to talk."

* * *

"All right, so the emperor's nephew knows you're here, and he's probably already discovered a couple of empty cells in the dungeon," Taws said. "That does turn up the pressure a bit."

"So what do we do?" Nils asked. "They'll have every guard in the castle looking for us."

"It might not be that bad," Sandri said. "Ri'sen won't want to make a scene, not with all his fancy guests here."

"He's sure to bar all the exits, though. Even *our* exit may be hard to reach."

"Well, we don't want to leave yet, do we?" Taws said. "So we can worry about that later. And you know, this could be a good thing."

"How?" Nils asked.

"Ri'sen's invested in our Miss Lady, yes? He'll probably be out searching himself. If we find him before he finds us, we can create an ambush." Taws produced a knife from his sleeve so fast Nils flinched. "Then I do what I came here to do."

"Actually, we need to talk about that," Nils said. "Kara'ni has agreed to remove Raeya's curse, but only if she can kill the emperor."

"What?" Taws said, gripping his knife in his four good fingers. "Tell me I heard that wrong."

"It's no big deal, is it?" Nils asked. "Your goal is the same. Does it really matter who delivers the final blow?"

"Of course it does," Taws said. "This man took over my homeland. You should understand now more than ever how much that devastated me. Countless Thrinians fell, and every year since my brothers and sisters have suffered and died because of him.

Now you want me to turn the job over to somebody else? A Galreyvan, no less?"

Nils looked to Kara'ni. "Can we compromise here?" he said. "Can't assisting in his death be enough?"

Kara'ni's eyes were hard. "Never."

"Well, somebody has to budge. I don't care who kills him, we just need to get it done so we can leave."

"Are you serious, Nils?" Taws asked, and Nils found himself backing up a step. Taws looked as dangerous as the spellweaver, only he was brandishing a knife. "You've known this lady for what, an hour? And you have to think about this? *Fives,* I don't even know what we're arguing about. I don't need your permission to do this. Come on, Sandri. Let's go."

"What? But Taws—" Sandri started.

"This is how it is, love. Unless you'd rather stay with them."

"Taws, hang on," Nils said. "I'm sorry, I didn't mean to—Taws!"

Taws didn't listen, just headed straight for the stairs. Sandri hovered behind, looking torn. "I...I'm sorry Nils," she said. "Be safe, all right?"

"Sandri, wait," Nils pleaded as she followed Tawson down the stairs. "We can figure this out!"

Neither of them looked back, and they disappeared into the darkness of the theatre below, taking a large chunk of Nils' resolve with them. "What do we do now?" he asked the emptiness in front of him.

"You get moving," Kara'ni said. "You have a bargain to keep, and now there's competition."

Nils turned around to face her. "You want me to work against Taws?"

"I don't care a mite about you or that Thrinian," Kara'ni said. "Just get me to that *kragraven* emperor, or maybe I'll take your girly's life instead."

Nils stepped forward. "Don't you dare threaten her."

Kara'ni didn't back down, and stared him in the face. "Then get moving."

Nils scowled and turned away. What had he done, releasing this woman? Raeya was right; he never should've trusted her.

"Taws and Sandri were our best bet for getting to Ri'sen," he said. "They have all the experience, *and* no one here will recognize them. What can we do? The wrong person sees any of us, and we're done."

"I have a thought," Raeya said. "We are in a storage room above a theatre just now, and I'm pretty sure we're surrounded by costumes."

"Oh," Nils said, looking around. "That...that is a thought, yes."

Raeya opened one of the chests on the floor. "There, see? Wigs. We can do this."

Nils moved closer to her. "I'd prefer you waited here," he said in a low voice. "It will be safer."

"I'm coming with you," she replied. "We need to watch each other's backs."

"Yes," Kara'ni said, rummaging through another chest, pulling out a straight black wig. "Wouldn't want the spellweaver to sneak up behind you."

Nils released a breath. "Fine," he said to Raeya, then started looking for a wig for himself. There was a startlingly green one in the chest. *To act as Desna,* he realized. There was a golden-blonde wig for Pria, pale blue for Kirit, deep red for Raulen. So then the long black wig Kara'ni was putting on was probably...

Nils shuddered, feeling another jolt from the stone.

"Are you all right?" Raeya asked.

"Fine," he said, grabbing a dark brown wig and shoving it on his head. "Just ready to be done with all this."

40 WEAVER'S STONE

"Ah, I missed having long hair," Raeya said, tousling the chestnut waves that fell over her shoulders. "I'm sorry, Nils, but I'm going to let my own hair grow back out."

"Why are you apologizing? You can grow it down to your toes if it makes you happy," Nils said, throwing glances this way and that. Even with disguises, he hated walking out in the open like this. This section of the castle was still eerily empty due to the hour, but that almost made him more uneasy. Would morning arrive soon, bringing a flood of activity with it? It felt like ages since he'd seen a window.

"In all seriousness," Raeya said softly, "I *am* sorry for what happened with your friend. It was all on my account."

Nils threw a quick glance behind them where Kara'ni walked with her new straight hair. She almost looked more intimidating now, in spite of the clean clothes she'd picked from the costume rack.

"We don't have to go through with this, you know," Raeya whispered. "We can try to lose her and regroup with the others."

"But your curse—"

"I know. I desperately want to be rid of it, but there *are* worse things."

Her words were tempting. Nils had released a monster, and what was he going to do without Taws and Sandri? Would they ever forgive him? Would he have to try to make the journey home without them? Fives, he wasn't sure he would've made it out of Chanterey on his own, or even the *manor*. And Taws was right: what was he thinking, giving Kara'ni his allegiance? Taws had done so much for him, and Nils was ready to brush him aside for some murderous spellweaving criminal?

No, not for her. For the woman who walked beside him.

Nils took a breath. "We'll just...see how it plays out," he said. "I'm not ready to give up."

There was a sound around the next corner, and Nils led his small party off in another direction. "You know," Kara'ni said from behind, "if you avoid everyone you hear coming, we'll never know if it was the emperor or not."

"Yes, but we don't want to meet him head-on, do we?" Nils said. "Even with different clothes and hair, he'll recognize your faces quickly enough. We need to be careful."

"Hm. I have an idea," Raeya said. "You've heard that if you're lost, it's better to stay put, right? Because otherwise you and the ones trying to find you might just keep making circles around each other?"

"Yes," Nils said.

"Well, we could be doing the same thing with the emperor, *and* we don't want him to see us. So what if we find a good vantage point and wait and see if he passes by? Such as, up there?"

They had just passed into an open area of the castle, and Raeya pointed to an overlook on the floor above them. There weren't many wall-lamps there, and it would be a decently sheltered place to watch from.

"Yes, we could try that." Thank Desna someone was having good ideas tonight.

They made their way up to the floor above and settled down low behind the banister, peeking through to look out on the castle interior. They could see an impressive amount of floor from here, both across from and below them. Kara'ni sat farther down, looking off toward the other side, leaving Nils and Raeya with some privacy. It felt dangerous, being any sort of alone with her. Nils did his best to stay focused on their task, but then this was Raeya he was sitting next to. It didn't take long for her to start talking.

"I noticed you're wearing my bracelet," she said.

"Oh," Nils said. "Sorry, I meant to give it back sooner." He jumped to unfasten it, but that tiny clasp was so hard to undo with one hand.

"It's fine," Raeya said. "I'd like you to keep it for now. I'm just glad to know it wasn't lost."

"Are you sure?"

"Yes."

Nils tried to settle back in, but he was plagued by embarrassment now. What did she think about him wearing her jewelry?

"Also, I...I again must say that I'm sorry, Nils," Raeya said. "You were right from the start that I wasn't your true love, but I wouldn't listen. I understand too well now how you must've felt being trapped in the manor, right down to finding yourself half-betrothed against your will."

Nils let his eyes do another sweep of the floor, still empty. "Has Isek...mistreated you?" he asked.

"You mean besides kidnapping me and bringing me here to serve the emperor, as an *assassin* of all things?" Raeya sighed. "No. He said he wouldn't force me to marry him, even though he desires it. He went out of his way to be kind, constantly looking out for me and seeing that I was well-cared-for. He even brought me books." She laughed. "Of course none of that changes what he's done."

"Well, I'm sorry too," Nils said. "You were right about him, and yet I...I tried to set you up with him."

"I know."

Nils turned to her. "You do?"

"You were painfully obvious."

Nils winced. And here he thought she was the naive one.

"Although, if I'm being honest," Raeya said, "you nearly succeeded."

Nils swallowed. "I was only thinking of myself. If I'd had any idea who he really was, I never would've—"

"It's all right," Raeya said. "I know you meant no harm. I told you I'm a good judge of these things, didn't I? Even if I was...disappointed that you weren't who I expected you would be, I could tell you had a good heart underneath, which is something of note. I feel like the more people I meet, the less I can say that about."

"Fewer," Nils said, then clapped a hand over his mouth.

"Hm? Ah, yes, you're right. *Fewer* I can say that about. Thank you."

"Did you just...thank me for correcting you?"

"Of course. Now I'll be less likely to make a mistake like that in the future. Who wouldn't be thankful?"

Nils blinked. *Gods. I really do love her.*

"Nils, you seem...different than you were before."

Nils shifted. "Different how?"

"At the manor I thought you wanted nothing more than to be rid of me, but now...well, we both know what happened when you found me in my room—"

"That was nothing," Nils spit out.

"It didn't seem like nothing."

"Well, it was."

"I'm not convinced," Raeya said. "And even besides that—I mean, you're *here* for one thing. My father let you leave the manor; you could've gone anywhere, so why did you choose to come here? I imagine my father offered you some exorbitant reward, but you don't seem the type to go to such lengths for that, especially with how much you hated him, so then why—?"

"W-why does it matter?" Nils said. Had Raeya moved closer? It suddenly felt like she was so close. "Raeya, you know that I'm not your—"

Movement below. Nils and Raeya got their eyes back on the floor just as four figures began ascending the staircase that would take them to the platform across from where they sat. The divide between platforms was large; could they stay hidden? It mattered a great deal, because the four figures were Ri'sen, Isek, and two guards. The emperor and his nephew looked like they were having a heated discussion, and Nils didn't have to guess the source of their agitation.

More movement caught Nils' eye, farther down the same platform. Taws and Sandri.

Fives. Do they know they're about to run straight into Ri'sen and his guards?

Nils stood, forgetting himself. He had to warn them somehow, but...No, they were all right. They hid themselves around a bend, so then they must've known who was coming. They were preparing to pounce.

"Nils, they're going to see you!" Raeya hissed, and she was right. Isek looked straight in his direction, then back at his uncle, then did a double take.

Darkness of Hearthnight, Nils thought. *Can he recognize my face from there?*

It didn't matter. At that moment, he and Ri'sen passed the place where Taws and Sandri were hiding, and Taws went straight for the emperor.

Ri'sen cried out, and Nils felt the shout echo inside his chest, penetrating his bones. A guard was on Taws even before his knife connected, and his aim was thrown off; he'd only hit the emperor's arm. Sandri leapt upon the guard, knocking him flat on his back in spite of the difference in size between them, freeing Taws to strike again, but Ri'sen had a sword in hand now. Isek had drawn a long knife, and worse—he was chanting.

Nils tried to shout across the chasm, but a hand with sharp fingernails latched itself over his mouth.

"Hush," Kara'ni said in his ear. "When your friend fails, we'll want the opportunity to strike by surprise."

Nils shook the spellweaver off of him. "I have to help," he said, watching the scene unfold with pins of agony spiking him every instant. Fives, this was all his fault. All because he wanted to help Raeya, to free her from her curse. Now, if he disappointed Kara'ni, she might just kill them both, but at this moment...

Taws needed his help. The man who'd kept Nils from breaking in the pit, who'd walked with him through the darkest time in his life, needed his help.

Taws and Isek were dueling now, a fight of knives and slashes. *Don't let him touch your knife,* Nils pleaded toward his friend. *Don't let it happen. Please, Desna.*

The emperor was retreating with his single guard, while the other guard was busy dying as Sandri put a blade through his neck. Nils cringed, searching for *any* way to help Taws. There, farther down. There was a bridge that crossed the chamber, connecting his platform to the other. He started to move.

A hand gripped his shoulder. "Where are you going, boy?" Kara'ni hissed. "The emperor's going the other way, and he only has one guard. Now's the time to strike!"

"Then go strike yourself," Nils said, pulling free. "I've got to get to Taws. He needs—"

There was a shout, and Nils looked back across the gulf. Taws had taken a hit, but...he was all right, still fighting. Just a surface wound.

"Let's go," Raeya said, and she and Nils started sprinting for the bridge, keeping watch on the other side as best they could. Sandri was trying to help Taws, but Isek parried her knife and threw her into the wall where she fell to the floor.

Gods, oh gods.

Taws yelled, charging at Isek, who reached for his hand—

No. No. Don't let him touch your knife!

He didn't. He struck Tawson's wrist, and his knife fell to the floor with a clang, his grip simply not strong enough with his missing finger. Nils would've been relieved no spell was cast, but now his friend was unarmed. Nils was almost to the bridge. Almost there...

Taws dodged a swipe from Isek, then another. He had a second knife on him, Nils knew. He could pull it if he could only get a break, or...

No, he was trying to take Isek's knife. To disarm him and use his own weapon against him. Isek dodged once, but then slowed, almost as if he *wanted*...

"No!"

Nils' shout seemed to fill the chamber, but it was too late. Tawson grabbed Isek's knife, then plunged it into his own chest, his eyes blank. Isek had cursed his own knife.

Nils and Raeya were on the bridge now, and as Tawson crumpled, Isek looked toward them, once-familiar eyes now uncommonly fierce. It may have taken him an extra second, but he could tell who they were.

"Nils," he growled, then he shouted. "What have you done? Why did you have to come here!"

Isek retrieved his knife from Taws' chest, the blade coated red, and Nils felt his heart sink even while it beat for all its life. What was he going to do when he reached Isek? He didn't know, but he ran all the same, ran for the fruitless hope of helping Taws, bleeding on the floor, and Sandri, lying helpless behind...

No...where was Sandri?

Isek grunted, his breath fleeing his lungs as Sandri's arm wrapped about his shoulders from behind. Her other arm plunged a knife into his back for a second time. She let him drop to his knees, then ran to Taws.

"Tawsey," she breathed, crouching over him. "Tawsey!"

Nils almost froze in front of Isek, who was panting on his hands and knees. It was stupid. The most stupid feeling Nils had ever felt, but yet he couldn't shake it. A feeling that not just one of his friends was dying on the floor, but two. He forced himself to keep moving until he reached Taws and Sandri.

Taws did not look good. Blood soaked his shirt, and his face was twisted in agony. Sandri pressed her hands into the wound. "What do I do, Nils?" she asked, tears dropping from her eyes. "Oh, gods."

Nils looked around. Raeya had stopped by Isek, looking horrified, and Kara'ni stood back by the bridge. Why hadn't she followed the emperor? Well, Nils would take it.

"Kara'ni," he said, not leaving any room in his voice for refusal, "help Sandri move Taws somewhere safe. Do it, and I promise I'll get you to the emperor. If not, then torture and kill me all you like, but I won't help you."

Kara'ni looked irritated, but she did it. Nils would've done it himself, but there was a pull he couldn't ignore any longer. Raeya must've felt it too, because she knelt down beside Isek who now lay upon the floor. Nils went and joined her.

Isek looked up at them, his breaths ragged and harsh. "Raeya," he said. "I...I'm sorry. And Nils...I'm sorry, too."

"What do you mean, you're sorry?" Nils said, fighting the irrational emotion that pricked at his eyes. Raeya was trembling beside him.

"I had a choice," he said. "I was sent to...to bring Raeya here, to bind her to myself, but I...Raeya, I never expected to fall so completely for you. Even so, I chose to serve my emperor. This was not what was best for you. I knew that, but even so..."

He winced against his pain, and Nils felt the thrumming of the stone, reaching out to him.

What would I even do with it? he asked himself. *What could I even do? I don't know how—*

"Nils, I...I'm glad you were the one...who turned out to be her true love. You've put her before yourself. You are...a better man than I."

Nils clenched his fists against the shaking in his hands, his arms. He didn't have the heart to tell Isek that he was wrong, that he wasn't—

"Being an agent and assassin for the emperor…is a solitary job. I never got close to people except with the intention of manipulating them, but you…you were different. I nearly killed you, and yet…I think you and I could've been true friends."

Stop, Nils begged. He couldn't take it. He was supposed to hate this man, so why—why did it hurt so much?

"Raeya," Isek said, looking at her. "I am a selfish man to the end. I…I wonder, if you could find it in your heart to…to kiss me, just once. I would rather my life end in sweetness than in pain."

A sob broke Raeya's voice, and she shook her head. "I can't," she said. "Isek, I can't. I couldn't bear the thought of having killed you. It's too much."

Isek managed a small smile. "I see. Then go, both of you. Hurry, and…escape."

"No," Nils said, finally managing a word. "No one should be left to die alone."

"Nils," he said, "some people would rather die alone…than have those they care about watch the light leave their eyes."

Nils took in a sharp breath, the pain in his lungs bringing him clarity. No matter what he said, Isek was not an entirely selfish man.

"Raeya," Nils said, "let's go."

Raeya rubbed at her eyes, tears streaming down her face. She gripped Isek's hand, then got up and left with Nils, neither of them daring to look back. They walked, then they ran.

* * *

It wasn't hard to find where the girls had taken Taws.

Blood splattered the floor, and Nils and Raeya found them barricaded in a storeroom. Sandri had Taws' head resting in her lap, and Nils would've rather found his friend's face still twisted in pain. Instead, he was frighteningly still, his skin drained of color.

"Is he—"

"He's still breathing," Sandri answered, "but he…he—"

"He's beyond saving by ordinary means," Kara'ni said coolly. "Unless you have a weaver and chrysolin, he's going to die."

Nils didn't have to think about his next action. He pulled the weaver's stone out of his sock, and thrust it toward Kara'ni. "Take it," he said. "Save him."

He heard Sandri gasp, and Kara'ni eyed the stone with astonishment, then looked back at Nils. "I cannot."

Nils fought the urge to throw the fiving stone at her face. "I don't care how little you care about us, you *will*—"

"I said *I cannot*," Kara'ni spat at him. "I am incompatible with healing spells. I tried it once—you can guess on whom—and it only made him bleed faster."

"Then what can we do?" Sandri asked in agony.

Kara'ni kept a level gaze on Nils. "Perhaps one of you could try it."

"I'll do it," Sandri said without hesitation. "Give it to me."

Nils held the stone out to Sandri, and she snatched it from his hand.

"Do you feel anything?" Kara'ni asked her.

"Like what?"

"If you have to ask—"

"Like what?"

"Tingling on your skin."

Sandri rolled the stone around in her fingers. "I...don't feel anything."

"Then you are not a weaver."

Sandri looked up at her. "But...but Taws—"

"You need someone else," Kara'ni said, sounding almost amused. Sandri followed her gaze, and soon all eyes were on Nils.

"Nils?" Sandri asked. "Can you—?"

This moment had been inevitable, hadn't it? Ever since he'd touched that fiving stone, he'd been unable to part with it, like he knew deep inside he was going to have to use it one day. But...could he do it? Could he paint his veins black with a fallen god's power? Mark himself a heretic and embrace the darkness?

Nils remembered Tawson's hand on his back, pushing him forward in the tunnel beneath the church. He remembered his words, ringing in his mind as he fought the darkness to reach Raeya in the dungeon, and came to a strange realization.

He wasn't afraid of the darkness anymore.

Nils took the stone back from Sandri. "How do I do it?" he asked.

Kara'ni smiled. "I'll teach you. You hold a godjewel, and so you use it like any other godjewel. You pray."

Nils swallowed. "To Lyare."

Kara'ni nodded. "Invoke his name first, keeping the stone in contact with your skin. Then, present to him your target while you touch it with your hand, again making skin contact. Some weavers can only transfer their spells to people through objects, but if you possess the power to heal, than the direct method is more likely. Regardless, you don't need to say a name, just a simple word—man, knife, stone—will do, as long as you picture the person or thing in your mind. Once identified, you weave your spell around your target. The specifics, what you want to happen and how you want it to be achieved. You must weave these under and over, stressing one syllable but not the next. Rhyming is unnecessary, though many find it helps their focus. Then, you cut your threads with a breath, and finish with the traditional ending of a prayer: 'In your name, Lyare, let it be done.' Your stone will disintegrate.

"Take care," she went on. "Words have meaning. If you use a word inaccurately, your spell will fail, but you will still lose your stone. If you try to weave a spell for which you are not suited, well, that may be less forgiving. You may find it has unpleasant side effects."

"How do I know if I am suited to a spell?" Nils asked.

"You don't," Kara'ni replied, "until you try."

Nils took a breath, staring at the black surface of the weaver's stone in his hand. He knew himself to be a quick learner, and he was accurate with words to a fault, but—

"Shall I give you an example?" Kara'ni asked. "I prefer my native tongue, but this should serve well enough: *Lyare. I ask that you shall see this girl, and bind her to a weaver's soul. A weaver same in age as she. The only one that she may kiss. If any other she shall kiss, his death will lie upon her lips.*" She paused to take a breath. "*In your name, Lyare, let it be done.*"

Nils glowered, and he could almost feel Raeya tense up beside him. It was her curse.

"Your turn," Kara'ni said with a cruel grin.

Nils looked to Taws, to Sandri. "He's dying, Nils," Sandri said. "Don't worry about what might happen. It can't be any worse."

Nils nodded, then knelt by his friend and put a hand on his forehead. He half expected to find Tawson cold, but he was warm. Still alive. Nils clenched the stone tightly in his hand, rehearsed the words in his mind, then breathed in, and spoke.

"Lyare. I ask that you shall see this man, then close his wound and save his life. Restore him to his health again." He took a deep breath. *"In your name, Lyare, let it be done."*

* * *

Whiteness. So bright, Nils shielded his eyes until they could adjust. All around him, whiteness.

"Nils."

He knew that voice. The voice from his dreams. He could never turn around to look, always frozen. This time would be no different, but still he tried—

He turned. Was this…not a dream?

"Nils, well done."

Nils stared at a man he'd never seen before, and could hardly fathom he was real. He wore long robes of black and white and was crowned with long white hair. His eyes were vibrant purple beneath black brows and lashes. In the middle of his chest was a large amulet of some sort, a black stone, not too shiny.

Lyare's Chrysolin Heart.

Nils jumped back. "Who are you?" he asked.

"I am exactly who you think I am."

"But, white hair…your hair is black."

"I do not expect humans to be correct in their perceptions of me."

"Where am I? Send me back. Taws—I need to help Taws."

"You have not left his side, child. Have peace. Our time here will not exist in your realm."

"Send me back anyway," Nils said. He wanted nothing to do with this monster, this—

"Fallen god?"

"Stop that. Why am I here?"

"You hold all of the godjewels, and you carry my power, now active inside of you. A link has been made between us. However, once your chrysolin disintegrates, I won't be able to speak with you unless you obtain more, and retain Raeya Dreygard's bracelet."

All of the godjewels...

"You've spoken with someone like this before," Nils said. "Anseph."

"Yes. I told him the truth, and sadly it killed him."

"What truth? Pria's innocence?"

"Are you sure you wish to know?"

"I'm not going to go around preaching *your* innocence, if that's what you're worried about. You are darkness itself."

"This is the truth: I am not. I am rest and renewal, though even those who still revere me have forgotten that."

"The other gods threw you from power and removed your season from the world when you refused to relinquish your hold."

Lyare shook his head. "I gave it up. My season, my godhood. What choice did I have? My appointed time had been corrupted. My darkness could provide rest no longer, only pain and fear."

"Then why didn't you just let go after your week was up, like you were supposed to?"

"Humans think gods immune to trouble. We are not. When it came time for Pria to take over, she would not wake from her slumber. She had fallen ill, plagued by dark forces you wouldn't understand. When a god is not in power, we sleep, restoring ourselves. Thus, I was the only one awake. With great effort I managed to rouse Raulen, who went at once in search of a cure for Pria's ailment. He saved her, but it took much time. Too much. The damage could not be undone. I knew that if I ever took power again, it would only bring atrocities. So I stepped back, never to take my place at the pedestal again."

Nils' head felt heavy, his chest tight, almost like he wasn't breathing in this strange place. "Why are you telling me this?"

"I thought I was doing good for humanity, but...I did not foresee the consequences of my actions. I simply want one of you to know, and maybe...maybe it could help in some small way."

"To know what?"

"That in relinquishing my place as god, I caused my power to overflow. It had lost its natural outlet, and so it finds its way into humans, even to this day."

"Spellweavers."

Lyare nodded. "I have no control over whom it chooses, or how it will affect them. Most...use it for darkness.

"There is more," he went on, taking a step closer to Nils, who stepped back out of his reach. Lyare frowned at him. "You are so tired," he said. "All of you. You labor, and you toil, and you take no rest. Not the deep rest that you need. I...I cannot help myself. I still long to give it to you." He tried once more to reach out to Nils.

"Don't touch me."

Lyare retracted his hand. "Your lives are a shadow of what they are meant to be, Nils Tenning."

"Maybe," Nils said, "but I don't believe a word of anything else you've said. You won't convince me that you're blameless."

"Very well," Lyare said. "Perhaps it is better for you that way."

"Send me back. I don't want to hear any more of this."

"As you wish."

41 EMPEROR RI'SEN

The change was so abrupt, Nils felt like he'd fallen.

He gasped for air, fighting the spinning in his head. Had that…had that been real?

A voice. "Taws? Tawsey?"

Nils snapped to attention.

Taws still lay in front of him, half in Sandri's lap. Nils' hand was on his forehead, and…

And Taws was stirring.

He opened his eyes. "Sands?" he said. "What happened?"

"Tawsey!" Sandri cried, crushing him in an embrace. "Oh, bless you, Nils, you did it. Desna bless you till the end of time."

"Wait," Tawson said, sitting up. "I…I remember…" he put a hand to his chest, then looked down. "Unholy fives," he said.

"You tried to take Isek's knife," Nils explained, beaming at his friend. He was alive—Taws was alive! "But he'd cursed it. You stabbed yourself."

"Then how…"

Nils' smile faded. He looked down at his arm, tugged up his sleeve just enough…

Black veins marred his pale skin. The world sunk around Nils, taking all heat and color with it.

"Fives," Taws whispered. "Nils, you…"

Nils couldn't look up. Couldn't look at him, or Sandri. His eyes were fixed on the symbol of his shame. Raeya stood behind him— gods, he could never look at her again. Even though he wasn't her true love, there was some small part of him that had refused to let go, that clung to each warm gesture from her, lit up each time she spoke his name.

But that was before he'd defiled himself. Even that final, stubborn piece knew better than to hope now. He would not regret saving Taws, but he would not be disillusioned either. From now on, he was alone.

"Nils."

He ignored Tawson's voice, still wouldn't look at him, but then…

Tawson hugged him. "I can never repay you for what you just did, brother," he said.

Nils took in a shaky breath. "But Taws, I…I'm…"

"The bravest man I've ever known, with a heart as big as his brain. Why do you think I was so confident sending you into Dreygard's manor?"

Nils broke, hot tears streaming down his face.

"It's going to be all right," Taws said.

"You betcha it is," Sandri said, throwing her arms around him when Taws moved back. "Thank you, Nils. *I* can never repay you, either."

Nils sniffed, rubbing his sleeve over his eyes. Stupidly, all he could do was nod.

"Boy," came a harsh voice to the right. Nils looked up at Kara'ni. "Congratulations on claiming your power. Now get me to Ri'sen before somebody finds us."

"Listen here, lady," Taws said, trying to stand, but he wobbled and Sandri caught him.

"What is it?" Nils asked. "Did I do something wrong?"

"He's just weak," Kara'ni said. "You would be too after losing so much blood. Sit, Thrinian. You won't be fighting the emperor."

Begrudgingly, Taws let Sandri lower him back to the floor. "Darkness of Hearthnight. If I can't go, then...take this," Taws said, fishing his spare knife from his boot and holding it out to Nils. "Don't give me that look. I know you won't want to use it, but...you never know. At least I can say my knife was present when that dog fell."

Nils didn't want to, but he accepted it, sliding it into his own boot. He didn't have to use it. He could just carry it, for Taws.

"The gods be with you, brother."

Nils nodded.

"We'll go back to the theatre," Sandri said. "Find us there afterward, yeah?"

Nils nodded again, then stood to leave, trying to walk quickly past Raeya without meeting her eyes.

"Wait," she said, grabbing his wrist. Right over his veins. "I'm still coming with you."

"Raeya—"

"You won't change my mind."

* * *

Back in the halls, the trio slunk off quickly, away from the place where Isek had fallen. It would be swarming with guards by now. Nils hoped to find *one* guard, not fifty.

"Do you know where we're going, young spellweaver?" Kara'ni asked. "We lost the emperor, thanks to that deviation."

"We don't need to find him," Nils said, removing his cloak. At some point he'd lost his wig too, but luckily he didn't need it anymore. "We'll let him come to us. That is, Raeya, if you don't mind…"

"I'm not thrilled about aiding *her,*" Raeya said, "but if all you need is for me to be seen, I can do that."

"All right. Be ready to take off your disguise."

★ ★ ★

Running.

From one corridor to another, then ducking out of sight, finding a way to evade the guard that pursued them until they slipped away.

Then finding another guard, and repeating the process.

Every watchman in the castle was looking for a young lady with red hair, so one glance at Raeya had them all stirred up. Emperor Ri'sen was sure to hear about it, and he would come with his own entourage, Nils was certain. They'd passed a row of windows on their mad flight, showing a lightening sky; if Ri'sen didn't want all of his guests to witness his castle out of control, he'd come to stop them with haste.

The trick would be getting him alone.

"Does it really matter if he has a couple guards?" Nils asked, panting as they took a ten-second break in a stairwell.

"Yes," Kara'ni replied. "And you'd better find him soon, boy. I've been trapped in a confined space for a long time, and if I pass out from exertion it's on your head."

"Noted," Nils said.

They made their way to the top of the stairs, jogged down the next hall, then halted abruptly at the sound of voices. Someone was speaking Galreyvan, and by the tone of his voice he was giving orders. Also, he was angry.

"That's him," Raeya whispered.

Nils nodded, so accustomed to the tension in his body that he didn't notice it anymore. He crouched down low, then carefully peeked around the corner.

There were several men in the hallway wearing Ri'sen's colors, along with Ri'sen himself. Most dispersed from him with their orders, but one followed as he turned and strode right toward them.

Nils pulled back and pressed himself against the wall. "Now's the time," he said in a tight whisper.

"Should I show myself?" Raeya asked.

"Not yet. Let the other guards get farther away, or we'll be overwhelmed."

Raeya nodded, and Nils' heartbeats thundered in his chest as he counted seconds, guessing when Ri'sen would reach them. Would he pass, or turn right into the hallway where they stood? If he was too close when he saw them, they wouldn't be able to outrun him...

"Head back to the stairwell," Nils said, "quickly."

Raeya and Kara'ni started back down the hall, Nils right behind them. A shadow passed—Ri'sen—and another—the guard—

"Hey!"

Nils winced. The guard had spotted them.

"Stop there!" he shouted again.

"Keep running!" Nils urged, gaining speed as the guard's shadow began to loom over him. "To the sides!"

The women each swerved to one side of the stairs, and Nils ducked and veered to Raeya's side just before the guard could grab him, leaving the man off-balance. Before he could steady himself, Nils threw all of his weight at him and sent him crashing down the stairs where he hit the wall at the bottom hard enough to knock him unconscious.

Nils turned, not having time to properly appreciate what had just happened. Ri'sen was standing in their hallway now, hand on his sword.

"Raeya, dear child," he sneered. "So much trouble you have caused." He took a step forward, but paused when Kara'ni brushed past Nils, pulling the black wig off her head, letting her dark brown waves of hair flow free.

"Hello, Suloron," she purred, and she pulled something from inside her shirt.

A small, black stone. How long had she—

Ri'sen muttered what could've only been a curse, then turned and ran, leaving his sword in its sheath. Kara'ni chased after him, and after exchanging a quick look, Nils and Raeya followed.

Ri'sen ran across to the next hall, down a flight of stairs, and off to the right. Kara'ni showed nothing of the exertion about which she'd complained, staying right on his heels.

"Get that door!" she shouted back at Nils just as she grabbed Ri'sen's cloak. There was only one door she could've meant, a large wooden one on their left, so Nils heaved it open and Kara'ni threw the emperor inside.

It was a relatively large chamber, perhaps a council room of some kind, or—no, it was a chapel. There was an altar on a dais at the front, and two rows of benches preceding it. A mural on the wall depicted a god with long, black hair. Once they were all inside, Kara'ni bolted the door behind them. Ri'sen drew his sword, stepping backward toward the altar to afford himself some space.

"You shouldn't have let me go, Kara'ni," Ri'sen said, throwing off his cloak. A dark stain on his sleeve marked where Taws had struck his arm. He wore a brave grin, but his eyes danced with fear. "I won't let you touch me again."

"You face two spellweavers, and one just as deadly," Kara'ni replied. "How long can you evade all three?"

Nils and Raeya took that as a cue, each taking a position in a side aisle while Kara'ni strode up the middle. Nils and Raeya had no intention of fighting, but Ri'sen didn't know that. He glanced between the three of them, continuing to step backward until his back hit the dais.

"Well, lucky for me I know which is the least dangerous," Ri'sen said. "That mask was always a silly precaution."

He fled toward Raeya, and Nils swore, but Kara'ni proved just as fast as the emperor. She sprinted between the benches and reached Raeya at nearly the same time he did—

But not quite fast enough to stop him from grabbing her. "Let me pass," he said to Kara'ni, holding his sword across Raeya's neck.

Kara'ni cackled. "You know me better than this, *Ni Sol'emi*. You think I care if she dies?"

Ri'sen growled, holding Raeya before him like a shield while she squirmed in his grasp. Would he kill her, his prized assassin? Did he know he'd already lost Isek?

Ri'sen backed up toward the dais, taking Raeya up onto the platform with him, while Kara'ni walked after them with absolute calm. Nils circled around the rows of benches to approach from the other side. *Gods, we never should have followed her.* There was nothing he could do now, but the drive to do *something* had him reaching for his boot, pulling Tawson's knife, an object foreign to his skin.

Kara'ni had the emperor and Raeya effectively trapped on the stage, but she couldn't touch Ri'sen without him striking her hands, and she would have to hold him long enough to chant a spell. If they delayed too long, someone would find them here. Nils wracked his brain for a solution that didn't involve dismemberment, trying frantically to find a way to make him release Raeya—

But then Raeya moved. It happened so fast, he almost missed it. She grabbed Ri'sen's sword-hand in both of hers, then yanked downward and ducked to the side, gripping his wrist with all her might as she slid under his arm.

"Now!" she shouted to Kara'ni, who was already moving in. She kicked Ri'sen's sword from his hand, then latched onto his other arm.

"Keep him restrained, girl," she ordered Raeya while the emperor cursed and pulled against the two of them. "Nils, guard the door!"

Nils scrambled to obey, and Kara'ni started chanting in Galreyvan, a rhythm familiar and strange all at once. Could she and Raeya hold him? Ri'sen was unquestionably stronger, and until Kara'ni finished chanting—

Raeya squealed, and Nils stopped, turning back to them. Ri'sen had thrown her off and grabbed Kara'ni with his free hand, yanking at her hair, but she kept right on chanting. Raeya got up and grabbed his arm again, trying to pull him off of Kara'ni.

And Nils...why was he heading toward the door? It was barred, and Ri'sen wasn't going anywhere. Even besides that, why was he taking orders from a spellweaver?

He started back toward Raeya, but the room went silent. Kara'ni finished her curse, and Ri'sen stilled. Nils stood, staring. Was it...over?

Over, except for watching the emperor kill himself in whatever gruesome fashion Kara'ni had devised. Nils didn't care to see, but Raeya was still up on the dais, holding Ri'sen's arm. Nils approached with quiet steps, afraid to break the overpowering silence of the room. As he came up on the platform, he could see the vacant look in Ri'sen's eyes. Kara'ni was grinning at him, disregardful of the blood running down from her scalp. She still held his other hand, almost affectionately.

"Ah, dear Suloron, *Ni Sol'emi,*" she said. She loosened the ties on the vambrace he wore on his forearm, pulling it off. There were three weaver's stones embedded inside. "I plotted for years what sort of spell would be best to end your life. In these last moments, I found one all the more appropriate."

She lowered her voice, almost a whisper. Nils got the impression she had forgotten he and Raeya were there. "What you don't know, *Ni Sol'emi,*" she said, "is that *I* was the one who gave your pet her curse, and now my power shall kill you two times over."

Two times over? What did she—

Kara'ni released the emperor's hand, and Raeya screamed. She tried to pull back, but Ri'sen was now gripping her arm. "No, no!" she begged.

"Be a good girl, now," Kara'ni said, getting behind Raeya to keep her from breaking free. "You hate this man too, don't you? Think of it as a kiss goodbye."

"No!" Raeya screamed again as Ri'sen secured her other arm, pulling closer to her, and Nils lost all sense of himself. He couldn't, he *wouldn't* let her endure this, a trauma as real for her as Gen Rill had been for him. There was only one way to stop it now.

He gripped Tawson's knife like a lifeline and ran at Emperor Ri'sen, shouting as he swung his arm and drove the blade into his neck.

Ri'sen jerked, still trying to obey the curse's pull, but his breath caught with every inhale. He staggered, grunting, until his grip finally gave out and he fell to the floor, gasping until he fell still.

Raeya stared down at the body at her feet, a few flecks of its blood on her cheek. Nils fell to his knees.

Inside, he fell further. He thought himself already in the depths, becoming a spellweaver, and now this? He'd done it. He'd killed a man. Nils, who would've gladly lived his entire life in a schoolhouse teaching children with a stack of dusty books in his arms, now wove dark magic and slew emperors with knives.

"What have you done?"

Nils wondered the same thing, but that vicious cry came from Kara'ni. She knelt before him, grabbing his shirt and pulling him toward her. "He was *mine*. Had I not made myself clear? I will never, *never* remove that girl's curse now. She can carry it to her grave."

Nils' muscles clenched tight, and he ripped the spellweaver's hands off of him. "I've had enough with your fiving petty attitude!" he shouted back at her. "Raeya doesn't even have anything to do with this! You were the one in the wrong, forcing her to kill with the power *you* gave her for an honest, innocent mistake. She deserves nothing of this, and you've scarred her enough. Stop hiding behind your heartache and release her, you black-hearted witch!"

Kara'ni stilled, but not as one who'd felt the shock of reality, or the peace of a cleared mind. No, she stilled like the trees right before the onset of a storm.

"Somebody will pay for this," she said, voice low and dangerous.

"Then let it be me. Remove her curse, and I'll submit. You can do as you please with my life."

Kara'ni cocked her head at Nils. "You'd give your life solely to free her from my spell?"

Nils took a breath, solidifying his thoughts. What was his life worth now? What could he do with it from here? If he returned home, he'd be sentenced to death the moment his wrists were seen. Even if he managed to hide them for a time, he had no tags, no identity. And no *home* to return to. The schoolhouse was gone, his family was gone, and even *he* wouldn't want his own company. At least this way, Raeya could live a normal life.

"Yes," he whispered.

Kara'ni smiled. "I can do as I please, you say. That gives me an idea. As pleasurable as it would be to kill you, I think I shall bind you to myself instead, and harvest a most obedient servant." She retrieved Ri'sen's vambrace from where it had fallen beside her, caressing the stones inside. "A spellweaver will prove most useful."

Nils shut his eyes. "So be it."

"No."

Raeya's voice. Nils opened his eyes, and found a sword held at Kara'ni's throat. Emperor Ri'sen's sword, in Raeya's grasp. "I'll keep it," she said. "I'll keep my curse. Just leave him be."

"Raeya, what are you doing?" Nils said. "I'm trying to save you!"

"And it's about time somebody saved you!" Raeya said. "Since you arrived here you've done nothing but sacrifice yourself for the people you care about. My sacrifice is small in comparison, but it's my turn to make it."

"You don't have the spine to kill me, girl," Kara'ni snapped at her.

"Under normal circumstances, perhaps not," Raeya admitted, "but for him? You don't want to test me." The edge of the blade grazed Kara'ni's neck, loosing a trickle of blood from her skin. "Leave now, and never bother us again," Raeya said. "The emperor is dead, and you're free. That's more than you deserve. In fact, I'm tempted to say that your *life* is more than you deserve, but I don't believe I have the right to make such judgments."

Kara'ni growled, clenching the vambrace in her hand. "Fine," she said. Raeya kept the sword close to her neck while she stood and turned to face her. "I will leave, but you had both better pray that we never cross paths again."

"I shall pray so every day," Raeya said, "and you may just want to do the same."

Raeya moved her blade just enough, and Kara'ni left with a disgusted huff, throwing one last haughty glare at Nils before disappearing from his line of sight. Nils stared at the empty space in front of him until something else came into his view. Orange hair, soft skin, blue-gray eyes.

A trembling hand touched his. "Nils. We need to go."

* * *

Nils and Raeya found their way back to the theatre through a castle that wasn't quiet anymore. The noise aided their passage, alerting them to the location of guards searching frantically for their emperor.

When they arrived at the theatre, Nils ascended to the loft on leaden feet. Sandri was keeping watch, and Taws sprang up from where he'd been resting when Nils appeared.

"Nils!" he said, bounding over to him. He seemed to be recovering well. "What happened?"

"I'm sorry, Taws," Nils said, "but your knife got left behind."

"Where?"

"In the emperor's neck. But I thought you might accept this as a replacement."

Raeya came around Nils, holding out Ri'sen's sword. Elation flickered on Tawson's face as he reached for it, but when he took in Nils and Raeya's expressions, their sullied clothing, he grew solemn. He took the sword without comment.

"I take it things are heating up out there?" he asked.

Nils nodded.

"Rest a moment," Taws said. "We'll leave when you're ready." He went to sit with Sandri on the stairs, and Nils and Raeya sat on one of the costume chests at the back of the room.

Nils stared down at his arms resting in his lap. "It isn't fair," he said. "I'm nothing and no one to you at my best, and at my worst…I have blackened wrists and bloody hands. Raeya, that you should be bound to me by your curse…I wanted to free you."

"You don't understand, Nils," Raeya said. "I don't need to be freed. Yes, there is the risk of others like Ri'sen endeavoring to use me, or of dishonorable men killing themselves and leaving me with the scars, but if you're worried about the fact that I can kiss only you, don't be." She smiled. "You're the only one I will ever want to kiss."

"But Raeya, I'm not—"

"Not my true love, I know. It turns out I don't have one, which means I get to choose, doesn't it?"

"So then why—"

"Why you? A spellweaver, a killer? You are neither of those things, Nils. You are a true friend, and a savior. As far as your claim of being *nothing* and *no one,* that couldn't be further from the truth. I have seen plenty now to know what sort of man you are, and I'd be hard-pressed to find another who measures up, whether townsman or king. Now, let me ask you something: Do you love me?"

Nils blinked, and his face grew hot. *Really? After all I just went through, I'm still going to blush?* "Yes," he confessed.

"Good." Raeya kissed him, and Nils breathed in a gasp, then stilled, and let his eyes close.

People said death was peaceful. Raeya's kiss wouldn't bring him death, but in the midst of terrible chaos, he'd never known such peace.

Raeya drew back only slightly, speaking her words onto his lips. "I love you, too."

42 HOME

Two weeks later, Nils sat with Raeya at the edge of the forest in Borlund, looking out on the fields and hills of their own country. While they still had some distance to travel, in a way it already felt like they were home. They could relax a little with the border crossing behind them.

Taws and Sandri had gone ahead to scout out a route, and Nils and Raeya took the opportunity to rest and have a moment to themselves. Nils held Raeya's hand in his own, moving his thumb in circles on her impossibly soft skin. Her head rested on his shoulder, and he leaned into her, staring down at their intertwined fingers. Every touch sparked a feeling he couldn't believe hadn't been there before.

He let his eyes fall to their wrists, pressed tightly together. Raeya's bracelet, now returned to her, gleamed in Pria's sunlight, touching Nils' skin at the place where his sleeve was pushed up just enough to reveal his weaver's veins. He gripped Raeya's hand a little tighter.

"How long will it take before someone notices?" he said quietly.

Raeya didn't have to ask what he meant. "We'll make sure nobody ever does. Cuffs are in style; you'll be fine."

Nils scowled. "I guess I'll have to get some before we return to the manor. And here I'd hoped I could avoid stooping to a noble's sense of fashion."

Raeya chuckled. "You'll look positively dashing, dear. But around me, you can dress however you please, with nothing to hide." She lifted Nils' hand to her face, lightly kissing his wrist.

"Raeya—"

"A symbol of your devotion to your friends," she said. "It's a shame you have to hide it at all."

"Raeya."

Nils pulled her close and kissed her. Once was never enough, so he brushed her hair aside with his fingers, then gently tilted her face to kiss her cheek and just below her ear. He moved to her neck, and Raeya sighed.

"Careful, Nils," she said. "You might make my skin blossom."

Nils snorted, then laughed into her shoulder while Raeya giggled and held him tight.

Yes, this place felt like home.

Nils sat up and looked at her, the question that had circled his mind for two weeks finally reaching his tongue. "Raeya Dre—"

He paused, stuck on that word. It seemed so simple out here in the wilderness, but once they got back, the reality of who Raeya was, and of who Nils would become, couldn't be ignored. If he wanted to stay with her, he'd one day find himself responsible for an entire province of people in desperate need, people who'd been caught up in Raeya's curse without knowing it. With Ri'sen gone, could Chanterey flourish again? Even if a spellweaver shepherded it?

Nils wasn't trained in leadership, or eager to take hold of it, but he had one advantage over Feren Dreygard: he cared. He cared about the plight of the people, and he wanted to see their lives improved. But becoming the domiseer? Gods, it was almost unimaginable.

Yes, this was a question he couldn't take back once it left his tongue, and one that would put him on a path he never expected nor wanted. The manor, his prison, would be his home. Feren Dreygard would be his *father-in-law.* And his daughter…

His daughter. He looked into her eyes, and he no longer saw the domiseer in them. They were simply Raeya's. If she was here beside him, then maybe all the rest…

Raeya raised a brow at him. "Dreygard?" she prompted.

Nils made up his mind. "I hate your last name," he said. "Would you consider taking mine instead?"

Raeya stared, then pressed her hands over her mouth. "Nils," she gasped, voice muffled by her fingers. "Do you mean—"

She cut off, turning worried. "Oh, but my father," she said. "Nils, I never managed to convince him that we should be married. I don't think I made any progress at all."

"That won't be a problem."

"Why not?"

Nils scratched the back of his head. "Well, at the time I didn't think we'd ever get to this point, but…your dad said he'd consider me worthy if I succeeded in bringing you back and taking down the emperor."

"He *did?*"

"Yes."

"That's wonderful!" Raeya gushed, throwing her arms around Nils' neck and hugging him tightly. "Finally, I'll be Mrs. Raeya Oakander."

"Oh, ah…it's Tenning, actually."

"What?"

"My last name is Tenning."

Raeya leaned back and stared at him. "Pria's Eyes, Nils. You made up *three last names?*"

"Just two. The third is the true one."

"Is it really?" Raeya snipped. "Because it matters quite a lot, my dear future husband. I won't spend my life with a fake surname."

"I promise."

Raeya huffed. "Raeya Tenning. Well, lucky for you," she said, smiling and drawing closer again, "I like the sound of that."

"So do I!"

Nils jumped at Tawson's voice. "Taws!" he said, scrambling to his feet. "How long were you listening?"

"Sands and I got back just in time to hear your eloquent proposal," Tawson said, draping one arm around Nils' shoulders and the other around Raeya's. "Congratulations, you two!"

Nils shrugged him off with a grimace, but was caught up in a hug from Sandri instead. "Way to go, Nilsey!" she said.

Nils sighed, and gave up, smiling. "Thanks," he said.

Sandri hugged Raeya next, and Taws replaced his arm around Nils. "If you need anything, brother—*anything*—you just let me know, all right? There are lots of Thrinians in Chanterey who know who I am, and any of them will gladly give you aid at my word, too."

"Thank you, Taws," Nils said. "I'm, um, sorry I mistook you for a gang leader."

Taws laughed. "Don't worry; that's closer to the truth these days. And what about you? Seems I'll be calling you *Lord* Nils from now on."

"Gods, no," Nils said. "Don't ever call me that."

Taws laughed again. "You can't escape it forever. Once you're domiseer, you're Lord Tenning, my friend."

"Maybe so, but at least give me a break until then."

"If you insist, my lord."

Nils shoved Taws, who grinned before turning to Sandri.

"Is it our turn now?" he asked her.

"What do you mean?" she replied.

"Our beloved friends here have declared their love for one another. But do you think you can stand the thought of staying by the side of a former royal?"

Sandri crossed her arms. "That was a pretty big secret to hide, and I'm not convinced you ever would've told me had you not been exposed."

"Fair," Taws said with a nod, "but listen, Sandri." He took one of her hands. "Even if I *was* still some lofty prince in a palace, if the gods allowed me to meet you in that life, I'd *still* want you for my girl. You've got cleverness to rival the best, a heart of diamond, and gods, you're beautiful. So don't try and tell me we're not a match. You're mine, and I'm yours, and that's all there is to it."

Sandri's eyes went wide, then she looked like she might cry. "Oh, Tawsey," she said, jumping into his arms. "You know I'll never leave your side, not for anything!"

Raeya let out a quiet squeal of delight beside Nils, watching the couple with her hands clasped in front of her face. "They have the most beautiful story," she whispered. "A forgotten prince and a townswoman."

"As beautiful as a thief and a domiseer's daughter?" Nils asked.

Raeya turned to him with a smile. "You mean schoolteacher, don't you, dear?"

"Oh boy," Nils said. Taws and Sandri had begun kissing as though Nils and Raeya were just part of the scenery. "They, uh, might be at this a while. We'll be lucky if we ever make it back to Chanterey at this rate."

"Think of it this way," Raeya said, taking Nils by the hand and leading him a short distance away. "The longer it takes, the more time we'll have together before we have a chaperone again."

Nils smiled, everything feeling a bit surreal. He'd just asked a girl to marry him, and she'd accepted. What would his mother think if she could see him now?

That was a stupid question. She'd be ecstatic. He could almost hear her gleeful teasing now. *Nils, my reclusive child, out on an adventure with his friends, becoming betrothed to the domiseer's daughter? Pria's Diamond Eyes, it's a miracle! And with a domiseer's wealth and estate, you can have enough children to fill a few schoolhouses.*

Nils cringed at the last part. Best not think that far ahead yet.

If only you could've met her, Mom. You would've loved her.

Raeya's fingers brushed his, and Nils looked down at their hands. His wrist was still exposed. Every time those dark veins caught his eye, it became harder to look away. They sucked in every thought, forced him to dwell only on them, to remember...

"Nils?" Raeya said.

"Sorry," he said. "I just can't help worrying about how this will affect us. How it will affect you. I could be dragging you into disaster with me, if I'm discovered."

"I won't let it happen," Raeya said. "Even if someone finds out, I won't let anyone touch you, not even the king. He *owes* you. If Tawson is right about Ri'sen's heir, then in taking him out you've effectively saved our whole country from another war with Galreyva."

"Well, that remains to be seen," Nils said. But it was worth hoping.

* * *

It wasn't supposed to go this way.

Nils stood across from Feren Dreygard, eyes cold and hard as ever. He was supposed to depose this man. To expose his villainy and bring an end to his reign. So how was it he'd saved his life, secured his reign, and was about to discuss plans to marry his daughter? When Nils thought about it, he couldn't imagine much worse of a failure. It was strange, then, that he stood with what felt like confidence.

"I didn't expect I would see you again," Dreygard said. "A thief, and an ungrateful townsman of the lowest sort. Still, for saving my daughter's life, I suppose I'll have to overlook your…deficiencies, and allow you to be wed, assuming you both desire it."

Nils frowned. The domiseer said that as though bringing it up for the first time. Nils looked around. There were two guards in the meeting room with them, but no one else. Even so, he could sense it. Dreygard was still taking precautions in case he was being watched. Well, Nils had to credit him for his thoroughness.

"We do," he said.

Dreygard was either unsurprised or simply resigned to the idea. "So be it," he said with no change to his face. Nils wondered how he'd feel about this if he knew Nils and Raeya weren't actually soulmates, but they'd both decided to hide that detail.

"As my future heir," Dreygard went on, "your training begins immediately. You will complete whatever tasks I assign, and you will shadow me whenever I command it."

Nils nodded, wincing on the inside. He and the domiseer were about to spend an uncomfortable amount of time together.

"Your position also entitles you to a certain amount of input," Dreygard said. "I believe you take issue with how the towns are currently managed?"

"Yes," Nils said.

"Then that can be an area of focus for you, if you prove proficient enough. What might you suggest up front?"

So direct, Nils thought. It was a good thing he'd thought about this so much. "Start funding schools and educating your populace, for one thing," Nils said. "Then abolish your taskers. Let people choose jobs for themselves, and ones that suit their skills whenever possible."

"Many jobs that need to be done aren't attractive," Dreygard said. "How do you propose to get workers for those? Let's say, coal miners, for instance?"

"Your people are impoverished," Nils said, "to a desperate level. Offer fair compensation for the work, and people will sign up to do it. Proper safety equipment wouldn't hurt either."

"And where do we get the funds to raise wages and provide equipment?"

"Well, you have a ridiculously superfluous rug in your entryway, as well as many other luxury items throughout the estate. Selling those could be a good start."

Lord Dreygard raised an eyebrow. "My rug?"

"Why not?" Nils said. "It won't kill you to walk on a bare floor, but it might just kill a miner when his unprotected lantern flame explodes. If you can't make sacrifices, then you can't expect your province to grow."

The domiseer already looked fatigued. Nils should probably keep his lectures to a minimum, or the man's patience wouldn't last long.

You also don't have to scramble to meet the demands of a foreign emperor anymore, which will free up some resources, Nils wanted to add, but it seemed that topic couldn't be broached without complete privacy. Word of Ri'sen's death had reached the manor long before Nils had, so Dreygard knew he'd been successful. Not that that required any acknowledgment, or any word of thanks for defeating his overlord and saving his daughter, it would seem.

"We'll resume our discussions tomorrow," Dreygard said. "Use the rest of the day to settle in."

Nils nodded, and the domiseer paused, then almost reluctantly held out his hand. Nils stared at it. He'd despised this man, more than anything, and he couldn't say he'd warmed up to him in these last few months. But...something had changed, and it wasn't the domiseer.

It was Nils. He'd done unspeakable things to achieve his goals too, hadn't he? How could he look down on this man when he knew full well that the domiseer had clean wrists under his sleeves while Nils did not? It was only blindness that had led Nils to believe he had any right to judge him in the first place. As much as he hated it, the world was not as black and white as he once thought.

Nils took the domiseer's hand, grasping it firmly. It felt like Lord Dreygard held the handshake a moment longer than natural, and Nils was acutely aware of his gaze on the newly-purchased leather cuff that resided on Nils' forearm. Dreygard met his eyes, then let go, blessedly dismissing Nils from the room.

Nils rubbed his wrist as he walked out into the manor where Raeya met him, accompanied by Tilda.

"How did it go?" Raeya asked.

"Fine."

"Fine?" Raeya said. "Anything else to say? As in, has he approved our betrothal?"

Nils smiled. "Yes."

"Oh, Nils!" Raeya said, embracing him. "Ah, we have so much to plan. Where, when, oh, and what shall I wear? Pria's Eyes, I'll be up all night thinking about this."

"Try to get *some* rest," Nils said. "There's no rush."

"No rush? Are you mad?" Raeya asked, and her smile was mischievous, sending a tingle down Nils' spine.

"Oh, there's something else I need to tell you," Raeya said, growing serious. "Several letters came in while I was gone. The work Jarik and I did toward securing supplies for the towns is still going through. Everyone who offered to fund the project remains on board. No one knows what happened, or who Jarik—well, you know."

Nils wasn't sure what to say. It was good news, but just hearing that name…it filled him with something hard to identify, and he could see it reflected on Raeya's face as well. For all that Jarik had been…could they still mourn him?

Lord Dreygard's voice interrupted them from across the room. "Raeya."

"One moment, Father," Raeya called to him, then whispered to Nils. "There is much I need to discuss with him," she said, "but…he's my father. Regardless of what he's done, I think I've already forgiven him in my heart."

Nils nodded, understanding. Raeya smiled, then kissed him on the cheek before going to the domiseer. Tilda lingered behind.

"Lad," she said, "I never liked you."

"So I noticed," Nils replied.

"You vexed my lady more than you know when you showed up. You were rude, insensitive, and…Blessed Pria, you should've seen the state she was in when she made me cut her hair. It was horrible. She winced with every snip of the shears. But, you've surprised me several times now, and…"

Tilda trailed off, and Nils noticed with some discomfort that she was starting to cry.

"And…you brought her…back to us." She sniffed, and took Nils' hand, pressing it in hers. "Thank you. In the end, you're just who she needed. The gods chose you rightly after all."

Tilda nodded as though affirming herself, then scurried off after Raeya, leaving Nils to stare after her in bewilderment.

"Soulmate!"

Nils flinched at the nickname, not needing to wonder who had come to assault his emotions next. Bern stood with Captain Clerrit, who offered a nod of greeting. They were both alive and well, along with Tilda. Dreygard had kept his word.

Bern sauntered over. "There's a fancy new room for you. Even fancier than the last; I seen it myself."

"*I've* seen," Nils corrected.

"What? No you haven't. But I'll take you when you're ready."

Nils sighed, but smiled. "Sure. Let's go."

As he followed Bern, he noticed himself rubbing his cuffs again, the new leather smooth under his skin. He'd been without the weaver's stone for a long time now, and yet…it still seemed like he felt a gentle thrumming now and then, something running through his veins. He took a deep breath, trying to shove it off, but his mind was already whirring.

Even if no one sees my wrists, at some point my aging will slow…

Stop it, he told himself. *I've already made my choices. I…I can make this work.*

Even with his greatest effort, there was one thought that always lingered, hovering at the back of his mind. He'd told no one about his encounter, his *connection* with Lyare. He would have to tell Raeya soon, but…what would she think? Nils didn't even know what to think. He didn't want to believe the words that were spoken, but…could a god lie? Even a fallen one? They were words that vindicated Nils' decision to wield Lyare's power, and yet to accept them and all that they meant...Nils would rather they were false.

Maybe none of it was real, just a brush with madness, as Kara'ni had said of Anseph. Whatever the case, one thing was certain: Nils did not desire this link with Lyare, and he would do everything he could to avoid accessing it. Thankfully, that only required that he never touch a weaver's stone ever again.

ACKNOWLEDGMENTS

First off, I have to say a big thank you to James, my husband and alpha reader for life. It means the world to me to have somebody to bounce story ideas and random line edits off of, even at eleven o'clock at night, especially when I know that somebody will take them seriously and can respond from his own experience as an author and storyteller. You're the best.

Next, another big thank you to Aunt Wendy, Lisabeth, and Sarah, my wonderful beta readers. I appreciate so much how you've each encouraged me and offered your insights to help make this story stronger. It's great to have readers among my family and friends who are not only willing to help in this way but who are genuinely invested in the project and excited to see it moving forward. Love you guys!

And a massive thank you to my readers—that's you!—for reading and supporting my work. I absolutely love to share stories with you, and there's nothing better than hearing that I've made someone smile or inspired someone with something I've written. I hope any sparks of inspiration make their way into your own artwork, whatever form that may take.

As always, I thank God most of all, because without Him, nothing is possible.

About the Author

Shannen L. Colton is a professional daydreamer (read: fantasy author) who writes from Upstate New York. She enjoys a quiet life with her family and cats.

shannenlcolton.com

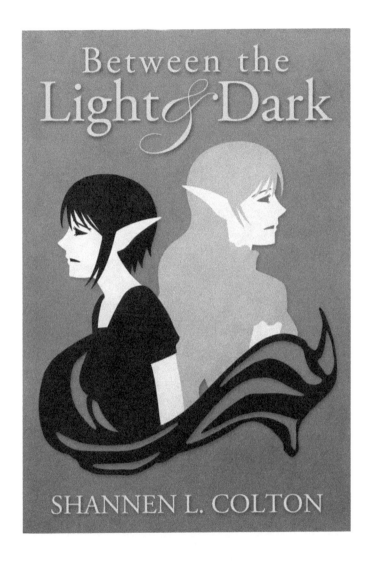

One would think a **damsel in distress** would be in *less distress*
after she's **rescued.**

But that all depends on *who rescues her.*